The Northland Chronicles:
Desolation's Wake

Henry J. Olsen

For Carol
We're in this together

"A razor has charms to smooth a savage beard."

DESOLATION'S WAKE

Prologue

They were all Rovers now.

Rover weaved in and out of the row of hedges. The boiling vat of gold that was the late-summer sky poured down onto his yellow fur, casting his lithe, four-legged body in hues of pale red and burnt orange. As his shadow grew long, his life grew short.

Leaving the hedges behind, Rover trotted through the lush prairie grass beside the pond. The prairie grass rose to heights that only nine years before would've been unthinkable in a Minneapolis park.

Did Rover have a family? Did he have puppies to care for? Had he once had an owner?

Did any of these questions matter?

No. No, they didn't.

Rover toed the edge of the pond, cautiously extending his golden muzzle for a drink. He lapped the pristine water with his tongue.

Rover was a dog. A dog that might have once had a name.

They were all Rovers now.

A slender wooden shaft, tipped with a sharp metal head, penetrated Rover's skull. Rover collapsed with a tortured yelp, hitting the pond water and sending ripples across the surface.

On the other side of the pond Weston Bridges emerged from the underbrush. He slung his crossbow over his back and circled the pond to Rover's corpse.

Rover was destined to become the protein in Weston's dinner.

Weston yanked his crossbow bolt from the golden retriever's head. Like the squirrels, rabbits, deer, moose, bears, and cats in the city, the dog was nothing but a meal now. After slipping the steel-tipped bolt into his quiver, Weston cradled the dead beast in his arms and began home. He didn't care that the bloodied body would sully his camouflage jacket. Minneapolis had plenty of unused clothing. A new jacket, free for the taking, was only a trip to Gander Mountain away.

Weston cut through a ragged patch of sawtooth sunflowers towards the sidewalk. The sun was low, clinging to the horizon like a stray bead of pancake batter sizzling on the edge of a griddle. Darkness would soon follow.

Night near the University of Minnesota was no longer what it had once been. Weston sauntered by the dilapidated student rental lots, which looked only vaguely more run-down than they had during his college days. He passed by fraternities and sororities, vestiges of that Greek life of which he'd never been a part.

Every time he walked these streets the memories returned. Memories of parties. Of one night stands. Of wild times with even wilder people.

Where were his classmates now? They were all either enjoying heaven or burning in hell. At least they weren't lonely.

In the distance ahead flowed the mighty Mississippi, impassive and strong. On this side of the great river's bank lay the university, now nothing but a decaying collection of lecture halls, dormitories, and chemistry labs. Across the river dozens of vacant offices and apartments rose up from the earth, together forming a downtown skyline.

Above the jagged backdrop lorded Target Tower, the tallest of the city's skyscrapers. Visible for miles, the tower's ominous presence reached every corner of the city. Though no one had known at the time, the construction of the resplendent ninety-story monolith had ultimately served as the city's last wasteful gasp. Now, like the pyramids of Egypt and the Coliseum of Rome, the tower stood as a grim tribute to a failed civilization.

Home wasn't far now. There Weston would skin and cook the dog. With proper preparation and lots of salt the meat would keep for several days. If it went bad sooner than expected Weston could hunt for more.

All things considered, summer was the easiest time to make ends meet. Game was abundant and more fruit-bearing trees blossomed with each passing year.

Yet even given the gifts of summer, preparing for winter was an annual challenge. Last winter Weston had run extremely short on food. He'd been so hungry that the leather on his boots had made him salivate. In the end he'd survived thanks to dumb luck, stumbling upon a black bear hibernating within the university's network of underground tunnels. The dormant bear had made an easy target. Its sinewy flesh and juicy fat had helped him push through those final weeks before the snow finally melted.

He hoped to do better this winter. Even with the recent influx of angry-looking men into the city, men who were claiming a large share of the available game, Weston felt confident he'd be better prepared than last year. If the unwelcome outsiders made game scare, Weston could rely on his potato and cabbage patch to tide him over.

Indeed, a disturbing number of men now inhabited the city. Many of them wore green vests and carried guns, which they fired indiscriminately. Weston was sick of the racket. Minneapolis was his city. His alone.

Weston stopped and cocked his head.

Voices. Two men approached. They ambled down the overgrown street, chatting.

Weston darted into the nearest driveway and hid behind a rusting Toyota Camry. The car's tires had deteriorated and lost their air, leaving the chassis to rest on the metal rims. Tall grass and weeds protruded from the pavement beneath the car, smothering it in a blanket of green.

The voices drew nearer, becoming clear.

"He's coming. I'm sure."

"But what makes you so sure, sir? We haven't heard anything since losing Bogues on Mallard Island."

"Osborne has no choice. He comes here or he dies. Osborne won't die willingly."

Weston peered over the car at the two men. Their features were hard to discern in the darkness. One had a thicker build than the other. The bright ember of a cigar hovered near his mouth.

"But we can't be certain he found the documents in that crazy old bat's underground bunker," the cigar smoker said.

"Don't speak lightly of Professor Singh, Lieutenant," replied the other. "He was a capable researcher. He saw the risks of living in our world and acted accordingly."

Crouching behind the car, Weston set down his kill and laid his crossbow across his thighs. Better to kill than be killed, if it came to that.

"And what of your army, sir?" the cigar smoker asked.

"This is a job only I can accomplish," replied the other. "I trust you to lead in my absence."

"I won't let you down. When will you go into hiding?"

"I have preparations to make that will take some time. I'd best take my leave tonight."

"Should I put the army on lockdown immediately?"

"Not yet. Wait until ..."

A mosquito buzzed in Weston's ear. He swatted, silencing it. If only the pesky bloodsuckers had disappeared with their human hosts.

Keeping to the middle of the street, the two men passed the driveway where Weston hid. It was too late for Weston to move. Only the cover of the grass and the darkness concealed him.

"We'll communicate by messages, left in the house we agreed upon, or by radio if there's an emergency," the cigar smoker said, stopping in the street. "Is there anything else I need to know?"

The other took one more step and swung around. His eyes fell not far from where Weston knelt. "There is. Three men know about Osborne. The first is Ramses Brushnell."

"The radio guy?"

"Right. The other two are a pair of men who just returned from Duluth."

"Ah, those two. I heard they ran out of gas on the edge of town."

"You heard correctly."

"And what of these three men, sir?"

"I may have a special mission for one or more of them. I'll let you know should the need to execute it arises."

Weston anxiously held his breath as the two men continued down the street. He remained silent until an inexplicable sight ripped the air from his lungs.

White lights materialized above the downtown skyline. More brilliant than stars, the lights flared to life in sets of three. Each new set appeared above the last, forming a trio of vertical columns in the sky.

At the columns' apex a red light flickered into being. It pulsated ominously, like a flaming crimson star.

An involuntary gasp escaped Weston's throat as he stumbled, falling backwards, his crossbow clattering onto the blacktop.

It was Target Tower. The dead tower had sprung to life for the first time in nine years. But how?

"We have ourselves a spy, Lieutenant," said the other, drawing a pistol as he approached Weston.

The smoking man tossed the red ember of his cigar to the ground and produced a handgun.

"Look!" Weston cried out, pointing to the orgasmic explosions of light. "The Tower!"

The cigar smoker craned his neck and looked over his shoulder. "I'll be damned ..." he uttered.

The other, not so easily distracted, paced forward, pistol in hand. Weston fumbled for his crossbow.

A deafening crack split the air. Weston felt a sharp pain in his neck. A pain worse than when he'd broken his arm on the playground. Worse than when he'd taken a baseball bat to his kneecap.

He sprawled across the driveway. A warm, wet stream of goo trickled down his neck. His breathing grew labored, the path between his mouth and lungs severed.

Was this the end?

He lay there, choking on his own blood, oddly transfixed by the majesty of Target Tower. It reminded him of Christmas. Not the desperately hungry Christmas of last year, but the Christmases of his youth, filled with presents, family, and warmth.

The two men stood over him, blocking his view of that radiant pillar.

"Nice shot, sir," the cigar smoker said. "He wasn't mistaken about Target Tower. The whole thing is lit up to the nines."

The other didn't look back at the tower. "It was a terrible shot. I was shooting to kill. I'll need to practice my marksmanship before Osborne arrives. I wouldn't want to let him down."

"What about this guy?" the cigar smoker asked.

"Put him out of his misery or let him choke on his own blood. The choice is yours."

Weston tried to offer his opinion, but only gasps and gurgles came from his throat.

The cigar smoker pressed his pistol to the bridge of Weston's nose. "You're lucky we have plenty of bullets," he said.

Weston closed his eyes. The pistol's muzzle felt cool against his forehead, until a volcanic blast of heat erupted from the steel barrel.

PART ONE

Chapter 1

January 3rd, 2027
Post Status: Public

Hello, world. Ryota here. Welcome to my new blog, *Ryota in the Minneapple.*

* * *

MINNESOTA WAS KNOWN as the land of 10,000 lakes. The largest of these lakes, Lake Superior, was expansive enough to devour the former state of West Virginia and still have room left for dessert. From there the lakes only got smaller. Many of them were nothing but backyard mud holes, not even specks on the map.

Most of the lakes had been carved into the earth by glaciers during the last ice age, thousands of years before. Though young on a geological scale, the lakes had existed long before the rise of man and had continued to thrive in the aftermath of mankind's fall. If anything the lakes were in better shape now than a decade ago. Water shortages were a thing of the past.

Lakes. Numbers. Estimates. Since departing from Mallard Island a week ago, Nathan had entertained random thoughts such as these. Abstract ideas kept his mind off the eerie quiet, broken only by the steady clopping of hooves on the rough highways and the medley of bird song that escaped from the surrounding woodland.

Nathan's companion, John Osborne, never a talkative man, had become even less chatty since leaving Mallard Island. On the island John had learned that he might only have a month to live.

The professor's message, delivered from beyond the grave, had put it like this: John had to find a power source known as the Northland Core, which was possibly hidden in Minneapolis. Without the core John's bionic left arm would tap into his body's metabolism for energy. It would leech away his stores of muscle and fat until he had nothing left to give.

Minneapolis, the city of Nathan's birth, was John's last hope.

Nathan's other steadfast companion was Mumford. Of an even quieter breed than John, Mumford was content to idle away his free hours, feasting on roadside vegetation and leaving tvapa pies in the middle of the road.

To hear John tell it, Mumford and the rest of his kind were secretly plotting to take over the world. Nathan couldn't see the sense in this claim. Mumford was not a human but a tvapa, a hardy pack animal with the body and antlers of a moose but the head of a Holstein. Mumford could hardly be expected to speak, much less scheme of world domination.

Nathan cracked a relieved smile at the realization that Duluth was only a few miles away. The city would spare him from discovering firsthand how long he could walk in silence before losing his sanity.

Among the vast, sparsely populated wilderness of Minnesota, only Duluth could legitimately claim to be a city. The capital of the Republic of Minnesota, Duluth served as a beacon of civilization, leading the way forward through an age of darkness. The Republic had already managed to establish a new currency that was largely accepted throughout the region. Even small villages like Nathan's hometown of Frontier View, which presently had little use for paper money, saw the existence of currency as a positive development.

But there was still much darkness to overcome. Blocks of abandoned houses stretched over the city's rolling hills. Like tombstones, the houses represented lives that had once been but now were no longer.

Businesses and public offices had fared no better. On the roof of a Cub Foods grocery store lay a car, upturned so that its tires faced the sky. Nathan guessed that it had been deposited there by a tornado. Guessing was all one could do when faced with random, unexplained destruction.

The edge of downtown was where the city finally came to life. People and horse-drawn carriages bustled past, all easily overtaking Nathan and his two companions. Mumford, slow as he was hardy, trudged ahead. A hindrance in summer, Mumford's plodding steadiness paid dividends when the snows came. Even in the middle of a Minnesota blizzard, Mumford could lumber forward as though it were a pleasant midsummer afternoon.

The sun fell fast as they passed by the familiar stores, restaurants, and bars of downtown. Soon they would need to decide where to hole up for the night.

On one hand, they needed to make haste. It would be foolhardy to waste even a couple hours that they could use to journey south. Then again, they had no idea when they would next pass through a real, living, breathing city. This would be their last opportunity to enjoy the city life for the foreseeable future, and in John's case, perhaps …

Nathan shook the thought away. Some ideas were better left unvoiced, even within the private chambers of one's own mind.

In any case, the decision was John's. Nathan was just about to ask what they should do when John spoke first.

"We'll stay in Duluth tonight."

"Are you sure?" Nathan asked.

"I'm sure."

Without further discussion, Nathan, John, and Mumford guided their cart towards the Lakefront Inn, the hotel they'd stayed at during their last visit to Duluth.

Despite the weeds that dominated its parking lot, the Lakefront Inn was clean, comfortable, and inviting. Nathan recognized the beige door of the room they'd checked into last time. And just beside it was the room where …

"John, are you worried about bumping into those guys with the car?" Nathan asked. A few weeks ago they'd departed Duluth under dire circumstances. Two men with a car, who'd been staying in the adjacent room, had assaulted John over a game of darts. In the aftermath Nathan had found John unconscious outside the bar. He'd managed to drag John's limp body to their cart and get them out of Duluth, but not without the help of cover fire provided by a mysterious guardian angel hidden amongst the shadows.

"I doubt they're still here. But if they are and they're still looking for trouble, we'll deal with them." John gave Nathan a sidelong glance. "It'll be a fair fight this time."

"I suppose ..." Nathan said, unconvinced. He'd barely escaped the two men the first time. That their black Honda was no longer in the parking lot was a relief.

Leaving Mumford and the cart outside, Nathan and John stepped into the hotel's lobby. They were greeted by the familiar metallic ring of the door chime.

"Just a moment," a female voice called from the doorway behind the counter.

Nathan waited patiently at the counter. John remained off to the side, examining a faded poster advertising Hawaii.

Looks like I'm in charge of booking a room again, Nathan thought. During their last visit he'd felt jittery about talking with the clerk. Now he knew exactly what he was doing.

After a brief wait, the same energetic brunette who'd assisted them last time emerged from the back room. When her eyes met Nathan's, she cocked her head and blinked — once, twice, three times — as though struggling to recognize a long lost relative.

"I wasn't expecting to see you two back here," she said.

"You weren't?" Nathan asked, confused. Had he and John given the clerk a reason not to expect their return?

"Oh, it's just that after your sister left, I figured you two probably wouldn't be back."

Nathan's jaw nearly hit the counter. "Sister?"

"Yeah, your sister, Emiko."

"Emiko?" Nathan said, bracing both arms on the counter. "Emiko was here?

"You didn't know? Emiko told me that you and your friend had left, but would come back to pick her up a few weeks later. That was the day after you two arrived. I let her stay in the same room you'd been staying in."

"She was here in Duluth at the same time we were?" Nathan exclaimed.

The clerk nodded. "You didn't know she was here?"

"No!" Nathan shouted, raising his hands above his head.

The clerk's eyes opened wide.

John loudly cleared his throat, drawing Nathan's attention. Silently he mouthed, "Calm down."

Nathan glanced back and forth at his arms before letting them fall to his sides. He closed his eyes and took a deep breath. There had to be an explanation for all of this.

"How long did she stay here?" he asked.

The clerk eyed a calendar on the wall. "She left about a week ago. She was a sweet girl, you know, and extremely helpful. I miss having her around."

"Emiko was helpful?" Nathan asked, struggling not to shout. "What did she help with?"

"Oh, you know, tidying the rooms, sweeping floors, washing sheets, tending the animals, that kind of thing." She counted the chores on her fingers.

"You mean ... you mean she helped you clean the hotel?"

"She sure did." The clerk smiled.

"Loons over the moon!" Nathan exclaimed under his breath. Emiko, cleaning? That she had been in Duluth was shocking enough. To hear that she had willingly done housework — and in a many-roomed hotel, no less — was like hearing that a family of blue whales had been spotted in Lake Superior.

As Nathan stood there, awestruck, he noticed the clerk trying to swallow a giggle.

"Did I say something funny?" he asked.

"No, it's nothing." She composed herself.

"Nothing?"

"It's just, well, I've never heard anyone say that before."

Nathan cocked an eyebrow. "Say what?"

"Loons over the moon." The clerk giggled. "It's cute."

"Oh," Nathan said flatly. Did he really sound that silly? He'd never given much thought to the phrase, much less thought about how others perceived it. In fact he couldn't remember when he'd started saying it, either.

John stepped in front of the counter and gave the clerk his trademark hard stare.

"How did she leave?" he asked.

"Well, that was the strangest part. There were a couple of other men here, with a car ..."

Nathan gulped audibly. Those two men were the last people he wanted to see. *Escaping from them once was enough, thank you very much*, he thought.

The clerk stopped speaking. She and John stared at Nathan.

"What?" he asked.

"You made a weird noise," the clerk said. "I thought maybe you had something to say."

"Oh? No, no, go ahead," he said, shaking his head.

"So, anyway, there were those two men. Just as they were checking out, I spotted Emiko crawling into the trunk of that old black Honda they were driving. I didn't have a clue what she was doing then, and I still don't now. But she seemed like a girl who knew how to take care of herself, so I let her go and didn't say a peep about it to the men."

"And where were they headed?" John asked.

"They wouldn't say. They had a few secrets they were unwilling to share. They were decent enough customers but I can't say I was too fond of them. Something about how they walked around here, like they owned the place, rubbed me the wrong way."

John looked to Nathan. "You have any other questions?"

Nathan shook his head. His mind, still finding it difficult to accept that Emiko had been here, was drawing a blank. His brain needed more time to hammer this one out.

"Are we gonna stay here?" he asked John.

"I don't see why not." John rested an elbow on the counter. "Do you have any vacancies?" he asked the clerk.

"Sure do. In fact, the room you had last time is open. How would that suit you?"

"It'd suit us fine," John said. "How much is it again?"

The clerk smiled at John. "Just one night?"

"Yeah."

"Well, I'll tell you what," the clerk said, shifting her smile toward Nathan, who forced himself to meet her gaze. "I'll let you stay here on the house. It's the least I can do to repay you for Emiko's help." She leaned over the counter and whispered, "Just don't let the manager know."

"Sure thing," Nathan said. Who was he to turn down a free room?

The clerk grabbed a key from under the counter and pressed it into Nathan's palm. She raised a finger to her lips and shot him a wink.

"Do you remember where the room is, or would you like me to remind you?" she asked.

Nathan rubbed the back of his neck, flashing an awkward smile. "I think we can find it."

"Suit yourself. If you need anything you know where to find me."

"You got it."

Nathan pushed through the lobby door and stepped back into the parking lot. "You go check out the room," he said to John, dangling the key from his fingers. "I'll take Mumford up to the stable."

John snatched the keys. "If you sent me off alone with that beast, chances are only one of us would return alive."

Nathan rolled his eyes. He would never understand the animosity John had for Mumford.

"Look at him," John scoffed, glaring at the impassive tvapa. "He's plotting to overthrow the Republic of Minnesota as we speak."

Nathan shrugged off John's remarks. "I'll see you in the room." He took Mumford's reigns and led the tvapa up the hill towards the hotel's stable. Already he was dreaming up excuses he could use to pay the clerk another visit.

Chapter 2

January 4th, 2027
Post Status: Public

Hello again, world! Sorry — I planned to write more yesterday before getting sidetracked, as parents always do. My daughter Emiko skinned her knee on the living room carpet and Superdad was called to the rescue. It only took a pink Band-Aid and a kiss for the owie for her to go back to tearing up the house. I, on the other hand, did not return to this blog. Funny how that happens.

So, why am I a here? My resolution for the new year is to actively maintain a blog. It sounds fun. I think the last time I had a blog was in high school. (Is MySpace still around? I can't imagine what I wrote about back then. It's probably better that I don't go looking for it.)

This blog will help me share things with family and friends. I'm terrible about keeping up with email. Now I can easily let the whole world know about the latest happenings in the Kanno household!

I just heard Danielle pull into the driveway. I'd better go see if she needs help bringing in the groceries. Every time I see our Subaru full of those brown grocery bags, I think of how lucky we are to be eating well. I know there are many other families who aren't so fortunate.

I'll try to post again soon.

* * *

THE KEY TURNED smoothly in the lock and John swung open the door. Nothing about the room had changed. Two beds, neatly made. A wooden dresser. An unadorned white desk. It was as unremarkable a hotel room as John had ever seen.

John sat on the edge of the bed nearest the door. He was glad Nathan had volunteered to deal with Mumford. Although he didn't actually believe that tvapas were planning an armed rebellion, he still preferred to keep his distance. When Mumford was around, John's boots always seemed to land ankle-deep in fresh tvapa pies.

John glanced out the window at the fading sunlight, at another day gone. They were at the midpoint of their journey, still a week away from Minneapolis. The professor's energy-recharging device had given John's bionic arm four weeks' worth of juice. Seven days had already passed since then, and it would take another seven or so to get to the city. That would leave two weeks to search for the Northland Core, the device which would hopefully keep his bionic arm charged indefinitely.

Would two weeks be enough time? John brushed his fingers through the hairs of his left arm, which he now knew was called SPEAR — Speed and Precision Enhanced Arm Replacement. Though he'd learned the arm's name, he still knew nothing of its inner workings. Sure, it could hit harder than a wrecking ball and throw objects with laser-precision, but what made it tick? Were there other functions he was unaware of? And why was it given to him of all people?

Another question still unanswered was whether or not using the arm would cut into the month of charge he'd been given. John had resolved to avoid using the arm's abilities until he found the core. To do otherwise would be foolish.

With a grunt of discontent, John pushed himself up from the bed to survey the room. Maybe his good friend Gideon had left behind more than a Bible.

John had been just as taken aback as Nathan to hear that Emiko had stayed here. Yet the more he thought about it the less surprising it seemed. Emiko was headstrong and had a fierce independent streak. She knew how to survive in the wilderness and she had been irate when John had agreed to take Nathan on this journey but not her.

She must've decided to follow them. But why did she stop in Duluth and not continue on to Mallard Island? Did it have something to do with those two Honda-driving goons?

Opening a desk drawer, John was greeted by the gentle tumbling sound of a rolling object. A bronze rifle cartridge spun into view and clacked against the drawer's front panel.

Someone had traded bullets for the Gideon's Bible.

John plucked the shell from the drawer and held it in his open palm. Had Emiko left this here? If she had, it meant she'd swapped her pea-shooting Ruger .22 for a real gun.

The door knob rattled. Nathan entered the room. He had one backpack hanging from his shoulders and another cradled in his arms. John waited until Nathan had set both bulky packs on the carpeted floor before sharing his discovery.

"Look at this." He held the bullet for Nathan to see.

"It's a rifle shell." Nathan shrugged. "What of it?"

"This got me thinking." John rotated the bullet between his thumb and forefingers. "You told me that on the night I collapsed in front of the bar, a mysterious shooter helped you escape — a real marksman, who shot the guns out of our assailants' hands, right?"

"Yeah. It was impressive. What about it?"

"Who's the best shooter you know?"

Nathan raised an eyebrow. "I'm pretty sure it's you, John."

John couldn't help but grin at that. The kid spoke the truth. But he was missing the point.

"Fair enough. Let me ask another question. Who is the greatest huntress you know?"

"Huntress? Well, I sometimes call Emiko the great huntress of Frontier View, but ..." Nathan's eyes flickered with understanding. "You think Emiko was the one who helped us out?"

"Bingo," John said.

"But Emiko uses a .22. That's definitely bigger than a .22 round."

"Emiko *used* a .22," John corrected. "We don't know what kind of rifle she's packing now. This looks like a .30-06 cartridge — popular ammunition, especially for snipers."

Nathan plopped himself onto the bed and cradled his head with his knuckles. He seemed unsure what to make of the theory. Maybe he just needed to hear more evidence.

"If your sister was the shooter, it would give her a motive to stay here and spy on those two men. If she saw them attacking us, she would want to know why."

"Her curiosity must've led her into the trunk of their car," Nathan replied.

John nodded. Nathan and his sister were both inquisitive, though their curiosity often expressed itself in different ways. Nathan was a bookworm; Emiko liked diving right into the thick of it and getting her hands dirty. John favored a more Emiko-like approach to solving problems, but recognized both methods had their place. Nathan's fondness for words had already proved invaluable on this quest.

Nathan ran a hand through his thick black hair. "Emiko was here. She probably saved us. Then she hopped in a car and disappeared. So, what do we do?"

"I have to go to Minneapolis. You have to decide for yourse —"

"I'm going with you, John." Nathan looked him straight in the eye.

"You sure?"

"Absolutely. I mean, of course I'm worried about Emiko, but I have no idea where I'd even begin looking for her. For all I know she could be in Minneapolis."

"Why would she be there?"

"Why wouldn't she be there? It's as good a place as any to begin the search."

John smiled grimly. "To Minneapolis, then."

"To Minneapolis." Nathan forced a smile. "Together."

This has to be rough on him, John thought. Still, he was confident that Nathan could persevere. Nathan and his sister were tough, solid, and resilient, just like the veins of iron ore that coursed through the hills of northern Minnesota.

Outside the sky was growing dark. Soon Duluth would bask in an artificial glow unique to its streets. Lit by both gas lamps and electric bulbs, Duluth was the only city for hundreds of miles with any nightlife to speak of.

"So, we leave for Minneapolis tomorrow?" Nathan asked.

"We do," John said, his eyes focused on the crumbling parking lot beyond the glass window.

"Planning to visit the bars again tonight?"

John looked over his shoulder to see Nathan shooting him a sly grin.

"I'm not sure the Drunken Loon would welcome me back. Not after what happened last time." John examined the .30-06 round thoughtfully for a few seconds before setting it on the windowsill. "We'll get some dinner and call it an early night. Minneapolis is waiting."

Chapter 3

January 7th, 2027
Post Status: Public

As I write this, Nathan is in the living room playing with the Samsung Æther that jolly old Saint Nick gave him for Christmas. It's a nifty toy. When I tried it I really felt like I was controlling the gameplay by manipulating the holographic image.

Nathan probably didn't need my help setting up the machine — he's a smart kid — but I gave him a hand anyway. And I'm glad I did, because it helped me understand how the device works.

It's pretty simple, really. A box, about the size of one of my chemistry books, projects holographic images upward, showing the player a variety of 3D objects. The player manipulates these objects to affect the action on the TV. Thus, the hologram essentially functions as a three dimensional touch screen.

However, the hologram is not actually responding to the player's touch. That's what the two cameras are for. One camera sits below the player, focused on his arms and hands. The other camera, placed below the TV, captures the player's entire body. Together the two cameras record the player's movements. The Æther's processor then renders new holograms (and TV images) in real-time. The processor is fast enough that there's no lag whatsoever, creating the illusion that the player is using the hologram itself to control the action.

The technology remains imperfect. The biggest issue is that the 3D projector's display angle is quite limited, meaning that from my point of view it looks like Nathan is wildly flailing his arms in the air, fending off an invisible swarm of angry bees.

I just hope he doesn't stumble and hurt himself. His younger sister does enough of that for the two of them.

Hmm … when I was Nathan's age, I would've been playing Super Nintendo. We sure have come a long way. (Yet despite all our technological progress, it still took me ten minutes to find and type the character "Æ." Some things never change.)

* * *

QUIETER THAN THE northern wilderness and more isolated than Emiko's hometown, Minneapolis was a city of small wonders.

Emiko rose with the morning sun. Her mouth opened in a cat-like yawn as she stretched her arms above her head. Cheerful robin songs filtered through the bedroom window. The fresh scents of summer dew and prairie grass teased her nose.

Today was going to be a good one. After greeting her with a morning this pleasant how could it not be?

Emiko threw off her sheets and hopped out of bed. The soft carpeting massaged her bare feet as she walked over to the dresser. From the folded stacks of clothing inside she selected a sleeveless black top and a loose-fitting pair of blue jeans. After changing, Emiko appraised herself in the bedside mirror. Wearing the sleeveless top, she looked like a real American teenager. Her face was clean, with none of the streaks of dirt that in the past had often graced it. Her black hair was as long as ever, coming down well below her shoulders. She would need to cut it soon.

She collected her M1903 Springfield rifle from underneath the bed. She slipped its strap over her head and let it hang from her back. Long and bulky as it was, the rifle, a gift from her father, had come to feel like an extension of her body. After pocketing the folding knife and a handful of rifle rounds from her nightstand, she sauntered through the halls towards the front door.

It was time for breakfast.

A week had passed since Emiko had decided to make this house her home. Like all the surrounding homes, this one had been full of dust, mice, cobwebs, and spiders. Unlike the other homes, however, this one had contained no dead bodies. Emiko didn't like disturbing the eternal sleep of the dead.

Reclaiming the single-story house from the years of neglect had been hard work. She'd swept every room from top to bottom, save for the basement, which she'd decided would be more trouble than it was worth. If her time working at the Lakefront Inn had taught her anything, it was the value of a clean room. And to think, just a few months ago she would've been content to live in filth. Maybe the change was just part of growing up.

She stepped outside, raising an arm to shield her eyes from the bright glare of the sun. She took cover in the shade of the front yard's lone maple tree and pondered where to start the day's hunt.

Since arriving in Minneapolis Emiko had fallen into a routine. She hunted in the morning and searched for the Restoration Army in the afternoon.

The hunting usually went well. The reconnaissance, not so well.

What was the Restoration Army? Emiko still didn't fully understand. Eavesdropping from her room in Duluth, she'd heard two soldiers named Smitty and Leonard talking about the revival of Minnesota, the return to a better age, and many more topics which she hadn't entirely grasped.

Politics were not Emiko's strong suit. The most heated disputes in her hometown had been about where barnyard animals could and couldn't roam. Still, it was clear that the men in green were up to no good. One group had kidnapped her and held her hostage at Sawbill Lake. Another pair had assaulted her brother Nathan and her friend Beard in Duluth.

What would the next soldiers she encountered do? Whatever their plans, Emiko hoped to stop them.

First, however, she had to eat. No one, not even Beard himself, could fight on an empty stomach.

The city had no shortage of game. Humans had vanished. Animals, both domestic and wild, had moved in. Squirrels both red and gray and a great variety of birds lurked in the trees. Joining these long-time residents were rabbits, gophers, deer, coyotes, and even wolves. These newcomers roamed the city streets freely, mingling with the stray cats and dogs that had rediscovered their feral instincts.

The larger game animals weren't of much use to Emiko. She had a strict policy of killing only what she could use. An adult deer was too heavy for her to carry home, much less prepare and eat before the meat spoiled. This restriction, self-imposed but important to her nonetheless, left Emiko to subsist on small game alone.

She ambled down the sidewalk, flanked on either side by lawns long untended. Bull thistle and teasel rose up to her chest. She hoped the growth spurt she was due for would soon leave the foliage closer to waist-level.

Something moved in the distance. Emiko shouldered her rifle, fell to one knee, and put the scope to her eye.

Black. Four legs. A dog. Though most dogs and cats were now just as wild as the rest of nature's denizens, Emiko still couldn't bring herself to gun them down.

She lowered the rifle and crossed the street, trampling patches of grass that had taken hold in the asphalt's cracks and fissures. Just a few short blocks away was a small park with a pond. A watering hole for animals large and small, the pond was the perfect place to stake out and wait for a fresh meal to arrive.

Once at the pond she sat down behind her hunting blind, a dark green tarp that she'd strung between two trees. The opaque plastic tarp hung about three feet off the ground. Its bottom edge just kissed the soft dirt below. In front of it she'd poked branches into the ground to break up the blind's outline. From behind it she could observe the comings and goings around the pond, confident that most passing creatures wouldn't notice her.

She peered over the blind, her rifle cradled in her arms, and waited. Patience was the essence of the hunt, a lesson her long days spent in the woods around Frontier View had taught her.

The blind was not without drawbacks. It left her back exposed, for one. Though the surrounding vegetation hid her well and she trusted her ears to detect any approaching creatures, she still worried that a person might sneak up behind her. Only the city's emptiness made her willing to accept this risk.

Wandering out from the tall brush, a thirsty coyote appeared at the pond's edge. More scavenger than hunter, the coyote was the size of a large dog. It had sharp ears, brown fur, and a grizzled white bib down its chest. Maybe it had come for a drink. Maybe it hoped to find a carcass or two to pick clean. In any case, the canine had chosen the wrong day to come to water.

Emiko raised the rifle to her shoulder. She watched the coyote through the scope as it waded into the shallow water. A coyote was the largest animal she could shoot without feeling wasteful. Though rough and sinewy, the animal's meat was surprisingly juicy and flavorful when cooked over an open flame. It reminded Emiko of duck.

She worked the bolt-action of her rifle, slowly chambering a round. She centered her sights on the coyote's head.

One shot would do it. She took a breath, held it in her chest, and pulled the trigger.

An explosion rang in her ears as the rifle pounded against her shoulder. The coyote collapsed, not making so much as a yelp as it slid into the pond. The bullet through its skull had snuffed out its life instantaneously, painlessly.

After re-slinging the rifle across her back, Emiko approached her kill. Blood gushed from the coyote's head wound, staining the clear water scarlet. Emiko took the carcass by its legs and dragged it onto dry land. She would field dress it, take what she could use, and leave the rest for scavengers. Such was the way of a hunter.

She closed her eyes. The coyote's sacrifice would feed her for days. Never would she forget that the gifts of the earth were what allowed her to live, to be alive.

With a clear conscience she took out her knife and cut into the beast's flesh.

Chapter 4

January 13th, 2027
Post Status: Private

Apparently I can use this blog as a journal, too. I just need to change the post status from public to private.

Hello, me.

I just got home from work. Throbbing migraine. The words revenue and grants won't stop ricocheting inside my skull.

My department had our winter meeting this afternoon. The department chair tore into me and my colleagues. We don't work hard enough! We need more grants! We waste too much time on projects with zero revenue potential!

He went on like that for over 20 minutes. It was all I could do not to walk out in the middle. We are professors at a public university for Christ's sake, not mercenaries for Pfizer! Isn't our mission to spread knowledge and undertake research for the common good?

His departmental goals are the antitheses of my reasons for having pursued a chemistry PhD.

Yet the sorry truth is that I won't make a fuss. I can't. I'm the newest addition to the faculty, and I'm sure the department would kick me to the curb without a second thought, tenure be damned. I slaved for years to get this position, and I'd be a fool to throw it away just because I don't see eye-to-eye with the department chair.

Were I still a bachelor perhaps I'd be willing to take the risk. However, I have Nathan, Emiko, and Danielle to consider. A job this secure and well-paying likely wouldn't come my way again, especially if I were to leave on contentious terms.

I'll just have to keep working and making my way up the ladder. Hopefully one day I can change things from the top.

But for today? Today I'll just pop a few aspirin and go to bed early.

* * *

WHAT WAS THE purpose of this meeting?

Ramses was in the Restoration Army's stable tending his horse Thunder when the call to assemble came. He made his way to the courtyard, which stood amid four university dormitories. The General had converted the brick-and-mortar dormitories, formerly occupied by students, into soldiers' barracks, a purpose for which they were surprisingly well suited.

Would the General deliver a speech? What plans did the General have for the Restoration Army? How much longer were they to remain in these improvised barracks? Would they mobilize soon? Though Ramses trusted the General's judgment he couldn't help but want answers. What knowledge-seeking man wouldn't?

Ramses waited under the summer sun, clad in his finest green vest and cleanest pair of khakis. Hundreds of his compatriots, perhaps a quarter of the army's total number, filled the courtyard. Most wore green, though a few of the newest recruits still lacked proper Restoration Army gear.

Looking around, Ramses was reminded as to just how youthful this fighting force was. The Restoration Army was mostly a collection of single men, many who had been nothing but children when the Desolation struck. The Desolation had stolen their futures, leaving them to struggle through a life now cold and purposeless.

But cold and purposeless their lives needed not be. In his singular wisdom, the General gave promise of a grand and illustrious future. Repaving the road to civilization would require hard work and perhaps even violence, but the results would speak for themselves. All blood spilled along the way would surely be forgiven.

The crowd was tense with impatience. A pair of fresh recruits behind Ramses openly questioned the purpose of the gathering. Ramses vehemently detested their insubordination. Though Ramses also wondered what the meeting was about, such thoughts were best left unspoken.

The growth of the army had been accelerating, Ramses realized. Many of the newest recruits had never met the General in person. Come to think of it, even Ramses himself hadn't heard from the General for a number of days. *No matter*, he thought. The General would appear today.

The mumbles and whispers grew faint as a pair of men approached, carrying a podium to the front of the crowd. The wooden platform thudded on the sidewalk as the men set it down. Two more men followed with a microphone and speaker. After positioning the speaker at the front of the podium and placing the microphone on top of it, the four men disappeared into the sea of troops.

A silence swept over the crowd, signaling the speaker's approach. Leaning forward for a better view, Ramses spotted a lone man striding assertively toward the podium. Clearly he was not intimidated by the gathering of men before him.

He was also clearly not the General.

He was Lieutenant Thurston Prince, one of the General's closest confidants, a man roughly forty years old. His broad chest was thrust forward, framed by his powerful shoulders. His neatly pressed green service uniform and meticulously shaved head accentuated his masculinity.

Why was Prince speaking today and not the General? Disappointment consumed Ramses. Still, if the General had sent

Lieutenant Prince to speak, Ramses had a responsibility to listen.

The lieutenant stepped onto the podium and claimed the microphone. Surveying the men assembled before him, he clicked the microphone on and cleared his throat.

"Men of the Restoration Army," he declared. "I come to you today with news both good and bad. Allow me to begin with the good. Yesterday we reached a grand milestone. Thanks to your stalwart recruiting efforts, our force is now officially two thousand members strong."

The crowd roared with approval. Though meager compared to the armies of old, relative to the current population of Minnesota — perhaps 70,000 men, women, and children — two thousand was a remarkable number.

"I trust this day will not soon be forgotten. When the new histories are written, these two thousand men will be remembered as the bravest of the brave. You men, gathered before me here and now, will be known far and wide as the heroes who restored this world to its former glory." The lieutenant shook his fist in the air. "We will bring peace, order, and justice back to this world. And when we do, the greatest of honors shall be yours: the honor of having had the vision to forge a new nation."

A thunderous cheer rose up from the assembly of men. The lieutenant raised a hand, calling for silence. The crowd immediately grew quiet.

What I wouldn't give to wield that kind of power and respect, Ramses mused. He hoped one day he would be the one standing on that podium.

The lieutenant lowered his hand and continued:

"And now the bad news. I'm sure a few of you are wondering why it is I, and not the General, who is speaking today. The General has undertaken a critical mission that only he is capable of completing. Because of the sensitive nature of this mission, I cannot provide more information at this time. Until he has successfully concluded this mission, he will be unable to perform his duties as leader of the Restoration Army. He has selected me to carry on in his stead until he returns."

What was this? A rumble of discontent rose from the ranks. How could the General do this? What was his important mission? Though the news caught Ramses just as unaware as the rest of the crowd, he kept his mouth shut. This was not the place to speak his mind.

Lieutenant Prince, to his credit, maintained his composure. Surely he had expected this reaction. He held his hand in the air again. After a momentary swell, the crowd's displeasure gradually subsided.

"The General has also requested that we maintain a low profile while he conducts his mission. We will scale back our city-wide patrols to the bare minimum. You will venture outside only when expressly permitted to do so."

The audience uttered a collective groan.

"I understand this will be a difficult time, but for the good of the Restoration Army, and for the bright future we seek to create, we must make this sacrifice for the General."

A wave of noisy discontent surged through the crowd. Would the lieutenant address the men's restlessness or let it settle on its own? Circumstances often forced leaders to opt for one of two imperfect choices. Were Ramses a leader, he too would have to bear the burden of choice. Though surely onerous at times, it was a responsibility no proud man would shirk.

"There is still much to do," the lieutenant shouted into the microphone. "Return to your barracks to await further instructions. You are dismissed."

The lieutenant knelt to set the microphone on the podium. He then smartly turned on his heel and walked away without looking back.

Ear-piercing feedback blared from the speaker, quickly intensifying. The same four men who had delivered the podium and speaker rushed forward to kill the power. After cutting the sound, they quickly hauled the podium and audio equipment away.

The assembly dispersed gradually, men trickling back to their respective quarters. Immersed in thought, Ramses waited until the courtyard was nearly empty before departing alone.

The General gone? Lieutenant Thurston Prince in charge? What was the General's compelling mission? Why hadn't the General announced his own departure? Perhaps a tearful goodbye would've been a touch dramatic. Still, it seemed odd that the General had left Lieutenant Prince in this awkward situation.

Ramses passed through the doorway of Centennial Hall and navigated the twisting corridors towards the privacy of his room. Lieutenant Prince's speech had given him much to consider.

Chapter 5

January 14th, 2027
Post Status: Public

Small update today: I added a short "About Me" page.

I didn't even know I could create one until Nathan showed me how. (I have no idea how he discovered this blog. I certainly didn't tell him about it. Perhaps I should be more careful about what I write here …)

Anyway, when I sat down to write about myself I realized I didn't have much to say, so I kept it short and to the point.

If you'd like to know more about me, please have a look. The link is in the upper left corner.

* * *

SINCE LEAVING FRONTIER VIEW, Nathan had passed through dozens of abandoned towns and villages. Each one had houses falling into disrepair and old cars rusting along the roadside. Seeing these unoccupied communities had only confirmed what he'd already known: that the world was now a god-forsaken place.

Yet for all Nathan had seen, nothing could've prepared him for Minneapolis. One part time capsule, one part nature sanctuary, Minneapolis was a dead city of a scale he had never before witnessed.

He and John ambled down the suburban streets, ahead of Mumford and the cart. Ash and maple trees lined the curbside. Having gone untrimmed for years, their canopies now cast shadows over the width of the street. Quack grass protruded from the pavement, giving way beneath Nathan's boots.

The houses were just as neglected as the streets. Vines snaked up faded siding and spread across rooftops. Sullen cars corroded in driveways, surrounded by thickets of burdock.

The outskirts of Duluth had been like this, too. The difference was that Minneapolis had no revitalized center to offset its desolate outer shell. The sheer absoluteness of the city's fall made loneliness of this place all the more palpable.

In the distance loomed the downtown skyline, ruled by the impossibly tall Target Tower, the crown jewel of Minneapolis. The tower had been the city's last major construction project before the Desolation. Nathan recalled watching it grow on the skyline, reaching higher month by month.

Like the people that built them, cities were supposed to have lives of their own, to react, adapt, and grow. Save for the encroaching flora and fauna, Minneapolis was just as Nathan remembered it. Every man-made aspect of the city had remained fixed for the last nine years. Were the souls of the departed still here, too? His spine tingled at the thought.

Better to focus on the present. Nathan and John had two weeks to find the Northland Core. Their only lead had already taken them as far as it would. Now they had an entire metropolis to search. Still, he and John made a good team. With a bit of luck they'd find it.

"Where to first?" Nathan asked.

"I'm not sure." John said. "This city is huge. The core could be anywhere. I say we start by checking military installations. Everything so far has pointed towards the military."

Nathan scratched his head. "I'm not sure the U.S. military had a presence in Minneapolis."

"How about energy companies? They might've been involved in developing the core, too."

"Energy companies ..." Nathan trailed off, frowning. "I don't know where they are, either."

John's features drew taut in disbelief. "You used to live here. Don't you know anything about your city?"

"I lived here when I was eight years old, John. My elementary school teachers didn't teach Power Plants 101."

John nodded. Though disappointed, he seemed to realize it was unreasonable to expect an eight-year-old to possess a working knowledge of the city.

"We could try looking around the university camps," Nathan said. "I know the university had close ties to the military. My dad used to complain about how the University of Minnesota was accepting too many grants from the Pentagon."

"He complained about it to you when you were eight?"

Nathan hesitated. "Not exactly."

"Not exactly?"

"Well, you see, I used to hack into the journal my father kept on his computer," Nathan admitted. "Actually, it was more of a blog. Or maybe a diary. Anyhow, he really should've used a stronger passwo —"

"So, you spied on your old man?" John grinned as though he'd heard that Jesus drank and gambled with the devil on Sundays.

"He should've used a more secure password!"

"I knew you had a dark side, kid," John said. "This proves it."

Nathan raised a palm to his forehead and groaned.

"Anyway, the university sounds like a good place to start," John said. "Lead the way."

Nathan nodded. His last trip to the university had been long ago, and he'd never visited without his parents to lead the way. He knew the main campus lay just across the Mississippi River from downtown. He could use Target Tower to close in and wing it from there.

"You know, my old house isn't far from the university," Nathan said, trying to sound nonchalant about the possibility of visiting his childhood home. "We could use it as our base of operations."

"It'd be as good a place as any. But are you sure you want to go back there? Your family left it behind for a reason."

Nathan considered. Like everything else in the city, his home would likely look just as it had the day his family left it in the spring of 2028. Would the eerie lack of change bother him?

"It should be alright," he said. "And unlike many of the other houses around here, it won't have dead bodies inside."

"Your house it is, then," John said.

Nathan studied the next street sign they passed. White letters on a green background read Silver Lake Rd. Confident he could find his house from here, he led John and Mumford south. They weaved past Silverwood Park, where his family had often picnicked, and a Rainbow Foods store that his mom had frequented for groceries.

They turned onto Nathan's block. Soon they arrived at his old address: 1013 39th Avenue.

"Here we are," Nathan announced. Years had passed since the yard had seen a lawn mower. The grass and weeds rose well above his waist. The ancient bur oak in front of the house, though tall as ever, seemed less imposing than Nathan remembered — probably the result of his own upward growth.

Fireweed had overtaken the empty driveway that had formerly been home to the family Subaru. The Subaru had carried Nathan's family north after the Desolation. Refueling the car had been easy at first. Abandoned vehicles, eager to share their gasoline, had littered the roads. But gasoline degraded quickly. Within a year the Subaru was choking on rotten fuel. Nathan still remembered the day when his dad burst through their cabin's door hours after dinnertime and announced that the car was a goner.

Behind the overgrown drive and the old oak stood the house itself. The sky blue, two-story house had aged better than most. The vinyl siding had retained its color well and the front windows were intact.

"We didn't come here to stare at it from the outside," John said.

"Oh, right." Nathan snapped out of his reverie. "Let's try the door."

After tying Mumford to the oak tree, Nathan and John walked up to the house. Fastened above the door frame was the number 101. The 3 had disappeared, perhaps snatched away by a squirrel.

The front door opened without a hitch. Nathan led John into the entryway. Though his mom would've insisted that they remove their shoes, Nathan made no such request of John. The house had already accumulated nine years of dust; the floor could handle a few additional boot prints.

The interior had the hot, dry smell of an attic long unopened. The unwelcome odors of death, rot, and decay were absent. Nathan's father, Ryota, had cleaned the house thoroughly before taking the family north. His fastidiousness was now paying dividends. Had he assumed that one day he and his family would return?

"Let me give you the tour," Nathan said.

John nodded indifferently.

They first went to the living room. The sofa and armchairs were positioned as Nathan remembered, all facing the television.

"We used to watch TV here," Nathan said. "And I used to play with my Samsung Æther."

"Samsung what?"

"Æther. It was a three-dimensional gaming system, my last Christmas present before the Desolation. Maybe by then you were already ..." Nathan still felt uncomfortable discussing the decade John had lost to a coma.

"Maybe," John muttered. "But games weren't my thing."

"Too busy playing football?"

"Something like that." A trace of a smile appeared on John's lips.

The next stop was the kitchen, which doubled as the dining area. A table draped with a dark blue cloth and surrounded by four wooden chairs stood in the room's center. Along the wall was a refrigerator, cracked open. Sunlight poured through a wide, two-paneled kitchen window, heavily streaked with water stains from snow and rain.

"We used to eat here as a family," Nathan said.

"Who did the cooking?"

"My mother and father were equally poor cooks." Nathan imagined his mother pulling a black-bottomed frozen pizza from the oven while the smoke alarm blared overhead. Attitudes towards food had changed much since then. These days preparing a meal required a person's full attention. Food was not to be wasted.

John poked his head into the refrigerator. "Empty," he muttered.

"What did you expect?" Nathan asked. Minneapolis' refrigerators were more likely to contain fungi, bacteria, or rats than edible food. Ryota had thoughtfully left the refrigerator door ajar to prevent mold.

"I heard McDonald's hamburgers and fries can survive for decades."

Nathan grimaced. "Even if they can I wouldn't eat them. If you really crave a burger and fries we can probably wrestle something up."

John shook his head. "It wouldn't be the same."

After briefly touring the other downstairs rooms, Nathan guided John up the stairs to his father's office and the family's bedrooms. He started with the bedroom at the far end of the hallway.

"This is my room," he said as he swept the door open. "Or maybe I should say it was my room?"

"Same difference," John offered. "So many books. It's like I'm back on Mallard Island."

"I wish I could've taken them all up north, but the Subaru was already overloaded."

John turned back into the hallway. Nathan lingered, taking in his bed with the Mega Man sheets, the Sakanachos figurine adorning his desk, his bookshelves lined with fantasy novels and manga, and the anime and video game posters taped to his walls. The kid who'd lived in this room had long since grown up.

He shut the door. Behind him, John was regarding a door in the middle of the hallway. A board was nailed over a hole near its handle.

John reached to open it.

"Don't," Nathan spit out, surprising even himself. "I'll try that one."

John let his arm drop. "Go ahead."

Nathan approached the door apprehensively. Could he turn that knob? Would the door open if he did? Closing his eyes tight, he reached out and twisted.

The knob didn't budge. Locked.

"This is the upstairs bathroom," he said, opening his eyes. "This is where ..."

"This is where?"

Nathan bit his lip. "This is where my mom died. After we buried her, my dad locked the door and threw away the key."

John stroked his chin thoughtfully. "Your father locked the door for a good reason. Let's move on."

Nathan nodded, moving down the hallway. After a brief glimpse into his parents' bedroom, he ushered John into his father's office. The office looked every bit the den of an overworked and underpaid university professor.

The curtains were closed, giving the room a cloistered feel. Hardcover textbooks and chemistry manuals lined the walls. File cabinets full of papers stood beside the windows. The room's centerpiece was an expansive work desk, topped with assorted papers, a plastic model of a water molecule, and a computer monitor.

"Come on," Nathan said, waving John in. "If we find anything useful in this house it'll be here."

He crossed the room and threw the curtains open, squinting into the afternoon sun that streamed through the window. He settled on closing the curtains halfway.

"You said your father was a chemistry professor?" John asked, inspecting the water molecule model he'd picked up from the desk.

"That's right." Nathan had been too young to fully understand his father's work, but he had a general idea. He imagined his father lecturing to students and working with test tubes. He used to wonder what sorts of enchanted potions his father could create by mixing different liquids. He now understood that chemistry was not magic.

Nathan eyed the monitor on the desk. This was where he'd hacked into his father's blog. If he could reread the blog again now, would he understand more? He recalled reading passages about himself, his mother, his sister, and the world at large, yet at the time he had been too young to comprehend all of his father's words.

Nathan knelt beside the desk. The black computer tower stood on the floor underneath. He pressed the power button.

Nothing happened.

Of course, he thought, realizing his stupidity. *No power.* Still, wasn't that how electronics had once worked, gadgets coming alive at the press of a button?

"I wouldn't expect there to be any power," John said, standing over Nathan.

Nathan pushed himself up from the floor, rising to his feet. "I didn't either. Just an old habit, I guess."

"Would the computer still work if it had a power source?"

Nathan furrowed his brow at the machine. "Hard to say. It'd depend on how well the individual components have held up. If we stumble across a solar panel or something like that I can give it another try."

"Sure." John grinned wryly. "Who knows? Maybe your dad knew something about the Northland Core."

"My dad working with the military?" Nathan shook his head. "I can't see it."

"Just joking," John said. "Say, look at this." He pointed to a spot on the desk.

Nathan leaned closer, his shadow stretching across the desk. "What about it?"

"The desk is covered in dust except for this rectangular area."

Nathan shifted so that his shadow didn't obstruct his view. He blinked in disbelief. Sure enough, there was a dust-free patch on the desk about the size of a notebook.

"Someone was here," John said. "And it wasn't long ago." He swiped a fingertip across the empty patch and held it up for Nathan to see. No dust.

"But who? And why?" Nathan raised an eyebrow.

John curled the fingers of his left hand into a loose fist. "We'll have to find out."

Chapter 6

January 17th, 2027
Post Status: Public

Quotes and photos on shared social media have reminded
me that today is Martin Luther King, Jr. Day.

It's easy to forget that Dr. King fought not only for
the rights of minorities, but for the rights of the
poor as well.

Poverty is a major problem. We talk about helping the
poor, only to turn a blind eye as we speed by the
shantytowns of homeless that have popped up on the
outskirts of our cities. Though the shantytown here in
Minneapolis is relatively small, on the fringes of
Chicago are tens of thousands living in squalor, their
numbers seeming to grow every time I drive down there
to visit my parents.

Is poverty a thing we can vanquish? Could MLK have
achieved the goals of his Poor People's Campaign if a
bullet hadn't struck him down?

That was nearly 60 years ago. There have been ups and
downs since then, yes, but the poor are now worse off
than ever.

I'm afraid to see what will happen if the situation
deteriorates further.

* * *

WHEN HE AWOKE the next morning, Nathan peered out the
window of his second floor bedroom. Dark charcoal clouds had
rolled in over the city, like a wool blanket smothering the
downtown skyline. The amorphous mass of gray swirled
around the colossal spire of Target Tower.

Nathan went downstairs. In the kitchen he discovered John had already prepared breakfast.

"What's on the menu?" he asked.

"A varmint I shot last night and a cabbage I found this morning."

"What kind of varmint?"

"The best kind."

Nathan frowned and cocked his head. "And where did you find cabbage?"

"There's a vegetable patch a few blocks over. Cabbage and potatoes. Looked like no one had tended it for a few weeks."

"I guess we're not the only ones in town."

"I guess not," John said. He gestured towards the back door with his thumb. "I made a fire pit in your backyard."

Nathan nodded. "You can do whatever you want back there. Weeds have overrun the lawn, anyway. Just let me know if you decide to do any interior redecorating."

"Don't count on it."

"Don't count on you asking, or don't count on you redecorating?"

John deflected the question with a shrug. He produced a pair of tin camping plates and divvied out two portions of meat and cabbage stew.

Taking a seat, Nathan noticed that the table cloth was now white. John must have replaced the old dark blue one. The redecoration had begun.

John handed Nathan a plate of stew. The stew meat was lean and pale — probably rabbit or squirrel, or maybe both. Only John knew for sure.

"What's the plan for today?" Nathan asked.

"We'll go look around the university," John said as he chewed. "See if we can dig up any information about the Northland Core or SPEAR."

"The university is big. We won't be able to explore it all in one day. We can start on the East Bank. Most of the physics and engineering buildings are there, I think. Later we can move on to the West Bank."

"And we can visit the Gaza Strip while we're at it," John said.

"Gaza Strip?" Nathan gave John a quizzical look. "Isn't that a place in the Middle East?"

John stared blankly across the table, his jaw working on a hunk of meat. Apparently he didn't intend to explain further.

Nathan quickly finished his stew. He pushed his plate to the middle of the table.

"I was thinking, while we're on campus we could stop by one of the libraries. We can research the city and determine other places where the Northland Core could be hidden."

"Good thinking." John stood up from the table and pushed in his chair. "You ready to set out?"

"I'd better take Mumford around back. He'll be less visible there. I don't know about you," Nathan said, narrowing his eyes at John, "but I wouldn't want anything to happen to Mumford while we're gone."

"Suit yourself," John said. "I'll meet you out front as soon as you're ready. Bring a gun and a raincoat."

* * *

Forty minutes later John and Nathan arrived at the edge of the university's East Bank campus. John wore a small backpack that held their rain jackets, a lamp, and other gear. His Colt Single Action Army revolver rode on his hip. Nathan carried only his Remington 870 12-gauge shotgun, strapped across his back.

"I didn't realize how many bars were here," Nathan said of Dinkytown, the quaint center of after-hours student life just north of the campus. "I thought university students spent all their time studying."

"Hardly," said John. Though he had forgone university to join the Marine Corps, enlisting hadn't precluded him from crashing a frat party or two. He never did figure out how students could get smashed on beer and liquor every night, year in and year out, and graduate with their livers intact.

Ahead stood a ten-foot-tall stone wall. It extended as far as John could see in either direction. Nathan led John to a gap in the wall, just wide enough to accommodate the two-lane road and the sidewalks that cut through it.

"Here we are," Nathan said with a melodramatic sweep of his arm. "The University of Minnesota, Twin Cities."

"Is there more than one University of Minnesota?" John asked.

"There were a few. Duluth had a campus, too. It's closed, of course, but the Republic of Minnesota has supposedly considered reopening it."

John gazed down the road that led deeper into the university grounds. In the United States he remembered, the value of a college degree had been plummeting by the year. Real skills, particularly those useful to the military, and connections to people in high places had far outvalued a diploma.

They continued along the uneven sidewalk, following a washed-out road that wound between classroom buildings. Most of the buildings were made of brick and stone. Granite arches embellished their facades. Fibrous ivy vines clung to the older buildings, many of which predated the First World War.

"Where are we going?" John asked.

"We should go to the campus mall. The most important buildings and offices are there."

They soon arrived at a field surrounded by untrimmed arbor vitae and dwarf cherry trees. What had once been a well-tended bluegrass carpet where students studied and lazed was now an unkempt confusion of goldenrod, asters, and prairie grasses.

"This is it — the mall." Nathan pointed to a building on the field's far side. "That's Smith Hall, where my dad worked."

"The chemistry building?"

Nathan nodded. "I doubt we'll find anything about the Northland Core there." He craned his neck, scanning the surrounding buildings. "The physics department was here, too, if I remember correctly. Buildings related to engineering would also be worth checking out. Let's take a look around."

They circled the mall, passing a couple of classroom halls before arriving at the Tate Laboratory of Physics. The entry facade was decorated with six stone pillars that rose to meet the roof. Behind the pillars were three sets of metal-framed doors.

"Let's go in," John said, climbing the stone staircase to the entrance.

Hairline fissures radiated throughout the windows set in the doors. Shards had broken loose, leaving behind jagged gaps. Aside from the doors and windows, however, the building's exterior had held up well. The centerpieces of the university had been built to last an eternity, and probably to withstand Soviet nuclear strikes, as well.

The building's interior was less impressive, emphasizing functionality over form. A dearth of windows left much of the entrance hall shrouded in darkness. The hall had a simple tile floor and plain, off-white walls. Opposite the entrance, doors opened into a lecture hall. Narrow corridors branched to the left and right.

"We need the lamp," John said.

Nathan rummaged through the pack on John's back. He extracted the lantern and a box of matches. John struck a match and lit the lantern. The flickering orange umbrella of light revealed a message scrawled across the wall: SPECIAL RELATIVITY IS DEAD. Rivulets of dried paint oozed down from the blotchy letters.

"That was Einstein's theory, right?" Nathan asked.

"I think so."

"Whoever wrote this message must have preferred quantum mechanics."

"I wouldn't know." John couldn't recall whether or not he'd taken a physics class in high school.

"I don't know much about physics either. Just bits and pieces." The halo of lantern light bobbed up and down as Nathan advanced. "Let's go check out the lecture hall."

John followed without protest.

The lecture hall was humongous, capable of seating over five hundred students. Only a blush of lantern light penetrated all the way to the lectern at the front of the room.

"I didn't know they could pack so many students into one room," Nathan said. He made his way down an aisle toward the lectern, passing through the ocean of seats.

John remained near the door. His surroundings grew dim as Nathan carried the lantern ahead.

"Aren't you coming?" Nathan called from halfway across the room.

"You go ahead," John replied.

Nathan stepped onto the podium. He circled behind the lectern and studied the papers atop it.

John waited in darkness. *Others have probably already combed through this building,* he thought. He wasn't the only one hunting for the Northland Core. His encounter with Gallagher on Mallard Island had made that clear. If the device were out in the open, someone would've found it long ago. He and Nathan needed to focus in on obscure locations, not obvious ones like this.

Nathan trudged back up the aisle toward John.

"Nothing down there," Nathan said. "Just some notes from an introductory physics lecture."

"Then let's move on." John pushed the exit door open, holding it for Nathan.

The two men explored the building, digging through the classrooms, offices, laboratories, and even the bathrooms. After an exhaustive search of the upper floors they descended into the basement. Dank hallways led to more labs and classrooms. Rounding a corner, John noticed a purple and yellow sign labeled "The Gopher Way." It pointed down a dark tunnel.

"What's the Gopher Way?" John asked.

"Minneapolis is freezing in winter. No one wants to walk outside. The Gopher Way is a complex of underground tunnels for getting from one building to the next. You want to check it out?"

"Maybe later. If we're going to move to another building I'd rather do it above ground. I want to get a better feel for the layout of this place."

"Then that's what we'll do," Nathan said.

Leaving the tunnel for another time, they proceeded back upstairs. As they drifted through the maze of hallways, moving closer to the front doors, John heard the unmistakable drumbeat of falling rain.

"Grab the rain coats out of my pack," he said.

Nathan obliged, fumbling around in the pack until he'd produced a black raincoat for John and a dark blue poncho for himself. John slipped into the black coat, which fit over both his backpack and revolver. Nathan's poncho similarly concealed the Remington shotgun strapped across his back. They stood beneath the protection of Tate Lab's stone overhang, staring into the curtain of rain.

"Where should we go next?" John asked.

"There's an engineering building somewhere around here," Nathan said. "We can go check it out."

John grunted his assent. They hurried along the edge of the campus mall, their eyes peeled for the engineering building. The rain spattered down into John's mouth and eyes. Though unpleasant, this summer squall was trivial compared to the painful blast of a Middle Eastern sandstorm. He was glad to have left his desert-hopping Marine lifestyle behind.

Nathan's fingers clasped John's forearm. "Over here," Nathan hissed, jerking John towards the row of shrubs that surrounded the mall.

"What?"

"Get down." Nathan released John's arm and dropped to one knee. He set the now snuffed-out lantern in the damp grass. "Over there." He pointed down the sidewalk.

John took a knee, feeling the chill of the rain-soaked grass through his Levis.

"Do you see it?" Nathan whispered.

John squinted. Through the rain, he had trouble seeing much of anything.

The object moved. A man in green clothes, perhaps? It was impossible to say for sure.

"I think it's a man," Nathan said.

"I think you're right." John rose to his feet. "We should go say hello."

Nathan gave him a look that urged caution. "Are you sure?"

"I'm sure." John gathered up the right side of his rain coat and tucked it under his belt, putting his Colt revolver within easy reach.

"Should I take out my shotgun?" Nathan asked.

"No, this should be enough. I don't want to scare our man away. Let's go."

They started toward the distant figure, unsure whether or not they'd already been spotted. They were fortunate that their black and blue raincoats blended into the day's overcast hues.

The figure wore a green rain jacket. What was he doing out here in the rain? And what was he doing in Minneapolis? No one would stay in this desolate city without good reason.

The figure craned his neck over his right shoulder. His eyes locked with John's. He stood frozen, gazing vacantly at John and Nathan. Suddenly he looked away and broke into a sprint.

"Come on!" John barked. He charged forward, his boots splashing through puddles.

Nathan soon pulled up alongside and steadily inched ahead. John rallied to keep pace, refusing to fall behind.

The fleeing man made a sharp left, disappearing behind a classroom building. John and Nathan reached the turn seconds later. John rounded the corner a half-step behind Nathan. Their target should've been just ahead, dashing down the sidewalk.

But he wasn't. He'd vanished.

John slowed to a jog. Nathan sprinted past, rushing full-steam down the sidewalk.

John trotted alongside the building, looking for doors, windows, or other nooks. He discovered an open window tucked behind a sprawling azalea bush. Easily accessible at ground level and wide enough for a man to climb through, the window was likely the key to the man's vanishing act.

John thrust himself through the window. Inside he found a classroom lined with rows of narrow tables that faced a black chalkboard. In the dim light he could make out one of those peculiar, elongated "S" symbols, written on the board in white chalk. Some kind of calculus formula.

John crossed the room towards the door. He'd never derived pleasure from mathematics. It had never been an integral part of his life.

He peered into the hallway. The unlit corridor was hopelessly dark. He could barely see the next door over, much less the end of the hall.

He cursed under his breath. Nathan had left their lantern by the physics building. By the time John returned with it their mystery man would be halfway to St. Paul.

As John was turning back into the classroom, he noticed another Gopher Way sign on the hallway's opposing wall. If the running man had gone down there, he could pop up to ground level from any number of places. No wonder they called it the Gopher Way.

John doubled back across the classroom, frowning disdainfully at the equation on the board before exiting through the window. The wind tugged at his shirtsleeves. Raindrops hurtled into his face as he stepped around the bush. He found Nathan waiting on the sidewalk.

"Lost him," Nathan sputtered, short of breath.

"Where did you go?"

"Straight down the sidewalk. I thought he might reappear further down the way." Nathan eyed the window behind the bush. "Find anything in there?"

"Only a math equation."

Nathan raised his eyebrows. "A math equation?"

John set off down the sidewalk. "Let's go back and reclaim our lantern before the rain ruins it."

"Oh!" Nathan perked up. "I almost forgot about it."

"I would've too, if it hadn't been too dark to see in there." John nodded sidelong at the building.

They retraced their path, soon arriving at the lantern. After picking it up they huddled underneath Tate Laboratory's overhang to escape the pounding wind and rain.

"Did you notice that guy's green rain jacket?" Nathan asked.

"What about it?"

"It was the same green that the men at Sawbill Lake and in Duluth wore."

John massaged his beard. Soaked with rain, it felt soft and smooth against his fingertips.

Was there a connection between this man, the men who'd kidnapped Nathan's sister at Sawbill Lake, and the two hoodlums he'd encountered at that bar in Duluth?

The possibility was too disturbing to simply dismiss.

Chapter 7

January 21st, 2027
Post Status: Public

On my drive home from work I saw a humongous LCD billboard advertising Pepsi SubZero, the new diet soft drink with "negative net calories."

Does anyone actually lose weight by drinking this stuff?

What a joke.

* * *

PLIP. PLIP. PLIP. PLIP.

Emiko awoke to a muffled palpitation, like the steady beat of a heart. She groggily rubbed the sleep from her tired eyes. On the ceiling she spied a dark circle. Droplets of water formed on it and lazily fell to the carpet below. She'd noticed the dark splotch before but had thought nothing of it. If she had realized it was a leak, she would've fixed it before the storm blew in.

The dull murmur of rain, now falling for the second straight day, was unrelenting. The storm made game scarce, the animals hunkering down to wait it out. Emiko hoped her dwindling cache of blueberries, wild carrots, and coyote meat would sustain her until the sky cleared.

Emiko curled up beneath her sheets and covered her ears with a pillow. As long as the rain continued she had little reason to get out of bed. More rest would do her good.

Plip. Plip. Plip. Plip.

She tossed and turned beneath the covers, searching for a comfortable position.

Plip. Plip. Plip. Plip.

With a groan of resignation, she tossed off the covers and hopped from bed. The insistent leak refused to let her sleep. She craned her neck back and scowled at the dark circle above.

The leak had pestered the wrong girl.

Emiko stomped out of the bedroom. She slipped into a pair of boots, put on a raincoat, and hurried down into the basement. She threaded her way through the dimly lit quagmire of cobwebs, dust bunnies, and mold. The tool she sought leaned against a concrete pillar.

An extendable ladder. Emiko hoisted it awkwardly with both hands, letting a portion of its weight rest on her right hip. Ladder in tow, she lumbered back through the basement, up the stairs, and into the backyard.

The storm had let up slightly. Emiko blinked to clear the mist from her eyes. Ominous gray clouds still swirled overhead, threatening to resume the downpour.

Emiko set one end of the ladder on the ground. She extended the ladder to its full length and rested the other end securely against the eaves. She scaled the rungs one by one, then scrambled onto the storm-slicked roof.

She crawled upward across the shingles. The light drizzle moistened her face; the breeze tugged at her long, black hair. Soon she reached the area above her bedroom. The source of the leak was readily apparent. A trio of shingles was missing, exposing the roof boards below.

The problem was clear. Now she had to resolve it. A hammer, a few nails, and a scrap of plywood to cover the hole would do the trick. She could find the materials in the basement.

She was scurrying back across the roof, eager to escape the dreary weather, when a shingle broke free and slipped out from beneath her foot. Losing traction, she tumbled towards the roof's edge.

She clawed and flailed, but it was no use. Rolling like a barrel she flew from the roof. Eyes to the sky, she plummeted to the ground.

Her ankle hit first. She screamed. Pain shot wildly through her back, legs, head, and neck.

Her chest constricted. She couldn't breathe. The angry sky glowered at her as she gulped for air. After what seemed like minutes her lungs finally recovered.

How long she lay there she couldn't say. The pain slowly receded from her neck, torso, and thighs until only a dull ache remained. The persistent touch of the rain was oddly soothing.

Could she move? She bent her knees, drawing in her legs one at a time. Slowly she sat upright. Though extremely sore, all of her muscles seemed to be working.

Planting her right leg, she attempted to push herself up. She yelped, collapsing onto her back, the ankle searing with pain.

Was it a sprain? A break? She didn't know.

She tried rising again, this time putting her weight on her left leg. Though tender and aching, her left calf and thigh supported her weight. She hopped to the back door on her good leg and stumbled into the house. A trail of mud formed behind her as she headed for the living room and flung herself onto the couch.

She gently removed the boot from her right foot and examined her ankle. It looked fine. She hoped that meant it wasn't broken.

Closer inspection revealed that the ankle had taken on a pinkish hue. Would it swell up soon? She had no idea. This was her first ankle injury. Her first serious injury of any kind.

What could she do? Ice was a common treatment for sprains, but there was no ice in summer.

She recalled her neighbor Cynthia instructing patients to elevate their injuries. Emiko slipped off her left boot and kicked her legs up on the couch's armrest. Soon the ankle started to numb over. She closed her eyes and drifted towards sleep, only dimly aware of the regular patter of droplets still leaking into the bedroom down the hallway.

Chapter 8

January 28th, 2027
Post Status: Public

President Hernandez gave his State of the Union address last night. I was hoping to write about it immediately afterwards, but then Emiko asked me to read her a bedtime story and I never made it back to my computer.

I should preface my thoughts by saying that although President Hernandez was not my choice in the 2024 election, I do sympathize with the position he's in.

His speech left me unimpressed. A few choice quotes:

"Hardship is a bridge on the road to prosperity."
"Hope for tomorrow lies within the seeds we plant today."
"This too shall pass."

All told, the speech was short on content and long on meaningless sound bites … which isn't to say there wasn't meaning to be found. The last quote is particularly telling: Mr. Hernandez feels just as helpless as the rest of us.

Because, really, what can he do? Unless he discovers a way to replenish the Ogallala Aquifer, I don't see how he can pull us out of this mess.

Of course, he said nothing of the mass of refugees flooding north. To acknowledge them would be to admit that there's a problem. That would be political suicide. But how can you fix a problem that you won't even discuss?

Mr. Hernandez must feel just as stymied as the rest of us. Perhaps next year, instead of giving a proper speech, he'll just stand on his podium and lead the citizens of this great nation in performing a rain dance.

* * *

UNRELENTING RAIN. Impenetrable clouds. Weed-ridden streets.

Once renowned for its hospitality, Minneapolis was extending no such warm greeting to its newest guest.

Aristotle journeyed toward the heart of Minneapolis along overgrown sidewalks and pock-marked streets. Raindrops pelted her raincoat. Water seeped through her jeans.

This was her first visit to the city. She was quickly realizing it was bigger than she'd thought. While it couldn't compare to Toronto — few cities could — clearly Minneapolis had once been a metropolis in its own right.

Once but no longer.

And there lay the key difference. While Toronto was recovering nicely, Minneapolis had been left to the whims of nature. Aristotle had yet to encounter a single human being.

What the city lacked in human life it made up for in human death. Aristotle knew she needed only to go explore the abandoned buildings to find the Desolation's fallen fruit. This was a city-sized graveyard, filled beyond capacity.

She was here for one reason: To find the General. Captain Griswold of the Toronto PD had told her that the General's base was here. Griswold's brief radio transmission had explained neither why he knew this, nor where within the city the General hid. All Aristotle knew was that Minneapolis was the place to look.

So she was here. This was what her life had come to — listening to hazy tips from her old boss and hunting mysterious men in dead cities.

She reached downtown, where banks, department stores, bars, clubs, offices, and apartments had once coexisted. Now only the concrete and rebar shells of these once thriving venues remained — and sometimes not even that much.

The wreckage of a Macy's department store stood before her. Significant chunks of the outer wall were simply missing, the stones chipped and cracked at strange angles. Waterfalls of rain spilled from the roof into what remained of the building's interior.

The Target shopping center across the street had fared little better. Sections of the roof had been twisted into impossible shapes, like grotesque steel fingers clawing at the blackened sky. The entire building looked as though it had just come out of a giant blender.

What had caused this destruction? Aristotle's first hypothesis was a nuclear strike, but she quickly ruled it out. The pattern of damage didn't fit the profile of a nuclear detonation. An ordinary bomb was another possibility, but in that case she would've seen a clear epicenter. Instead the destruction seemed to be chaotic and random, as though a whirling dervish had torn through the city.

A whirling dervish? That was it. Sometime after the Desolation a tornado must've blitzed through downtown, ripping up buildings and strewing them about like a toddler kicking towers of Lego bricks.

Aristotle kept moving. Leaving the tornado's brief but destructive path behind her, she soon came to what she recognized as Vikings Stadium. The stadium was a Euclidean nightmare, refusing to assume a describable shape. It had seven sides of various lengths, all covered by a roof of glass. An immense protrusion, like a rhinoceros' horn cast in concrete and steel, jutted out above the entrance. Etched upon the giant overhang was the face of a golden-haired Viking overlaying a map of Minnesota.

The stadium was the former home of the Minnesota Vikings, a team in the National Football League. Though Aristotle was no sports fan, even she knew of the unbreakable grip the NFL had once had over America's television audience. Despite all the dangers, concussions, injuries, scandals, and lawsuits, the NFL had remained the continent's most popular sports league until the very end.

Man's thirst for violence ran deep. The stadium, a temple of condoned violence, served as a reminder of this fact. Though she had no proof, Aristotle suspected that it was this same thirst, latent in the veins of mankind, that had led men to engineer and unleash an incurable virus of apocalyptic proportions. Indeed, for what purpose would people create the Desolation virus, if not to fulfill some deep-seated urge to inflict suffering?

Since the Desolation the world had become a wild and lawless place. Yet strangely enough, the total sum of violence had fallen sharply. There was no more war. There were no more world-rending bombs. Though often swift and brutal, post-Desolation violence rarely threatened more than a handful of men or women at a time. War and savagery, no longer institutionalized, were now individual pursuits.

Individuals could be dealt with. Aristotle had dealt with her fair share.

The rain continued to fall. The clouds overhead continued to churn like black buttermilk. Aristotle pressed on.

Somewhere in Minneapolis the General awaited.

Chapter 9

February 3rd, 2027
Post Status: Public

Emiko was bored this evening, so I walked to the convenience store and bought her a box of crayons. When I returned, before I'd even taken off my shoes she snatched the box from me and went into a drawing frenzy!

(At least she was considerate enough to draw on printer paper rather than the wallpaper.)

If I can recall how to use the portascanner, I'll consider uploading one of her lovely creations.

* * *

A MAN NEEDED take only one step inside a mess hall to understand the name's origin. Dimly lit and scuzzy, the Restoration Army's cafeteria was as foul as the pond scum clinging to the bottom of a canoe.

Cooks dished out slop from stain-ridden aluminum tubs. A pile of potato peels amassed in the kitchen's back corner. Hungry soldiers stood in line, holding breadcrumb-specked trays as they waited for servings of greasy mystery meat.

Ramses sat in the far corner of the mess hall, apart from the commotion, sipping a lukewarm cup of herbal tea. Rain pounded the windows, which were covered with translucent black plastic to hide the activity within. Lanterns strung above provided illumination.

Just as the barracks above had once been a student dormitory, this mess hall had once been a university cafeteria. Who would've thought that a university dormitory could serve so well as soldiers' quarters?

A few tables over from Ramses, soldiers spun tales of big guns, loose women, and wicked hangovers. All of it was banal, uninspired drivel. Weren't there more pressing concerns at hand?

Ramses finished his tea and clasped both hands around the cup. Tapping the empty cup with his fingers, he contemplated an issue most important.

Over a week had passed since anyone had last seen the General. Already rumors were spreading around the barracks: *The General was sick. Bedridden. Dead?* The most outrageous theory suggested that he was being held captive in Stillwater Prison, naked and starving, reaching out from his cell to beg for food.

The rumors were ludicrous. The General would never succumb so easily. Of that much Ramses was certain.

The mess hall's rear door opened and slammed shut. A moment later Lieutenant Thurston Prince rounded the corner.

Lieutenant Prince had taken charge of the army in the General's absence, though whether this was by design or chance no one could say. Indeed, one prevalent rumor was that Prince himself had locked the General in Stillwater Prison.

Prince walked towards the center of the room, riveting the attention of the surrounding men. Though he wore the Restoration Army's standard green fatigues, in recent days he had taken to adorning his head with an ocean blue beret.

The beret seemed a peculiar choice. None in the army wore hats unless circumstances called for helmets or other protective headgear. Like a jewel-laden crown the striking blue beret set Prince apart. Some had even taken to calling him the "Prince of Minneapolis." While Ramses was reluctant to engage in such tomfoolery, he had to admit the nickname was a stupendous fit.

Prince halted in the middle of the room. His presence commanded every eye in the mess hall. He cleared his throat.

"I'm looking for two men: Private Smith and Private Redding, recently returned from Duluth."

Heads turned as a chorus of whispers filled the room. Shortly, two men rose from the murmuring mass. Ramses recognized them as Smitty and Leonard, a pair who had just returned from looking for oil and recruiting new soldiers up north. Smitty was as big as a black bear, looming larger than even Lieutenant Prince. Leonard was thin as a fishing pole and had a gap between his front teeth wide enough to hold a cigarette. Supposedly they'd driven a car all the way down from Canada, only to have it run out of gas just on the outskirts of Minneapolis.

"Present, sir," Smitty said, standing at attention.

"You're Private Smith?" asked Prince.

"Correct, sir."

"And you must be Private Redding," Prince said, addressing Leonard.

"That's right, sir."

"Follow me. I have a special task for the two of you." Prince turned on his heel, expecting the two men to follow immediately.

Smitty and Leonard glanced at each other, then down at their trays full of food. Leonard gestured at his meal, silently pleading with Smitty. Smitty shook his head, mouthing "*No!*" as he pointed at the departing lieutenant. Leaving his tray, Smitty took off after the lieutenant. Leonard, after ruefully saluting his food, hurried behind.

The room remained silent as the three men crossed the mess hall and vanished around the corner. Soon the thud of the shutting door resounded throughout the room. Gradually, the messing soldiers returned to their meals and resumed their stale conversations of beer and women.

Ramses rested his elbows on the table, listening to the incessant rain as he glared at the bottom of his empty cup. Why had Prince chosen those two men for this special task? And why was Prince delegating orders to begin with?

Ramses had done everything the General had asked. He had confronted John Osborne and lived to tell about it. He had dutifully manned the radio room despite the excruciating boredom of the task. He had even taken charge of establishing the Restoration Army's first mounted unit!

No matter what he did, he never made any headway up the dual ladders of rank and respect. Worse yet, now that the General was gone there was no one left to ensure that his developing talents would be recognized and employed to their utmost.

Was there anything he could do to make himself more useful? Ramses recalled that, before going AWOL, the General had been expecting Osborne to come to Minneapolis. He'd even said he wanted Ramses to help usher Osborne into the city.

Was Osborne already here? And if so, was anyone doing anything about it?

Perhaps this was Ramses' chance to prove his worth.

Chapter 10

February 7th, 2027
Post Status: Public

Those hapless Vikings. They never fail to let me down.

We just got back from watching Super Bowl LXI at the Thompsons'.

Final score: New York Jets - 28, Minnesota Vikings - 27

The Vikings scored with two minutes left to take a six-point lead. Their first Super Bowl title was only seconds away. Not to be outdone, however, Jets quarterback Dylan White led a spectacular 80-yard drive, throwing the game-tying touchdown pass as time expired. Their kicker nailed the extra point and the Jets snatched a Super Bowl victory — their first since the days of Joe Namath.

The Vikes remain ringless. Even the lowly Lions won the big one a few years back! We Vikings fans just can't catch a break.

That said, I did enjoy the game, and I'm glad the NFL managed to solve its bankruptcy woes. For a while there I thought pro football was doomed. Those concussion lawsuits had the league on its knees. The switch to soft-shelled helmets with thick foam padding was a game changer, both for the league's finances and for the sport itself.

* * *

NOW FALLING FOR a third day, the rain refused to stop. Emiko remained on the living room couch, staring up at the white plaster ceiling and listening to the murmur of raindrops. The roof and walls kept her warm and dry, but how long would their protection last? With the way her luck was running, she expected the entire house would collapse around her any time now.

She flipped onto her side, facing the seat cushions. She was being over-dramatic. Still, her ankle was as swollen as a chipmunk's cheeks and her stomach was as empty as the Ogallala Aquifer. Maybe her dark thoughts were justified.

Hardship and tragedy had visited her before. She'd lost her mom to the Desolation virus. She'd lost her dad to cancer. She'd been kidnapped by a band of fearsome men. But never had she found herself physically incapable of performing the simplest of tasks. Right now she couldn't even walk properly. With no legs she had no hope.

Would she die here alone? Would she starve to death before her ankle recovered? What had made her think that she could come down to Minneapolis and survive on her own? Now more than ever, she recognized the value of companionship. She needed a Beard or a Nathan, a Pierre or a Cynthia, to help her through rough patches like these.

Her stomach churned, pining at the thought of Cynthia's pork bone soup. On a rainy day like today there was nothing more delicious than a bowl of that hearty broth. But pork bone soup wasn't to be served. Beard and Nathan weren't rushing to her rescue. As much as Emiko could've used the help, as much as she needed it, she would have no one to nurse her through this difficultly. Her fate depended solely on the health of her ankle.

Something salty, warm, and wet trickled from her eyes. The flow quickly grew into a raging flood, the likes of which not even the thickest of walls or sturdiest of roofs could've protected her from.

Chapter 11

February 14th, 2027
Post Status: Private

I don't have much time. I'll make this quick. Please excuse any typos. Although this is private, so really only my sober future self can blame me for any mistakes. Ha!

As you know today is Valentine's Day. Here in Minneapolis we're in the middle of a raging snowstorm. Terrible road conditions. A perfect excuse to not have a Valentine's Day gift, right?

Anyway, after spending most of the day locked in my office, I came downstairs to find salad and a bottle of Merlot already on the kitchen table. Danielle was standing over the stove, putting the finishing touches on beef medallions and mushrooms. It was just the two of us; Danielle had asked the neighbors to look after Emiko and Nathan for a few hours.

After I helped my wife set the table, we sat down to eat. The beef was fabulous. The best I've had in some time. Good wine, too.

But the best part was that all through dinner, Danielle had this look on her face, like she expected me to initiate something. Finally she couldn't take it anymore — she stepped out of the kitchen and returned a minute later with her gifts for me: a Gophers baseball cap and a black silk tie.

That's when I told her that I'd meant to buy her a gift but hadn't been able to, thanks to the blizzard. I also suggested that in Japanese culture men don't buy gifts for women on Valentine's Day. (True story!

Never mind that we don't live in Japan and that my parents' attempts to instill me with Japanese culture failed spectacularly …)

Danielle stared at me with utter disappointment. She stood up and flew from the kitchen.

The trap was set.

I waited a few minutes and then followed her out. I found her sitting on the couch in the living room and sat down next to her. I kept a solemn expression, like I understood what I'd done wrong and was contemplating my apology.

I put my hand on her leg, then took the jewelry case from a pocket and set it on her lap. She didn't understand at first, but when she realized what it was, she gave that "you sly devil" look.

(I'm lucky Danielle is so quick to forgive.)

She eagerly flipped the case open and pulled out the necklace inside, which I'd in fact bought weeks ago. As she examined it, I explained that the pendant held four birthstones:

- Aquamarine for Emiko
- Tanzanite for Nathan
- Peridot for her
- and Opal for myself

Certainly it was the most thoughtful gift I'd given her in quite some time.

Needless to say, now the bottle of wine is empty, the kids are still gone for another hour or two, and I just heard Danielle finish taking her shower. I'd better go!

* * *

WHEN THE DOWNPOUR finally ended, Nathan and John were no closer to finding the Northland Core than when it had begun.

After hopping out of bed and putting on a black t-shirt and blue jeans, Nathan went down to the kitchen. John was cooking breakfast over a propane stove they'd found in the basement. It smelled like more meat.

"Morning, John," Nathan said.

John grunted indistinctly in reply.

With a yawn, Nathan pushed back door open and stepped out to visit Mumford. He treaded carefully through the high grass, paying heed to avoid the landmine-like tvapa pies that Mumford frequently deposited.

Mumford was chomping away at the backyard's grass and weeds. Nathan scratched the docile beast between its moose-like antlers. A simple creature, the tvapa was content as long as he had enough to eat.

Nathan turned to go back inside, his left boot narrowly avoiding a fresh glob of tvapa excrement. Maybe there was a hint of truth to John's tvapa conspiracy theories.

Nathan smirked and shook his head. Though John's influence had rubbed off on him, there were matters on which their thinking diverged.

Their strategy for finding the Northland Core was one such matter. So far they'd spent most of their time scouring the university. Though they'd failed to find anything, Nathan still believed the U of M was the core's most likely hiding place.

His reasons were numerous. Many of the school's professors had fostered ties with the Pentagon. Furthermore, the man in the green jacket had clearly not been out on a pleasure stroll. Above all, however, Nathan simply had a nagging suspicion that the Northland Core was there. Irrational and inexplicable, the hunch was something Nathan himself couldn't understand, much less communicate to John.

John's frustration was growing evident. He was eager to take the search in a new direction. After consulting a map from one of the university libraries, he and Nathan had agreed that today they would scope out the offices of MinnePower, the utility that had managed the electricity needs of the entire metropolitan area.

On its face, MinnePower seemed an obvious choice. The Northland Core was a power source. Power companies dealt with power sources. By that logic, MinnePower should've at least known about the Northland Core.

On the other hand, utility companies and Pentagon research seemed unlikely bedfellows. Nathan doubted MinnePower had contributed to developing the Northland Core.

That said, it was John's life hanging in the balance, not Nathan's. Unless Nathan could verbalize his attraction to the university, he couldn't rightly oppose John's decision to expand the scope of their search.

Nathan reentered the kitchen to find breakfast ready. "Smells good," he said, taking a seat at the table.

"Meat and potatoes always smell good," John said. With a serving fork, he dished half the meat in the pan onto Nathan's plate.

Nathan attacked the meal. Though the meat had the taste and texture of venison, he couldn't say what it was for sure. When they were both finished Nathan got up from the table.

"Are you ready to head out?" he asked.

"Give me a minute. I left my gun and the map upstairs," John said.

"Could you grab my gun, too? It's beside my bed. I'll take care of clearing the table."

"It's a deal." John turned and left the kitchen.

Nathan stacked the plates and silverware in the sink. Though the house didn't have running water, force of habit dictated that he put them there. Maybe one day these old habits would again be rewarded. Today was not that day.

John came back down with his Colt at his hip and Nathan's Remington 870 in his hands. Nathan took the shotgun and slung it across his back.

"I'm ready," he said.

"Then let's go." John tipped his head towards the front door.

Outside, robins chirped overhead. Trekking through the city was more pleasant now that the clouds had broken and the rain had stopped. Nathan and John soon arrived in Dinkytown, the bar and restaurant district just north of campus.

Now seventeen, Nathan was almost old enough to be a university freshman. He could've been a student sipping on a hot cup of coffee in one of these cafes. If not for the Desolation ...

As they rounded the corner of a derelict bar John stopped abruptly. Offering no explanation, John clutched Nathan's arm and yanked him into bar's recessed entryway, a trapezoidal nook with a door set between two angled walls.

John leaned over to spy down the sidewalk. He quickly pulled his head back. "Two men in green are headed our way."

"Green? That can't be a coincidence."

John nodded. "They're still far off. I can't say if they spotted us or not. Let's wait and see what they do." He pulled his revolver from its holster.

Following John's cue, Nathan readied his shotgun. Though he didn't have much appetite for violence, it was best to be prepared.

John pressed his back against the wall, holding his pistol at the very edge of their cover. Nathan took a knee. The lower vantage point would make it easier to shoot around John, if it came to that.

John stole another glimpse around the wall.

"You've gotta be kidding me," he muttered.

"What?" Nathan whispered.

"A couple of old friends are coming to pay us a visit."

"Old friends?"

"You like riddles, right?"

Nathan frowned. "Only when they lead to buried treasure."

"Here's a hint: They drive a black Honda."

"John, that's not a riddle, that's ..." Nathan's mouth gaped open. Those two men? They were here?

John grinned darkly. "My thoughts exactly."

"So, what's the plan?"

"Check that door."

Nathan stood up and pulled the door's handle. The hinges creaked as it opened.

"It's unlocked," he said.

"In that case —"

A bullet slammed into the building, breaking loose a chunk of concrete. The chunk shattered on the sidewalk, throwing up a cloud of chalky white dust.

"Get inside!" John barked.

Nathan flung the door open and both men ducked inside.

"I think they recognized us," John said dryly.

"You *think* they recognized us?" Nathan exclaimed. "What now?"

"We'll split up and take cover. Find a place where you can watch my back. I'll do the same for you."

Nathan nodded. "They might try to come in another entrance."

"I know," John said as he dashed off.

The bar had two floors. A serving counter ran along the first floor's back wall. Two dead and decaying bodies, surrounded by empty liquor bottles, were slumped over the counter. There was no time to consider how they'd met their ends.

A table topped with playing cards and empty beer mugs occupied one corner. More chairs and tables filled out the rest of the space. Sunlight streamed in through windows installed high above, just below where the wall met the ceiling. A flight of stairs led up to the second floor, a railed loft.

John flew up the stairs. Nathan quickly scanned the first floor once more before heading up after him. The higher ground would work to their advantage.

"Decided to follow me, huh?" John said when Nathan reached the top of the stairs.

"Great minds think alike."

John looked over the loft's railing at the floor below. "What about ordinary minds?"

Nathan had no answer for that.

The second floor was also furnished with a serving counter. He ran behind the counter and fell to one knee. Tall enough to conceal his kneeling body, it was as good a hiding as he was likely to find.

Liquor bottles littered the counter, lined the rail beneath it, and cluttered the shelves behind it. All were dry. Booze went fast when faced with the world's end.

Where had John gone? Nathan adjusted his grip on his shotgun and poked his head over the counter. Among the obligatory tables and chairs he spotted a pool table and a pair of dartboards. Two narrow corridors presumably led to other rooms. Beyond the balcony's railing he could see a portion of the first floor, including the front door.

John raced into the room from one of the corridors. His eyes darted back and forth.

"John," Nathan hissed. "Over here."

John met Nathan's eye and nodded. He ran up to the counter and swung over it, his boots making surprisingly little sound as he landed. John was more acrobatic than his gruff, lumberjack-like appearance suggested.

"Glad you could join me," Nathan said

"We have trouble," John said, taking a knee.

"What?"

"This pub is a terrible place to defend. I've seen at least three entrances and there could be more. We should get out of here."

"Okay. Which exit?"

"Follow me." John kept low as he moved toward the end of the counter, his revolver at the ready.

The whoosh and thud of a door opening and closing came from downstairs. John raised a finger to his lips.

Their pursuers were here.

Nathan crawled along the space behind the counter until John signaled for him to stop. "Too late," he mouthed, shaking his head.

Nathan exhaled nervously through his nose. He clung to his shotgun. What could they do now?

Like a whooping crane gracefully lifting its head, John rose to his feet. He held his revolver beside face, inching upward until his eyes were just high enough to peep over the counter.

He quickly ducked back down. "The man downstairs has a shotgun," he whispered.

"I saw you up there," the man downstairs shouted. "Why don't you just give yourself up before this gets ugly?" Nathan recognized the voice. It was the bigger and broader of the two men.

"I don't know where the other guy is," John said into Nathan's ear. "I'm going to make some noise, but you need to stay quiet. They don't know you're behind this counter with me."

John pulled away and looked Nathan in the eye, seeking acknowledgment. Nathan gave a firm nod.

"Still sore about losing that game of darts?" John called back. "Come to think of it, you never did pay me my winnings."

The man spit loudly. "There's nothing I'd like better than to finish what I started in Duluth. But the game has changed. I have orders to bring you in alive."

"Is that right? I bet you're hoping I'll just give myself up?"

"It would make this easier."

We could surrender, Nathan thought, *but surrender isn't John's style.* Surrender didn't appeal to Nathan, either. They would get out of this jam. They always did.

"Come out with your hands up before I get angry," the man shouted. "And tell your little friend to come out of his hiding place, too."

John pointed at Nathan, then toward the closed end of the counter. Nathan nodded in understanding. John wanted him to stick tight to that end. There his back would be covered and he could gun down anyone who approached John. He crawled over and pressed himself up against the counter's inner wall. After checking that his shotgun's safety was off, he raised the butt of the gun to his shoulder.

John clambered in the opposite direction, moving for the counter's opening. From there he'd have a chance to get a clean shot at the man below. At least that's what Nathan assumed he was planning.

"Do you think I'm joking around?" the man bellowed from below. "Things are just going to get worse for you, Osborne. I don't care what kind of condition I drag you back in, as long as you're breathing. Surrender now and I guarantee we won't hurt you or your pal."

Crouching, John contorted his body around the counter's opening and fired a shot from his revolver. He quickly retreated and cursed under his breath.

"I'm not playing around, Osborne. Let me show you."

With a thunderous crack, a volley of buckshot ravaged the empty bottles on the counter. Nathan covered his head and closed his eyes as shards of glass rained down.

The explosion of shattering bottles gave way to gasps of agony. Nathan's eyes sprung.

John was clutching his leg. He was hit. But how?

The bottles, Nathan realized. They were like shrapnel. He cringed at the thought.

John was right. This position was indefensible. They had to move. Somewhere. Anywhere. Now.

A door slammed nearby. More men, more trouble. Nathan needed to know more. Clutching his shotgun, he cautiously rose to peer above the counter.

"No!" John mouthed. He jabbed his finger at the floor, urging Nathan to stay down, before grunting in pain and reaching for his wounded leg.

Nathan's eyes cleared the counter. He looked ahead, down at the first floor. The big man was there, his shotgun trained at the floor above. He didn't seem to have noticed Nathan.

"There are two of 'em back here," a second voice cried out. Nathan's head snapped to the right. Just across the counter stood the other man, tall and skinny.

The thin man flashed a toothy grin. He had a rifle in his hands. "Hey there, buddy. Remember me? Because I sure as the stink of a skunk remember you."

Nathan dropped back to the floor. A bullet whizzed overhead. He squeezed himself tight against the counter, his breaths raspy and shallow. Had John seen the second man there? Was that why he'd wanted Nathan to stay low?

Nathan was pinned down and John was wounded. Was it time to surrender?

"The General said we could take out the scrawny one, right?" the skinny man called to his partner downstairs.

"He said we could kill the Asian twerp and beat Osborne half to death if they didn't surrender. Do you think they're gonna surrender?"

"Don't look like it to me," the skinny man said cheerily.

Nathan gulped, looking to John. Though grimacing in pain, John had picked up his revolver and was taking aim.

"I can't see him," John growled. "He might be circling around to get a clear shot at you."

Nathan pressed the shotgun's stock to his shoulder and aimed above the counter. Where would the thin man pop up? Nathan would have to aim and fire as soon as the man showed his face. Were his reflexes up to the task?

"Keep steady," John said. "Breathe."

A bead of sweat rolled down Nathan's forehead. *Why would they kill me but not John?* he wondered.

It was the arm. They wanted John's arm. But why? What could they do with an arm?

A chill spread across Nathan's skin. He'd been shot at too many times. He just wanted all this violence and killing to end.

He heard a shot. His eyes darted back and forth. The skinny man had yet to appear.

There was a heavy thud downstairs. A body hitting the floor? But who?

"Smitty? Smitty? What the hell!" The thin man materialized on the opposite side of the counter. His rifle was drawn, but his attention was no longer on Nathan.

He screamed at a presence unseen: "Why the hell did you —?"

Nathan didn't think. His sights found the man. His finger pulled the trigger.

Fire burst out from the shotgun's muzzle. A skull-cracking explosion rang in Nathan's ears. Blood squirted from the man's head, splattering down onto John below. His limp body fell with a thump that reverberated through the floorboards.

Nathan stared blankly at the space where the man had stood.

He was safe. Or was he? He didn't understand what had happened. He'd gunned down one guy. Who had taken care of the other?

Footsteps approached from behind. John was looking over Nathan's head, above the counter.

"Looks like you boys were in a bit of trouble."

"You could say that," John replied, sounding unsure of himself as he studied the newcomer's face.

"Who is it, John?" Nathan blurted out, his blood still threatening to rupture his veins.

John's expression softened. He set down his revolver and put a hand on his wounded leg. "It's the last person I would've expected to meet in Minneapolis."

Chapter 12

February 16th, 2027
Post Status: Public

Today I attended a special lecture by Professor Kang, a friend from the biology department. The presentation was about genetically-modifying common working animals to thrive in different environments.

I agree with the project's rationale. Presently, making the north habitable requires considerable amounts of energy. As fossil fuels become scarce, lower-energy alternatives could become essential to our continued prosperity.

For instance, Dr. Kang notes that much of the developing world employs oxen for labor-intensive tasks. Oxen are very hardy, but they aren't particularly suited to cold temperatures. The solution? Dr. Kang proposes we isolate the genes that allow our furry, antlered friend, the moose, to survive Minnesota climes and insert them into the oxen's genetic code.

The project is still in its infancy. Although the idea is sound, I fear it will attract little interest until it's too late. By the time our cars stop running we won't have any energy left for bio-research.

My only other qualm? Dr. Kang should reconsider the name. "Taiga-Vegetation-Adapted Pack Animal" is a mouthful!

* * *

JOHN AND COLONEL KENNEDY STEARNS went way back. Stearns had been one of John's superiors in the Marine Corps. When John had joined the service, Stearns had been there to train him, to teach him, and to act as a mentor. Stearns had taken the foolish and headstrong youth known as John Osborne and molded him into the man he was today — confident, wise ... and maybe still a bit headstrong.

Their partnership had continued for many years, during which time Stearns had guided John and company through countless missions. In fact, it was Stearns who'd helmed that final sortie in Egypt, the one that had cost John his arm.

With each passing month, John's memories of his time as a marine grew more distant. Now, with Colonel Stearns standing before him, those memories surged back.

"Osborne?" the colonel said. "John Osborne? Is that really you?"

"It's me, sir," John said.

"Christ, with that beard I hardly recognized you!"

"I could say the same to you, Colonel." Indeed, the colonel had grown a well-tended beard of his own. Though shorter than John's and more gray than black, Stearns' beard lent him an air of righteous dignity.

"Just Stearns is alright. Hell, call me Kennedy if you like. We aren't in the service anymore."

Stearns paced around the outer edge of the counter toward John. Though his cheeks had sagged slightly and lines stretched across his brow, he still looked trim, fit, and ready for action. Streaks of black among his short silver hair offered a hint of youthfulness. He wore a faded blue button-up shirt. In his right hand he held a Desert Eagle semi-automatic.

"He was your colonel in the Marines?" Nathan asked, tilting his head back to get a clear look at Stearns.

"He sure was."

John realized he sounded like a schoolboy or a fresh recruit, but how could he not? It wasn't every day an admired old acquaintance emerged from the world's ruins.

"Can you stand up, John?" asked Stearns, taking a knee.

"I'm not sure." Seeing the colonel, John had nearly forgotten about the wound to his thigh. "I think there's a piece of glass in my thigh."

"Let's get you out from behind this counter and have a closer look." Stearns turned to Nathan. "Would you mind giving me a hand, son?"

With a nod, Nathan hopped to his feet.

"Let's haul him over to that table," said Stearns, pointing. He and Nathan took John by the shoulders and gently pulled him across the ground.

"What's your name, son?" Stearns asked.

"Nathan." Always wary of strangers, Nathan spoke tentatively, much like when he'd first met John.

Stearns and Nathan laid John's back against a heavy wooden chair. Stearns undid John's belt and slid his shredded jeans down to expose the wound. A credit card-sized chunk of glass jutted out from John's thigh.

"Looks nasty, but I think we can pull it out of there," said Stearns. "First, though ..." He stood up and approached the dead body beside the counter. That one, Nathan's kill, had been Leonard. The other man, on the first floor, had been Smitty. Not that names mattered in death.

Stearns knelt and ripped off the lifeless man's shirt sleeves. "These look clean," he said, returning to John's side. "We can use one as a cloth and the other as a bandage."

"That's quick thinking," John said.

"No one lasts very long on their own without it." Stearns smiled warmly.

"What about disinfectant?" Nathan asked.

Stearns draped the two sleeves over John's shins. He reached to his hip and produced a chrome flask. After twisting off the cap, he raised it to his lips and took a swig.

"God, that hits the spot. Whiskey. The only medicine a man needs," he said, smacking his lips. "Good for disinfecting wounds, cleaning guns, and for taking a load off." He handed the flask and a piece of cloth to Nathan. "Alright, son. Put a little whiskey on that cloth. After I extract the glass, I want you to gently dab the wound. Got it?"

Nathan nodded.

Stearns wrapped the remaining piece of cloth around his palm.

"I didn't know you were a drinker," John said.

"I suppose there were a lot of things you didn't know," Stearns replied. "Though you're right. I wasn't much of a drinker back then. Watching the world disintegrate changes a man."

John ran his hand across the hairs of his bionic arm. The Desolation had changed everything and everyone. He had never imagined Stearns sporting a shirt, a pair of jeans, and a beard. Especially the beard.

"This will hurt," Stearns said, his cloth-wrapped hand hovering over the embedded glass shard. "I'd consider gritting my teeth."

"I can take the pain," John said. He'd already lost an entire arm. This would be nothing in comparison.

Stearns grasped the splinter of glass and quickly but steadily pulled it free. John grunted reflexively. The pain passed in an instant.

Stearns examined the glass shard before tossing it over his head. It landed behind the counter with a clink.

The wound seeped crimson. Nathan dabbed it with the alcohol-soaked cloth. Though the whiskey burned, John refused to give the pain a voice.

"That should do the trick," Stearns said. He took his cloth and wrapped it around John's thigh like a bandage. "This will do for now. The wound was clean and the bleeding doesn't look serious, but we may want to stitch you up when we get a chance."

A silence enveloped the group. Stearns and Nathan seemed unsure how to address each other. John wanted nothing but a moment's rest.

He couldn't rest long. The Northland Core was waiting. With an injury limiting his mobility, finding the core would be difficult. He'd have to entrust Nathan to lead the search.

Maybe he would ask Stearns for help, too. Would the old colonel be willing to lend a hand? It was unclear what Stearns was doing in Minneapolis.

"Stearns," John said.

"Yeah?"

"We're holed up in a house not far from here. Could you help Nathan take me there?"

"Of course. It goes without saying. Just give me a moment to get my backpack. I dropped it before I rushed in."

"I appreciate it."

Stearns grinned. "Did you think I'd just abandon one of my best men, wounded on the battlefield?"

Chapter 13

February 18th, 2027
Post Status: Public

Danielle and I took the kids to Target Tower today.

The view was spectacular! We could see so much of the city. Nathan and Emiko had fun looking for our house among the stretches of suburbia below. And I could've sworn I saw the St. Croix River and Wisconsin in the distance …

We went up the tower late in the afternoon and stuck around to watch the sunset. It was a treat to watch the shadows grow longer and longer, before finally they engulfed the entire city.

We weren't allowed up onto the outside observation deck. It only opens when the weather is suitable. Once the temperatures are well above freezing, perhaps we'll make a return trip so that we can get the full experience.

Speaking of weather, the forecast says that a powerful cold front will blow through the North tonight. I can only imagine what it'll do to our heating bill.

* * *

THE WALK BACK TO Nathan's house was slow. Nathan and Stearns supported John, who limped along between them. By the time they reached the house Nathan's back and shoulders ached. He and Stearns helped John to the living room and laid him across a couch.

Nathan flopped into a leather reclining chair. He looked on as Stearns leaned his North Face backpack against the sofa and began unwrapping the makeshift bandages from John's thigh.

"Well, the good news is you're not going to bleed to death," Stearns said as he examined the wound. "The bad news is that this cut probably won't stay closed on its own. But if we can get our hands on the proper materials, I should be able to stitch it shut."

"Do we have any surgical thread?" John asked Nathan.

Nathan shook his head. "I don't think so. But there was a clinic a few blocks away. It might still have medical supplies."

John raised an eyebrow. "Wouldn't looters have picked it clean during the Desolation?"

"Maybe. But I think most people would've been snatching up pills to relieve fever and the other symptoms of the Desolation virus. We might still be able to scrounge up basic first aid supplies."

"Sounds like it's worth a look, in any case. Maybe we can find some proper bandages while we're at it," Stearns said "Can you lead the way there, son?"

"Sure." Nathan considered John's unbandaged leg. The wound was bleeding again, though the flow had slowed. "You won't stay here with John?" he asked Stearns.

"I'll be fine," John cut in. "Take Stearns with you. Maybe you can learn something from him." He looked Nathan straight in the eye. "We'll talk more about our situation here once you two get back.

"Got it," Nathan said. John was telling him not to reveal their reason for being in Minneapolis. "I'm ready when you are," he said to Stearns, who was rewrapping John's thigh with the bloodied cloth.

"Then let's go," Stearns said as he finished with the bandage. He gave John a hearty pat on the shoulder. "Get some rest. We'll be back before you know it."

Nathan and Stearns headed out the door, back into the late-summer heat. A turkey gobbled in the distance.

Nathan had rarely gone to this clinic as a child. He'd never understood why his father wouldn't take him there. Something to do with health insurance, he vaguely recalled. Still, he had passed by the clinic enough times to remember its location.

Also, every Halloween the nurse there had doled out full-sized candy bars, making it all the more unforgettable.

"So, this was your old neighborhood I take it?" Stearns asked.

"That's right."

"I bet the grass wasn't nearly as tall back then."

"And the tree branches didn't hang over the road, either."

"We're staying in your old house?"

"That's right. The house where I grew up."

"You must've been an elementary school student when the Desolation came."

Nathan nodded. "I was eight."

They walked to the end of the block and took a right. On the roadside they met a green car that had smashed head-on into a fire hydrant. The impact had crumpled the car's grille and front fender. Its mangled hood hung half-open, leaving the engine compartment exposed. The passage of time had ruined the car's paint job and rust had eaten holes through the doors. The fire hydrant, in contrast, had survived the crash intact, and its cheerful red paint had faded surprisingly little over the years.

Had a Desolation victim plowed into the hydrant in a suicide attempt? Or perhaps a couple of Desolation survivors had taken the vehicle for a joyride and "parked" it here, confident the destructive act would trigger no repercussions. The car's story was one of millions scattered throughout the city, most of which Nathan would never know.

He and Stearns continued past the car. The clinic was two blocks ahead.

"How long have you been in Minneapolis?" Nathan asked.

"Oh, I'd say about three or four weeks now. I'm just passing through. It's easy to lose track of the days, wandering the country like I do."

"You've been all across the country?" Nathan asked. Since the Desolation, he'd heard precious little news of the world beyond Minnesota.

Stearns reached for his hip flask, unscrewed the cap, and had a quick hit. He relished it with an "ah."

"I've been from Washington to Florida, and from Mexico to Maine. It's the same story everywhere. Empty cities, decaying factories, and pockets of survivors scraping by. It's a damn shame, I tell you." Stearns shook his head. "And to think I fought to protect this country, only to see it end up like this."

"So it's true, then? All the cities are empty, like Minneapolis?" Nathan asked.

"Oh, there are exceptions, to be sure. Denver is coming along. So is St. Louis. And Detroit too, ironically enough. God knows, before the Desolation, the Motor City was more forsaken than Pluto. Our friends north of the border in Toronto are also making a comeback. Still, recovery is slow. It can't help but be slow, I imagine, not after we lost so many people."

"I wish I could see the world," Nathan said.

"You still can, son." Stearns downed another mouthful of whiskey. "Too bad there isn't much to see anymore."

Nathan eyed the flask. "Where do you find the booze?"

"Whiskey is all over, son. You just need to know where to look. Would you like a hit?" Stearns extended his arm in offering.

"No, thanks."

"You a teetotaler?"

"A what?"

Stearns chuckled. "Now, there you go, making me feel old. A teetotaler is someone who doesn't drink."

Nathan shook his head. "I'm not. I just don't like the taste very much. Feels like fire going down my throat."

"That's just part of the charm, son. All part of the charm." After taking another swig Stearns slipped the flask back onto a hook along his belt.

They crossed a two-lane street. Just ahead was the clinic.

"By the way, I was wondering: How did you come to rescue me and John? Did you see us outside that bar?" Nathan asked.

"I did, in fact. I was minding my own business when I saw you two pinned down in that entryway. It wasn't clear what you were doing there until those two goons shot at you."

"Did you recognize John?"

"From that far away?" Stearns said incredulously. "Not a chance. I hadn't seen him in years. And that beard makes him look different than I remember."

"But then what made you decide to come into the bar?"

"Those soldiers. They're crawling all over this city. They mostly keep to themselves, but I had a run-in with a couple of them a few weeks ago that left a bad taste in my mouth. Once I saw they were involved, helping the non-aggressors — you and John, as it turned out — seemed like the right thing to do."

"So, the men in green vests are soldiers?" It was the first time Nathan had heard them explicitly referred to as such.

"It seems so. In fact there were a lot more of them milling about the city, causing a big ruckus, until a week or two ago. For whatever reason they've mostly disappeared. Maybe they got sick of Minneapolis and moved on to another city. Good riddance if you ask me."

"I see," Nathan said.

The thought hit him like a roaring black Honda: The two men in the bar were the same two that had allegedly driven off with Emiko in their trunk. Nathan was ashamed of himself for having not recognized the link sooner.

Was Emiko in Minneapolis? It suddenly seemed an incredibly strong possibility.

But what could he do? Nathan was already living in their childhood home, the one place she was most likely to visit. If she wasn't there, where else could he look? Minneapolis was huge. Two people could wander its streets for years without ever crossing paths. And then there was the matter of John. With his injury, he now needed Nathan's help more than ever.

Nathan's mountain of problems soared to new heights, yet he'd come no closer to determining how best to scale it.

"Son?"

"Huh?" Nathan said, twisting his neck to look at Stearns.

"Is this the place, son?" Stearns said, pointing with his thumb.

Separated from the sidewalk by a thick bramble of honeysuckle, the clinic looked much as Nathan remembered. Only the auburn paint had faded.

"This is it," Nathan said.

Stearns smiled. "Thought I'd lost you for a minute there. But no worries. I'm sure a guy your age has more dreams than he can fit into a day."

"Something like that," Nathan said.

If only Stearns had known the half of it.

Chapter 14

February 20th, 2027
Post Status: Public

Here in Minneapolis yesterday morning the police discovered a handful of dead on the streets — homeless who had succumbed to hypothermia during the big freeze. Thirteen deaths, last I heard.

I thought that was shocking. Then I talked to my parents.

Down in Chicago there are over 1,000 dead. Most of the dead were people living on the city's outskirts, people with insufficient clothing, food, and shelter who couldn't find respite from the cold. And that casualty count is only preliminary. The authorities are still combing through the shantytowns, turning up more corpses.

I know times are hard, but this? Couldn't we at least build proper shelter for these people?

This incident has brought a couple points to my attention.

First, if there are over one thousand dead, I have to wonder exactly how many refugees are living in and around Chicago. It's obviously far more than I had previously imagined.

My bigger concern, though, is the dearth of media coverage on the subject. This should be headline news! Yet I wouldn't have heard about it if not for my parents.

One thousand dead.

Last year, when terrorists unleashed chemical weapons in San Francisco's BART system, 104 lives were lost. As you'd expect, that attack immediately became front page news.

Yesterday's big freeze? A Baidu search turned up a number of articles, but it's hardly the talk of the nation.

We're looking at the greatest single day death toll in this country since the September 11th attacks, over 25 years ago.

The deaths are tragic. The eerie silence that surrounds them is terrifying.

* * *

JOHN LAY STRETCHED out across the couch. His revolver rested on the coffee table, still within reach. He didn't expect he'd need it. Minneapolis was more lifeless than the surface of Lake Ontario in the dead of winter.

The reappearance of Colonel Kennedy Stearns' was a veritable miracle. The colonel was from a long-lost life.

John remembered Stearns as a competent commander, one who had always kept an eye out for his men. Was Stearns still that man? Would he now keep an eye out for John and Nathan? Recruiting the old colonel to help search for the Northland Core could have unintended consequences. How would Nathan react? Would Stearns be a help or a hindrance? And there was still the matter of asking Stearns how he managed to arrive at just the right moment ...

John needed to talk with Nathan. A brief chat would settle the issue. Then they could move forward, either with or without Stearns.

Footsteps approached outside. John put a hand on his revolver.

Boots scuffed loudly up the front steps. The front door creaked open.

"Honey, we're home!" Stearns called out.

John relaxed and loosed his fingers from his revolver. Stearns had changed much since the Desolation.

The Stearns etched in John's memory was not a playful man. He gave orders and expected them to be followed. He was stern, fittingly enough, but reasonable. And he never blamed his subordinates for his own mistakes. Those qualities had earned him John's respect.

The Desolation had seemingly given Stearns a brighter outlook on life. Conversely, it had left John hard and callous. Why such divergent outcomes from the same event? Perhaps their differing experiences during the catastrophe held the answer.

John had missed the Desolation completely. After losing his arm in Egypt he had fallen into a coma and slept straight through the main apocalyptic event. By the time he awoke the world he'd known was no more. He'd become a stranger in his own land.

Stearns and Nathan entered the living room with bundles of medical supplies in their hands.

"We found more than we expected," Nathan said.

"I was surprised the place hadn't been picked over. Everyone else must've had the same thought and not even bothered to check," said Stearns. "I gotta say, this city is one of the creepiest I've been too. It's like a metropolis frozen in time, doubly so now that those soldier-types have vanished."

Nathan set an armful of supplies on the coffee table. "How are you holding up?"

"I'm fine," John said. "My leg is feeling better already."

"Really?" Nathan asked.

John remained silent. Immobilized on the couch, his leg did feel better, but he knew it would start throbbing if he changed position.

"The blood on your bandage is dry," Stearns said. "The wound might have clotted, but I'm afraid it'll open up again as soon as you move." He gently unwrapped he bandages.

"What's the verdict?" John asked.

"I think you'll pull through," Stearns said, patting John's calf. "But like I said, we'd better stitch you up."

"You're the boss," John said, feeling it strange not to address Stearns as "sir."

Nathan looked to Stearns. "You know how to stitch?"

"I sure do," Stearns replied. "You don't?"

Nathan shook his head.

"Well then why don't you pull up a chair and watch as I get to work on our friend John here."

"Sure thing," Nathan said, before bolting into the next room to get a chair.

"A good kid, that one," Stearns said once Nathan was gone. "Where'd you find him?"

"Up north," John replied.

"It's a wild world up there. Glad to see it can still produce decent people." Stearns repositioned himself on both knees, a comfortable stance for operating.

John said no more. Soon he would ask for a moment alone with Nathan. Though a greenhorn, Nathan was the only man alive who had John's absolute trust, the kind of trust that could be earned only in the heat of battle.

Stearns, too, had once been worthy of that trust. He would have to prove he still deserved it.

Nathan lumbered back into the room with one of the dining table chairs. He set it beside Stearns and took a seat.

"Don't get too comfortable there now, son," Stearns warned. "I want you to pay attention. I might ask for help."

"You got it," Nathan said.

"Are you ready to get started?" Stearns asked John.

"I'm ready."

"Then let's get to it. Could you hand me the bottle of antiseptic and a medical cloth, son?"

Nathan obliged, handing Stearns the materials from the coffee table.

Stearns blotted the cloth with the antiseptic solution and gently patted the wound. John gritted his teeth at the sting. A little pain now was a small price to pay if it meant staving off infection. An infection could cost John the leg. Losing a limb was never pleasant, as he well knew.

"It's best to clean a wound as soon as you can," Stearns instructed Nathan. "We poured some battlefield spirits on this one, but proper antiseptic is better if you have it, especially when you consider the zany strains of bacteria that could be lurking in these godforsaken cities."

Stearns finished cleaning the wound. He returned the bottle and blood-stained cloth to Nathan, who set them on the table.

"Thread and needle," Stearns said, holding out his open palm. Nathan promptly handed over the stitching supplies.

"Sorry to say, the one thing that eluded us was local anesthetic," Stearns warned John.

"I'll be fine. I've dealt with worse."

"I know."

How much did Stearns know? Stearns had said nothing of John's bionic arm, nor of that last, fateful mission he'd sent John on. Was he simply avoiding an awkward subject? Or was he hiding something?

"Lean in for a closer look," Stearns said, waving Nathan in. "This part is best learned by watching."

Nathan hunched forward in his chair, studying the thread and needle in Stearns' hand.

"Stitches actually do damage to the skin, but they help the long-term healing process by keeping everything in place," Stearns said, looking John in the eye. "Assuming the injured party doesn't overexert himself and rip them open, that is."

"You don't need to —"

John winced as the needle punctured his skin. There was another stab of pain as it pierced the opposing side, followed by the unsettling feeling of nylon threading through his flesh.

Stearns tied off the suture and had Nathan trim the excess thread. He then repeated the process. The space between the two flaps of skin grew smaller with each subsequent stitch.

After finishing the fifth stitch, he handed the needle and thread to Nathan.

"And that's how you close a wound," he said.

"Thanks. I understand the process, but I couldn't do it myself," Nathan said, his brow scrunched in concentration.

"Practice makes perfect, of course," Stearns said with a wink. "But I'd rather hope it's a long time before we again require needle and thread."

John gently drew the leg towards his chest. He was eager to get off the couch.

"Slow down there, Tex," Stearns said, putting his palm on John's chest. "You'll need to take it easy for a couple weeks. It's probably best if you use crutches until the wound has had some time to heal."

"Great," John muttered. He had a deadline to meet. He didn't have time to slow down.

"I think we have some crutches in the attic. I'll go check later," Nathan said.

Stearns removed his palm, letting John sit up. John tested the leg, seeing how the stitches would hold. Even moving gently, he could feel the thread tugging at his loose skin. Maybe crutches were a good idea.

"We'd better put a wrap around it, just in case there's any more bleeding," Stearns advised.

After they wrapped the wound, John slipped into a spare pair of Levi's. He hoped the blood would wash out of the old pair. Though easy to replace, jeans were a hassle to break in.

When they'd finished disposing of the bloody rags and tidying up the coffee table, John settled in on the sofa, set his hands on his thighs, and regarded Stearns.

"I can't tell you how much I appreciate the help, Stearns. I'm not sure what would've happened back at the bar if you hadn't been there to cover us."

"Anything for an old friend," Stearns said.

Friend? John had never thought of Colonel Stearns as a friend. A mentor, perhaps, but never a friend. Still, titles meant nothing now. Maybe Stearns was just a friend.

"Say, Stearns."

"What's on your mind?"

"Could you give me and Nathan a moment?" John said. "Not that I want to leave you out in the cold, but —"

"I understand, John. I just stepped back into your life today. If you two have things you need to discuss in private, that's fine," Stearns said graciously. "I'll go keep watch outside. Just don't forget I'm out there," he added with a chuckle.

"We appreciate it," John said.

"Not at all." With a friendly salute Stearns left the room. The door latch clicked softly as he stepped out of the house.

"So, what do you think?" John asked Nathan.

"He seems like a decent guy," Nathan said, leaning back in his chair. "Are you thinking about asking him to help us find the Northland Core?"

"Bingo," John said. He was glad to hear that Nathan was on the same page.

"Well, do you think he'd be helpful?" Nathan asked.

"I think so, especially since I'll be limping around. He could help us search, and he'll supply extra firepower if we run into any more goons."

"And do you trust him?"

Indeed, that was the big question.

"I need to clear the air with him," John said. "We have a history. It's a good history, but there are a few blanks that need filling in. We can bring him along slowly, feel him out, and I'll ask him some questions soon."

"Alright by me," said Nathan. "By the way, he told me how and why he helped us out in the bar."

"Yeah? What did he have to say?"

"That he saw us pinned down and wanted to help. I guess he's had troubles of his own with those men in green."

"His appearance was rather timely, don't you think?"

Nathan shrugged. "Not all coincidences are bad. Maybe we were due for a stroke of good luck."

John snorted in contempt. "A man can dream."

"One more thing." Nathan's expression turned serious. "I think Emiko might be in Minneapolis."

John saw the connection. "Those two goons were the ones that drove off with her, weren't they?"

"Right. It seems likely she came down here with them."

"Then she could very well be in the city. We can keep an eye out for her," John said. He wished he could promise more help.

Nathan nodded grimly. "That's all I can ask for."

"Who knows? Maybe she'll find us," John offered.

"Maybe," Nathan said. He glanced out the window. "Are you sure Stearns will want to join us? We're assuming he will but we haven't actually asked."

"I don't see why not." John massaged his uninjured thigh. "It seems he's doing the same thing I was before you and I met, just wandering around the country. Spending a couple weeks with us in Minneapolis will probably be the highlight of his year."

"Assuming everything goes well ..." Nathan said.

"It will," John said, though he too was uncertain. "It's settled then. I'll go back out and bring him in." He gingerly rose from the sofa. His thigh felt tight and sore.

"Relax. I got this," Nathan said, getting to his feet.

"No. I should go talk to him."

Nathan put a firm hand on John's shoulder. "Sit," he said. "I'll bring him in."

"Fine," John grunted. As much as he hated to admit it, the kid was right. His wound needed rest and relaxation. More than he could offer it.

Chapter 15

February 22nd, 2027
Post Status: Public

It seems I spoke too soon about the lack of media coverage surrounding the big freeze. Within hours of my post, reports of the catastrophe blew up all over CNN and other news sites. Currently the death count is reported at 1,322.

Perhaps journalists were waiting for concrete information to stream in before jumping on the story? The media does seem to be on a short leash these days … In any case, President Hernandez is now in Chicago assessing the damage and consoling the citizens. Tonight he plans to give a speech.

It's been a harsh, bitter winter. As I reflect upon the tragedy in Chicago, I find myself wondering how much more punishment our country can take.

Thank God spring is nearly here. Climatologists claim we'll see more rain this summer. We can only hope.

* * *

NATHAN GLIDED DOWN the front steps. He found Stearns across the street, leaning against an elm tree.

"That was awfully quick," Stearns said as Nathan approached. "You and John get enough time to yourselves?"

"We did," Nathan said, stopping at the curbside. "And we have a proposal for you. Why don't you come back inside and we'll talk it over?"

"I'm all ears. Not literally, of course. That would be unsightly. But anyhow, why don't you lead the way?"

"Of course."

They crossed the street and went back into the house. John was waiting on the living room couch.

"Do you want to do the talking or should I?" Nathan asked John once everyone had settled into their chairs.

"This is my show," John said. He turned to Stearns. "We're looking for something, and we could use your help. Are you interested?"

"I probably am," replied Stearns. "What did you have in mind?"

"You'd better make yourself comfortable," John said, "because it will take a while to tell you all about the Northland Core."

* * *

Stearns ruminated silently for a long time after John finished his story.

John understood. It was a tale that needed time to breathe. A bionic arm, a coma, a listless life of drifting, a kidnapping, and a quest to Mallard Island. With Nathan's help, John had told all.

"So, you're here to find this Northland Core. Is that right?" Stearns asked.

John nodded firmly.

Stearns continued. "You know, I always wondered what had happened to you after that disaster in Egypt. Truth is, you were airlifted from the battlefield and I never saw you again. I heard rumors that you'd been shot up something serious, but it was never clear what had happened until now. It was a mystery that troubled me to the very end, until the Desolation. After that my priorities changed a bit, as I'm sure you understand." Stearns drew his chin towards his chest, eyeing the ground. After a meditative pause his focus swung back onto John. "But anyhow, now everything makes sense."

"It does?" Nathan cut in.

"Sure. The Pentagon must've been sitting on this bionic tech, waiting for a worthy test subject. That honor just so happened to fall to John."

"Honor?" John grunted. As far as he was concerned, the bionic arm had deprived him of his best years and given him less than nothing in return.

"I see why you're angry, given how things unfolded, but I can't imagine the boys in the Pentagon expected you'd spend all these years in a coma. And then the Desolation on top of that?" Stearns shook his head. "Events transpired in a manner that no one could've predicted. You were a victim of unfortunate circumstances."

John dug his fingers into the sofa's armrest. Though he knew Stearns was probably right, he still yearned for a more substantial target to blame for his troubles. He'd been wronged too severely to just let bygones be bygones.

Nathan looked to Stearns. "So, will you help us?"

Stearns lips parted in a broad smile. "I thought that much was already assumed."

"So you're in?" John asked.

"I'm in."

And like that, John and Nathan's two-man team became a trio.

Outside, the sun drooped below the treetops, taking its final bow before leaving the world stage for the day. Though their search had stalled and John had sustained a debilitating leg injury, the addition of a third companion offered hope. Years from now, John would look back and recognize today as a turning point in the search for the Northland Core.

"Anyhow, the day is growing short. I reckon we'd best get ready for dinner. We can discuss our plan of action over a hot meal," Stearns said. "Nathan, would you mind showing me to your kitchen?"

"Sure thing." Nathan stood and made for the door. "It's right this way. We're a bit short on provisions, but we should be able to scrape a meal together."

"Certainly. We'll prepare a feast worthy of the occasion."

Nathan and Stearns went to the kitchen, leaving John to rest on the couch. How long would his wounded thigh hold him up? *Not long*, he decided. Hell, he would look for the Northland Core in a wheelchair if he had to.

That left only one question: Where to look next?

* * *

When the meal was ready, Nathan and Stearns returned to the living room. They stood on either side of John like a pair of human crutches and helped him into the kitchen.

Dinner was a simple affair of pan-seared venison and a collection of edible greens that Nathan had gathered while exploring the city. They ate by the amber light of a kerosene lamp. The meal didn't last long. Nathan soon forked the last morsel from his plate into his mouth. He waited for John and Stearns to catch up.

After shoveling his plate spotless, Stearns let out a hearty burp.

"Excuse me," he said, patting his belly. "It's just been awhile since I've enjoyed a delicious meal in good company."

"Burp all you like. I won't take offense," Nathan said.

"Bless your little heart for that," Stearns said. "So, shall we get down to business? You boys told me you'd been looking around the city. Where has your search taken you so far?"

"We've only had a chance to look around the university," Nathan said.

"Not a bad place to start. Have you looked anywhere else?"

"Not yet."

Stearns fingered his tidy gray beard. "You said you have about two weeks, right?"

"Less than that now," Nathan replied. The deadline sounded less ominous when Stearns omitted the consequences of not meeting it.

"Well, this is just my spontaneous thinking on the matter, but it seems to me that if this Northland Core were hidden in the university, someone would've found it already."

Nathan cocked his head. "What makes you say that?"

"I get the distinct impression that you two aren't the only ones looking for it."

"Oh?"

Stearns shook his index finger. "Those men in green vests have been looking for something."

"They have?" Nathan uttered, his tone more clueless than he'd intended.

Stearns nodded. "I reckon that's the case, at least."

"I think the colonel might have a point," John said. His fork clinked as he set it on his empty plate.

"Okay," Nathan replied, trying to keep his tone neutral. Faced with disagreement from two sides, he didn't feel comfortable mounting a counterargument. Moreover, he wasn't sure what his argument would be. Declaring that his gut told him that the Northland Core was in the university wouldn't get him far in a debate with two ex-marines.

"What do you suggest?" Nathan asked.

"Well, I don't suppose the good old U of M was the only place you two had in mind," Stearns said. "Where else were you planning to look?"

"Today we were headed for the offices of MinnePower, the electric utility," John said. He pointed to his bandaged thigh. "Then this happened."

"A power company ..." Stearns smacked his lips as he mulled it over. "Not a bad idea. But you boys mean to tell me you didn't get any more specific leads on that island? What was it again?"

"Mallard Island," Nathan said. "Most of the documentation we found there was destroyed before we could read it. Minneapolis is the only clue we have to go on."

"I see. Then this is going to be harder than I thought."

John chuckled grimly. "You're telling me."

"To the power company tomorrow, then?" Stearns asked.

John nodded.

"I guess so," said Nathan, shrugging.

Stearns looked to John. "I suppose you'll rest here while Nathan and I go scope it out then?"

"Hardly," John said. "I'm coming with."

Stearns' flask seemed to magically materialize in his hand. He took a hearty drink.

"You always were a crazy bastard, John Osborne," he said. "The three of us it is."

PART TWO

Chapter 16

March 4th, 2027
Post Status: Public

Tomorrow is Emiko's fifth birthday. I'm sure you know
what that means.

Birthday cake!

I've gathered all of the necessary materials. Now I
just have to mix and bake.

You'd think my chemistry knowledge would translate to
the kitchen. Yet as Danielle, Nathan, and Emiko can
attest, this is certainly not the case …

* * *

THOUGH THE RAIN had stopped days before, Emiko remained
alone in her cozy suburban home.

She was famished. Or at least she should have been
famished. After a couple of days without food her hunger had
subsided, as though her stomach had realized that it was
growling in vain. Taking this as a bad sign, Emiko struggled out
of bed and set out to hunt.

She limped out the front door, her rifle strapped across her
back. The long summer rain was now but a memory, recorded
only in the extra inches the weeds had shot up since the storm's
passing.

With her ankle as it was, large as a giant pine cone and dark
as a raspberry, Emiko was in no condition to stalk game. Unsure
she could make it to the pond, she settled on finding a hunting
spot closer to her house. She struggled along the sidewalk,
staggering towards a patch of grass at the end of the block.

She stepped a few feet into underbrush and sat down to
watch the intersection. Though not an ideal hunting spot, it did

allow observation of two separate roads. Sooner or later an unsuspecting animal would pass. She crossed her legs and set her rifle on her lap.

A creature soon appeared. A creature that walked upright on two legs and wore bright red.

A woman.

Emiko sunk her teeth into her lower lip. What to do? Humans were the most unpredictable creatures of all.

After double-checking that she was well hidden, Emiko gingerly rose onto one knee. If she had to she could take flight into the tall grass, even if it meant reinjuring her ankle.

The woman drew closer. She had brown hair, cut short. What was she doing in this city of bones? Was she in league with the Restoration Army? Though the woman's crimson sweater and indigo jeans contrasted sharply with the Restoration's Army earthy colors, Emiko dared make no assumptions.

Fearing the woman would spot her, Emiko withdrew deeper into the foliage to watch and wait.

* * *

Aristotle spotted the figure as it retreated into the cattails. It had looked like a child, maybe a girl, but what was a child doing here in Minneapolis, alone?

Or perhaps the girl wasn't alone. Aristotle slid her revolver from its holster and twisted the barrel, setting it to Snipe. She replaced the gun but kept her hand close, ready to draw, and made her approach.

The air was still. The high grass stood straight and proud. Somewhere within awaited the girl.

Aristotle cut into the underbrush. She didn't get far.

"Hold it," ordered a young female voice.

Aristotle froze mid-step. She waited for another command. When none came, she spoke:

"What do you want me to do next?"

Aristotle remained still, waiting for a reply. Was this girl armed? Dangerous? Aristotle was prepared to dive into the marshy thicket and draw her firearm. Hopefully it wouldn't come to that.

A few yards ahead, a young girl emerged from the cover of the grass. She had a deep bronze tan and black hair that hung well past her shoulders. Her hands clutched a long-barreled bolt-action rifle. The girl's black eyes and the rifle's steel muzzle were locked on the same target: Aristotle's head.

"What are you doing here?" the girl asked.

How much of the truth did this girl need to hear? Perhaps it was best to start from the end and work backwards.

"I saw you crouching over here and wanted to see what you were up to. I haven't seen many people here in the city."

"And before that?" the girl asked, narrowing her already fierce eyes.

"Before that?" Aristotle stalled. Though fundamentally simple, the answer wasn't exactly straightforward. "I'm looking for someone in the city," she said.

"Who?"

"A man who calls himself the General."

"The General," the girl said, slowly and deliberately, lending weight to the words. She readjusted the butt of her rifle against her shoulder. "And why are you looking for him?"

"To find out what he's doing, and to stop him if need be."

The girl eyed Aristotle from the far side of the rifle's barrel, assessing the risk her target presented. Finally, she brought the rifle down from her shoulder.

"I think we should talk."

Talk? Aristotle thought, heaving a silent sigh of relief. Of course they could talk. But what would a young girl like this — Aristotle guessed she was twelve or thirteen — have to say about the General?

"That would be great. Where?" Aristotle asked.

"My place."

"Are there others there?"

The girl hesitated before shaking her head.

Aristotle cocked an eyebrow. "You're here alone?"

"I'll show you where I live. Follow me."

Holding the rifle in both arms, the girl limped past Aristotle, wincing noticeably with every step.

"Are you okay?" Aristotle asked.

"I'm fine," the girl replied sharply, glancing back over her shoulder. "Now are you coming or not?"

Chapter 17

March 12th, 2027
Post Status: Private

The Subaru is such a handful.

The promotion material claimed it would get 64 miles
per gallon. Recently it's been getting closer to 55.
Very disappointing.

I was waiting to see if it would improve now that
winter is behind us, but Danielle won't have it. She
insists that I take it to the dealer for an immediate
tune-up.

I can sense that she's under a lot of stress these
days, but she hasn't told me why.

I don't think it's the car.

* * *

FROM THE OUTSIDE, the young girl's home looked as though it
hadn't been lived in for years. The yellow siding had faded, and
a number of shingles had detached from the roof. The exterior's
shabbiness concealed the fact that the girl was staying here. She
was hiding in plain sight.

Aristotle followed the girl through the front door. The
entryway was remarkably tidy and dust-free.

"Could you take off your boots?" the young girl asked as she
slipped out of her sneakers.

"Of course," Aristotle replied, taking a knee to untie her
laces.

After resting her rifle against the wall, the girl disappeared
into another room. She hobbled back in just as Aristotle was
slipping off her boots.

"Sorry, I don't have any drinks for us."

"Not a problem. I wasn't expecting a drink," Aristotle said, rising to her feet. "A place to sit will be more than enough."

The girl smiled. The expression accentuated the thinness of her face. Was she naturally scrawny, or was she hard-up for food? Given the girl's limp, Aristotle suspected the latter.

They went into the living room, also well-maintained. A sofa and coffee table invited guests to sit and enjoy a drink. An eclectic assortment of chairs circled the coffee table like Conestoga wagons around the campfire. A notebook lay on the table. Affixed to its well-worn leather cover were two pieces of masking tape. The words *World's End* were written across the tape in black marker.

A portrait perched on a windowsill caught Aristotle's eye. The photo depicted a family of three, two parents and a daughter. The parents stood side-by-side behind their daughter, each resting a hand on one of her shoulders. Clearly a product of her parents' genes, the daughter had pale blond hair and skin white as falling snow.

Aristotle's eyes shifted from the pale girl in the photo to the bronze-skinned, black-haired girl now before her. Both girls wore sleeveless black tops and dark jeans. Different girl, same outfit. The clothes had probably sat in a dresser, unworn for nine years, until recently. Hand-me-downs passed from the dead to the living.

They settled in. The girl sat in an upholstered chair by the coffee table. Aristotle took a seat on the far end of the sofa.

"Mind if I set my gun on the table?" Aristotle asked.

The girl considered for a moment before answering, "Go ahead."

Slowly and steadily, Aristotle drew her revolver from its holster. She set it beside the leather-bound notebook. The girl eyed the firearm with obvious interest.

"What kind of gun is that?"

"It's a custom model."

"A custom gun?" The girl's face lit up. "I didn't know there were custom guns."

"They're rare but not unheard of. Long ago many guns were crafted individually and fine-tuned to better suit their owners' needs, just like swords and knives. My revolver invokes that tradition."

"Neat." The girl ogled the gun as though it took all of her will not to reach out and touch it. "What's special about it?"

"A lot of things. It has a high caliber for a handgun, for one. And it can handle both standard rounds and shotshells."

"You can put shotgun shells in a handgun?"

"In this one you can. Small-gauge shells."

The girl cocked her head. "I thought handguns had that spiral shape inside the barrel, like rifles. Doesn't that make the shotgun shell spin and the buckshot come out wildly?"

"You're talking about rifling," Aristotle said, pleasantly surprised at the girl's knowledge. "And you're right, usually that would be the case. But this revolver has a clever solution to that problem. Maybe I can show you later." Aristotle nodded toward the doorway, where the girl had set down her rifle. "And how about your gun? I don't see many old bolt-action rifles like that around these days."

"It's an M1903 Springfield. It was used in the great wars of the 20th century."

"A real classic."

"Thanks. My dad gave it to me."

Aristotle adjusted her posture, crossing her legs just above the knee. "By the way, I never caught your name."

"Oh, sorry!" the girl exclaimed, raising a hand to her mouth in embarrassment. "My name is Emiko."

"Emiko." Aristotle's head bobbed in approval. "I like it."

"And you?"

"My name is Aristotle."

"Air-ih-sta-tol. What a long name!" Emiko eyed Aristotle with skepticism. "That can't be your real name."

Aristotle grinned. She liked this girl's spirit. "It's not the name my parents gave me. But it is my name now."

"I see."

Though Emiko clearly wasn't satisfied, she pressed the point no further. The cackle of a ring-necked pheasant filtered in through the window.

"Are you from Minneapolis?" Aristotle asked.

"I lived here until I was six. This is my first time back in the city since then."

Aristotle tilted her head towards the family portrait on the windowsill. "I noticed that this isn't your house."

"So?" Emiko retorted. "There are so many houses here. I figured I could choose one I liked." Her face cringed sourly. "One with no dead bodies inside."

"Why not live in your family's old house?"

Emiko bit the corner of her lip, shaking her head. "It would be weird without my family there."

"I'm sure it would," Aristotle said. After the Desolation, she'd fled the home that she'd shared with her mother and sister. Returning to it now would only stir up nightmares.

Aristotle reached for the notebook on the coffee table. "*World's End?* That's an interesting name to give your diary."

"It's not my diary."

Aristotle's fingers brushed the warm leather cover. "But it is a diary?"

Emiko sprang from her chair. "It was my father's diary," she said, hopping to the far end of the coffee table on her good leg and snatching the notebook from beneath Aristotle's fingers. "It's the only keepsake I have from my old house. And I'd prefer if you didn't read it."

"Point taken," Aristotle said. She'd hadn't meant to pry.

Emiko hobbled back to her chair and clutched the notebook to her chest. "You said you're looking for the General?"

"That's right."

"Why?" the girl prodded.

Why? How could such a simple question be so difficult to answer? Aristotle stared out one of the room's sash windows, at the large silver maple in the front yard. A pair of robins weaved around its wide brown trunk before disappearing into the endless blue sky.

"Because it's the right thing to do," Aristotle said.

"The right thing to do ..." Emiko repeated slowly, as though pondering a foreign concept. "And what have you found so far?"

"Not much. Only weeds, dust, and bones," Aristotle said. "And why are you looking for the General, Emiko?"

"Let's just say it's personal. Wherever there's trouble I seem to hear the General's name."

"That's very admirable of you."

"Admirable?" Emiko tilted her head to one side. "Like, something you admire?"

Aristotle nodded. "I think it's impressive that you're chasing after the General by yourself." She gave Emiko a concerned look. "You are living here alone, right?"

"I can take care of myself," Emiko said defiantly.

"I'm sure you can. But how would you feel about working together. I think we'd make a good team."

Emiko pondered the idea. A smile slowly stretched across her lips.

"I think I'd like that."

"Then it's settled. We'll search together. But first, we'd better eat something."

Emiko's stomach growled menacingly. "You have food?"

So she is hungry! Aristotle concluded. "I have a little. We can share it today. But we'll have to go hunting for more soon."

Chapter 18

March 18th, 2027
Post Status: Public

Gather your chairs and circle round, because Mr. Kanno
has big news for you today.

Danielle is pregnant! She told me just this afternoon.
I wasn't expecting another kid at this stage in my
life. I don't know what I can say besides …

Another child!

My hands are practically shaking with excitement. I'd
better say goodbye here before I write something
idiotic.

P.S. EXCELSIOR!

P.P.S. I'm done now. Really.

* * *

A CRUTCH UNDER each arm, John shuffled away from the
MinnePower Gas and Electric corporate office.

Four stories of broken windows topped by a caved-in roof,
the office had once managed the energy needs of the entire
Minneapolis-St. Paul metropolitan area. Now it was merely an
ugly punctuation mark dotting a fruitless search.

John, Nathan, and Stearns had combed the building for
information about the Northland Core. A long walk back home
was their only reward. The proceeded down the crumbling
asphalt of Hennepin Avenue.

"So, do you have any notions about our next step?" Stearns
asked.

John shook his head. "I don't. We'll have to take another look
at the map."

"I reckon it's gonna be an awfully difficult search if we just keep stabbing in the dark. A long, difficult search. And from what you've told me, time isn't on our side."

"That's right."

"And you don't have any other clues to go on? Didn't the professor, Professor ... what was his name again?"

"Professor Singh."

"Didn't the good Professor Singh up on the island — Muskrat Island, was it?"

"Mallard Island."

"Right." Stearns cleared his throat. "Well, didn't this island-bound professor give you any tips about where to find this Northland Core?"

"Nothing."

"I see," Stearns said, scratching his cheek. "Well, as Ma Stearns used to say, 'Nothing good comes easy.'"

John gave Stearns a sidelong stare. "Your mom used to say that?"

"You know, the truth is I'm not really sure anymore," Stearns said with a good-natured chuckle. "But it's too hokey of a line to utter without introduction. I was once a hard-ass marine just like you, you know."

"Once a marine, always a marine?"

"Some would say that, but me? I'm not so sure."

"Same here," John muttered.

John looked back at Nathan, who trudged along with his eyeballs pinned to his shoestrings, keeping unusually quiet. Although he'd actively engaged in today's search, now he seemed reluctant to speak his thoughts. Perhaps he felt uncomfortable sharing his opinions in Stearns' presence?

"Do you have any idea what we should do next, Nathan?" John asked over his shoulder.

Nathan didn't seem to hear.

"Nathan?" John repeated.

"Yeah?" Nathan's head jerked up.

"Have you thought about where we should look next?"

"Umm ... I've thought about it, but I haven't come up with anything." His face became downcast, as though he were admitting a great failure.

"Don't sweat it, kid. Stearns and I aren't doing any better. If you think of anything, don't hesitate to share."

Nathan forced a smile. "Sure thing, John."

What's eating him? The question gnawed at John as he continued down the sidewalk, planting both crutches with each step.

A murder of crows cawed from atop the rusty, sun-bleached sign of a garage, JIM'S AUTO REPAIR. The crows spread their dark wings and took flight. Their black bodies grew small against the mellowing late-afternoon sun. They veered towards the enigmatic behemoth on the Minneapolis skyline, Target Tower.

* * *

Later that evening Nathan, John, and Stearns gathered in the kitchen. A lamp, dangling by rope from an overhead light fixture, illuminated John and Stearns as they studied a map spread across the dining table. Despite Stearns' protestations, John remained on his feet, using the wooden crutches for support.

Nathan sat at the far end of the table, smiling at his friend's stubbornness. John refused to let his wounded leg keep him down.

Nathan looked to the stars outside, tapping his fingers on the table. A multitude of questions occupied his mind.

The first was obvious: Where was the Northland Core?

While John and Stearns jabbed fingers at the map, seemingly at random, Nathan returned to the logical foundations of the problem. What was the Northland Core? What kind of organization would've developed it? In what sort of facility would it be stored?

It seemed likely the Northland Core resided within a sizable facility. This wasn't a middle-school science fair project; it was a big-time, Pentagon-sponsored initiative. Additionally, the facility had to be well hidden. If the project hadn't been absolutely top secret, they would have found clues to its location by now. Finding the core by poring over the map seemed a long shot.

Another issue troubled Nathan. Since seeing the Northland Core documentation on Mallard Island, he'd had an unsettling feeling of déjà vu.

Was it possible he'd heard of the Northland Core when he was very young? Maybe his father had talked about it. But why would his father know about the Northland Core? And why would he talk about it in front of his son?

Nathan's father, Ryota Kanno, had been a chemistry professor at the university, and his work had undoubtedly involved Pentagon contracts. But the Northland Core seemed more like an endeavor of physics or engineering than one of chemistry. And besides, even if his father had helped develop the core, why would he have mentioned it to Nathan? No matter how Nathan contorted his synapses and neurons, the answers eluded him.

"Nathan?"

Stearns voice pulled him back into reality.

"Yeah?" he replied.

"Are you still with us, son? You look lost over there."

"Of course." Nathan grinned sheepishly. "I'm not going anywhere."

"Of course," Stearns repeated, a twinkle in his eye. "Do you have any thoughts on this matter?"

"About where to search tomorrow?"

"What else?" Stearns raised both of his bushy gray eyebrows. At times like this, the three of them brainstorming around the table, Stearns reminded Nathan of a bizarre, ex-Marine version of Pierre.

Nathan scratched the side of his neck. "I've been thinking, but I don't have any fresh ideas yet."

"No worries, son. Just don't be shy about speaking up if anything comes to mind. Got it?"

"Yes, sir," Nathan replied. Twice today he'd been told to speak his mind. He didn't need to hear it again.

"There's no need for the formality, son. Hell, you can call me grandpa, geezer, or even whitehead if you'd like. It's all the same to my prehistoric ears." As though to lend credence to this point, Stearns uncapped his flask and took a long draw of whiskey.

"Got it," Nathan said, rolling his eyes. He rose from his chair. "I'm going to check on Mumford," he said to John.

"Go ahead," John said. "Tell that brute I still have my eye on him."

"I'm sure that'll keep him in line."

Nathan made for the back door. Outside the air had the pleasant, not-too-humid crispness of an autumn evening. Though the calendar still said it was late summer, within a few weeks fall would officially arrive.

Minneapolis was cooler than Nathan remembered. No longer burdened with the heat created by people, cars, factories, and homes, the city had become a more hospitable place. He would never forget the heat waves that had smothered the city in those final years before the Desolation, turning it into a smoldering, insufferable hell. The Desolation had destroyed much, but the weather, at least, had taken a turn for the better.

Nathan walked across the yard to Mumford. Bats flitted through the darkness overhead, chasing insects for dinner. Or was it breakfast? Nathan supposed that to an animal a meal was a meal regardless of when it came.

Mumford munched on the grass, apparently content to loaf idly in the cool night air. Or perhaps the tvapa was plotting to take over the world, as John often joked. At least Nathan hoped John was joking …

Nathan ran his hand through Mumford's short, fuzzy hair. Through the kitchen window he saw John and Stearns still discussing where to begin tomorrow's search. All of the other rooms were dark.

In many cultures light represented hope. Though the city was dead and steeped in darkness, light still came from the moon and the stars above, from the constellations that Nathan's father had taught him long ago, from Hercules, Perseus, and Andromeda.

Would it be enough?

Chapter 19

April 27rd, 2027
Post Status: Public

The entire nation watches anxiously as farmers sow their seed corn.

The media offers constant updates. Streaming video shows tractors chugging up and down the fields, spreading those yellow seeds of hope across the earth.

In a way, I find all of this very strange. When I was young no one paid much attention to farmers and their crops. Sure, we would drive past the fields of emergent green stalks and admire how they seemed to shoot up inches overnight. And when harvest came my parents would buy fresh corn from the farmers market. But none of it was worth making a ruckus over. The corn was always there, quietly growing as we went about our business.

Now a media frenzy surrounds the corn-planting season. Will it grow? How will we find enough water to irrigate the fields? Will we harvest enough to feed everyone?

I suspect everything will work out in the end. It always does. Yet a part of me is wary.

* * *

THAT NIGHT A HEAVY FOG descended on the city. The dreary mass blotted out the sun, turning the morning colors into a wash of gray. Hazy specters hovered about the tops of the unlit lampposts.

Fog hid the hunted. It also hid the hunters.

Aristotle and Emiko set out into the earthbound clouds. Emiko, sporting a severe limp, gamely kept pace a step behind Aristotle.

"Weren't you going to show me how your gun works?" Emiko asked.

"I was. Why don't we find a place to sit so that I can demonstrate?"

The two women found a wrought-iron bench on the roadside, beside a twisted bus stop sign. Virginia creeper twined about the seat slats. Lavender asters sprouted up where the bench legs met the ground.

Aristotle unholstered her revolver and removed the bullets in its cylinder. "So, what do you want to know?"

"Everything," Emiko said, her eyes widening.

"Then let's start at the beginning. It's a four-chambered revolver."

Emiko rolled her eyes. "I can see *that*. I want to know what's special about it."

"Point taken." Aristotle flipped the revolver's chamber open and let the shells inside drop onto her lap. "There are four features that make this revolver unique. One of them I already mentioned."

"It only has four chambers."

"Right. And that brings us to the second feature: This revolver is chambered to fire both .55 caliber rifle rounds and 28-gauge shotgun shells."

"Those are big for a handgun, aren't they?"

"They are. Sounds like you really know your guns."

Emiko blushed. "Where I'm from you have to."

"Such is the way of the world these days. Anyway," Aristotle continued, "big bullets make for big recoil. To deal with this we have the third special feature: a muzzle brake and a series of springs and weights to dampen the kick. They're the main reason why the gun is so big."

"And the other reason?"

"Because a big gun will scare most men into submission long before you're forced to shoot them." Aristotle lifted the muzzle to her lips and blew across it.

"And the fourth special feature?" Emiko asked.

Aristotle had saved the best for last. "When we talked earlier, I mentioned that rifles use rifling, those little grooves inside the barrel. Shotguns, meanwhile, have smooth barrels."

"And most pistols also have grooves like rifles," Emiko added.

"True. But what if I told you the barrel of this gun could be both rifled and unrifled?"

Emiko pondered this for a while, before shrugging. "I have no idea how that would work."

"Most people wouldn't. Before seeing this revolver I probably wouldn't have believed it either," Aristotle admitted. "Let me show you the inside of the barrel. Don't worry — it's unloaded." She angled the barrel, trying to avoid pointing it directly at Emiko. No one wanted a gun in their face, not even an unloaded one.

"Do you see the rifling?" she asked.

"Yeah, I can see the grooves."

"Now watch carefully." Aristotle twisted the barrel. "How about now?"

"Oh, cool!" Emiko exclaimed. "When you did that, the spiraled grooves filled themselves in. Could you show me again?"

Aristotle rotated the barrel. The twist was a subtle movement of only a few degrees, just enough to let the rifled grooves slide in or out of place. She repeated the motion a few times to let Emiko see.

"Usually, a gunsmith scores grooves in a handgun's barrel. This revolver, on the other hand, lets me have my grooves and hide them too. That's why the barrel is a hair thicker than most guns — it needs space for the rifling to retreat when I switch to Spread mode."

"Spread mode. I like the sound of that." Emiko patted her hands against her thighs. "What's the other mode called?"

"Snipe mode."

"Can I try changing it myself?"

"Go ahead. It takes only a slight twist."

Emiko accepted the revolver carefully, as though it were a loaded flintlock pistol. She peered down the barrel and twisted. After repeating this a few times she returned the gun to Aristotle.

"Where can I get a gun like this?"

"You'd have to head up to Toronto, where my gunsmith is."

"Toronto! Isn't that in Canada?"

Aristotle nodded. "It'd be a long journey. Even if you made it, there's no guarantee that my gunsmith would build one for you. He's selective about who he'll work for."

Emiko spread her hands wide. "Does he make long-barreled versions, too?"

Aristotle shook her head. "He doesn't. Or at least he didn't when I got this one. He told me the twist barrel would be harder to implement in a rifle-length weapon. But perhaps he's figured it out since I last saw him."

"Maybe someday I'll go to Toronto with you and find out," Emiko said.

"Maybe you will."

Emiko squinted into the distance. Holding a finger to her lips, she pointed out into the fog.

Aristotle saw it, too. A brown, four-legged animal had materialized from the haze. A deer.

Dinner had arrived. Aristotle set her revolver to Snipe and steadied her aim.

* * *

Emiko and Aristotle prepared the deer's meat for storage. They found an empty ice chest in the basement. The chest would help protect the meat, if not keep it cool. Emiko wasn't confident they'd be able to eat all the meat before it spoiled, even if they dried and salted it. Still, after her recent deprivation, the risk of wasted meat didn't seem like so great a crime.

In the early afternoon, over generous portions of freshly seared venison, Emiko and Aristotle discussed their next move.

"So, where should we look for the General?" Aristotle asked. She sat perpendicular to Emiko at the table.

"Do you have any ideas?"

"I'm afraid I don't. My source told me I should look in Minneapolis — nothing beyond that." Aristotle ran a finger across the tablecloth. "How about you? Any hunches you haven't acted on yet?"

Emiko scrunched her brow together. "What do you mean?"

"Well, what brought you here in the first place?" Aristotle rested her palm on the table.

"I followed a couple of the General's men from Duluth."

Followed didn't tell the half of it, of course. Emiko had actually stowed away in the trunk of the men's car. Eventually the car stalled out on the outer limits of Minneapolis. After waiting until the men were long gone, Emiko pushed the rear seat forward and made her escape.

What would've happened if the two men had checked the trunk? Emiko had a feeling it was better she hadn't found out.

"And what were those men doing in Duluth?" Aristotle asked.

"They were looking for oil, and recruiting soldiers for an army."

"Recruitment ... Do you have any idea how large the General's force already is?"

"Well, not exactly. But I'd guess it's pretty big."

"Which means that the General would need a big place to house his troops."

"Sure, I guess that makes sense," Emiko said.

"So where can we find a place big enough to accommodate an army?"

Emiko dug her teeth into the corner of her lower lip. A large place? Target Tower? Vikings Stadium? But people didn't live in towers or stadiums.

"I don't know," she said with a defeated sigh.

"Didn't you used to live here?"

"Yeah," Emiko mumbled. But she'd left Minneapolis when she was six years old. What did a six-year-old know about a city's layout?

"Then think. Where in Minneapolis could a large group live? We're talking about an army. They'd need open space to train."

A large group? Open space to train? Emiko's first urge was to blurt out "Northeast Park," but she quickly thought better of it. She'd already scoped out the expansive park. A large group couldn't live there unless they'd looted tents from every Gander Mountain and REI store in the city.

She thought back to her youth. She had a fuzzy recollection of sitting in an open field, surrounded by buildings of gray stone and red brick, watching people herd past. But where was this place? Was it real or imagined?

It had to be real. She remembered her father taking her there.

That was it. Her father!

"How about the university?" she said eagerly.

"The University of Minnesota?" Aristotle tapped a finger against her temple. "That's a good idea. Lots of open space, and plenty of apartments. The General could even be housing men in the dormitories."

"Should we go there, then?"

"Do you know how to get there?"

Emiko offered a tentative nod. "I think so.

"Then tomorrow you'll lead the way."

Chapter 20

May 21st, 2027
Post Status: Private

Finals are over. I just posted the last of my students'
grades. You know what that means.

School's out for summer!

I've always found it odd that teachers look forward to
summer vacation just as much as their students.
Clearly no one actually wants to be at school. What
does it say about our education system that neither
those instructing nor those instructed wish to
participate?

Anyhow, the first weeks of my summer are already
planned out. In two days Nathan and I will set out for
the Boundary Waters Canoe Area, a few hours north of
Minneapolis. Our days will be spent canoeing across
pristine blue lakes, catching fresh walleye, and by
night we'll sit by the campfire, roast marshmallows,
and look up at the stars.

It'll be the perfect summer getaway.

* * *

WEEKS HAD PASSED since the General's disappearance. The
Restoration Army's activities had normalized. Well, mostly
normalized. Recruiters in other cities continued to bolster the
army's ranks, and soldiers in outposts spread across Minnesota
and its neighbors kept watch.

But in Minneapolis normal was not what it had been. The
army's main regiment was still on lockdown, stuck inside the
dormitories-turned-barracks.

Ramses carried on as the radio operator, a job as tedious and thankless as ever. When his shift at the receiver came to a close, he went to the Restoration Army's stable. Visiting the stable was the only bright spot in his day.

Ramses scratched Thunder between the ears. The stable's first occupant, Thunder was now one of three horses here. Though the General's long-term plan was to employ cars and trucks, and perhaps even tanks and airplanes, horses were an effective stopgap — faster, cleaner, and smarter than those brutish, genetically-modified freaks known as tvapas.

A fine horse you are, Thunder. The finest of them all, Ramses thought as he studied the noble steed's luminous black eyes. While manning the radio he often daydreamed of freeing Thunder from this oppressive stable and taking him on a heroic adventure to further the Restoration Army's cause.

"Private Brushnell?"

Ramses' eyes rolled toward the entryway. A young, fresh-faced recruit stood in the door frame. Dressed in Restoration Army green and more boy than man, the recruit panted for breath. He'd clearly sprinted here.

Were the newcomers getting younger, or was Ramses merely growing old? The truth perhaps lay somewhere in between.

"Yes, Private?" Ramses said.

"You are Ramses Brushnell, sir?"

"That I am." Ramses drew his shoulders back.

"Lieutenant Prince is looking for you, sir. He requests that you report to his office immediately."

"Understood, Private."

Ramses returned his attention to Thunder, brushing his fingers through the stallion's soft, flowing mane. At times he wondered if he'd been destined to be a horse trainer rather than a soldier. Unfortunately, given the state of the world, such a destiny could never be realized.

Ramses glanced back at the doorway. The boy hadn't budged.

"Is there anything else, Private?" Ramses asked.

"Sir, I thought I was to lead you to the lieutenant, sir," the boy stammered.

Did I once sound like this? Like a rambling idiot? Ramses wondered. No, it was unthinkable. Preposterous!

"I'm familiar with the location of the lieutenant's office, Private. I'll make my way there shortly."

"Understood, sir."

The boy stood at attention, hands at his sides, absolutely still.

"You are dismissed," Ramses said. "Go."

"Yes, sir." With a salute the boy vanished from the entryway.

Ramses sighed. What was becoming of the Restoration Army? It was admitting the lousiest of the lousy. When would the General return to provide more capable direction?

* * *

A few minutes later Ramses stepped into the lieutenant well-appointed office. Fog gathered outside the room's large, three-paneled window, obscuring the view. Tropical plants of the fake plastic variety lined the walls. Most discordant of all was the pink flamingo in the corner.

"Private Ramses Brushnell," said Lieutenant Prince, seated at his desk. "Just the man I was looking for."

Today Prince wore a beige shirt, much like a Boy Scout's uniform. A red neckerchief sat under the shirt's collar, held in place by a gold slide below his neck. Astride his head perched that ridiculous French beret.

"You called, sir?" Ramses said.

"I did. I don't imagine you'd have paid me a visit otherwise. Please, have a seat." Lieutenant Prince gestured at a leather chair in front of his desk. Ramses sat, sinking deep into the cushions. The seat had more give than a water bed.

Prince produced a case of cigars his desk drawer. "Would you care for one?" he asked.

"No, thank you, sir."

"Suit yourself."

After choosing a cigar, Prince pared off one end with a penknife and lit it with a stick match. He drew deeply from it, the business tip smoldering like a campfire ember. With a satisfied air he exhaled a curling tendril of smoke.

Ramses didn't know how to smoke a cigar, nor did he want to embarrass himself by trying. Still, he recognized the offer as an attempt to win his trust and favor. But to what end? Ramses waited patiently for Prince to speak.

"You've been with the Restoration Army for some time now, Brushnell. Over a year, if I'm not mistaken."

"That's correct, sir."

Prince held his cigar between his fingers thoughtfully, studying Ramses.

"I have a question for you, Brushnell."

"Yes, sir?"

"What are you fighting for?"

Ramses didn't hesitate. "I'm fighting for the future of mankind, sir."

"I see." Prince flicked his cigar over the ashtray on his desk. "But I'm curious as to where your loyalties lie. Do you fight for mankind? Or do you fight for the General?"

Ramses straightened his posture. "The General fights for mankind, sir."

Prince sucked on his cigar. He gazed at Ramses through the smoke.

"Say you could only choose one, mankind or the General. Which would it be?"

What was Prince getting at? Ramses resisted the impulse to squirm in his chair.

"Speak your mind, Private," Prince encouraged. "Your answer won't leave this room."

Though the words were meant to reassure, they only made Ramses wonder about the consequences of an incorrect answer.

"I would choose to stay true to the stated purpose of the Restoration Army, sir. The good of mankind stands above all else. But, again, I see no conflict of interest between the General and the goals of the Restoration Army — goals which the General himself laid out."

Lieutenant Prince nodded contemplatively. He stubbed out his cigar in the ashtray.

"Then that will be all, Private. You're free to return to your duties."

"Thank you, sir."

Ramses stood. His eyes lingered on the garish pink flamingo as he approached the door. He reached for the doorknob.

"Take care now, Private Brushnell," Prince said.

Ramses looked back over his shoulder. "I always do, sir." He stepped out, carefully shutting the door, and headed backs towards the stable.

Why had Prince asked him those questions? Was the lieutenant testing his loyalty? Ramses didn't know how to handle the situation. But he knew someone who would.

Chapter 21

June 23rd, 2027
Post Status: Public

Endless days without rain. Insufferable dry heat.
Fields of yellowed grass.

This is summer. And what a miserable summer it is.

* * *

THE UNIVERSITY OF MINNESOTA was more expansive than Aristotle had imagined. It had three campuses, one on either bank of the Mississippi River and a third in the neighboring city of St. Paul. How many students had once studied here? Ten thousand? Fifty thousand? Neither number would've come as a surprise.

Now the university was empty. Aristotle and Emiko meandered across the fog-covered East Bank campus. For all Aristotle knew they could've been the only two living souls on the university grounds.

"Do you know where the dormitories are?" Aristotle asked.

"I'm not sure. Maybe we can find a map," Emiko suggested.

Aristotle nodded. She wondered why she hadn't thought to work with a partner before now. Had she just not found a suitable match? Or had her experiences with the Toronto PD soured her on the idea?

Emiko pointed ahead. "That sign has a map." Though she clearly wanted to sprint to the sign, her ankle limited her to a brisk, uneven shuffle. Aristotle followed behind.

The map was engraved in a three-by-five-foot metal panel, soldered between two steel posts.

"It looks like there are dormitories down here," Emiko said, indicating a location on the campus' south-east corner.

"Four dormitories, to be exact," Aristotle said. "Let's go."

They crossed the campus, passing classrooms and lecture halls. The old, stately buildings blended seamlessly into the fog, their granite walls fading in and out of the gray.

Soon they reached Washington Avenue. Car access had been blocked off and two sets of light rail tracks had been laid into the pavement. The route cut through campus and spanned the Mississippi River. Between the campus mall and the student union a train rested on the rails, still connected to the dead power grid above. Aristotle and Emiko crossed the tracks by way of a footbridge.

"We're almost there," Emiko said, just above a whisper. "Should we be careful?"

"I suppose we should." Though the dorms might have been empty, it was best to assume they weren't.

They crept through the fog, veering past a towering concrete building. The tower rose both up and out, reaching over a dozen stories into the sky. Glass-enclosed elevated walkways extended from its body like branches from a tree, connecting it to adjacent buildings. A sign indicated that it was called Moos Tower.

Emiko stopped at one of the tower's many corners. She peeked around.

"I think I see a dormitory."

"What does it look like?"

"Um ... it looks like the other buildings here. It's six stories tall and made of brick."

"Any sign of activity?"

"Not really. I see a big fat squirrel, and lots of fog, and —"

Emiko recoiled from the corner, leaving her sentence unfinished.

"And?" Aristotle prompted. "What else did you see?"

"I think ..." Emiko spoke in a hushed voice. "I think I saw someone in one of the windows.

"Inside the dormitory?"

Emiko nodded.

"What did they look like?" Aristotle asked.

"I don't know. I turned away as soon as I saw them," Emiko said. "Do you want to take a look?"

"Can you describe where you saw them?"

"He was in one of the windows. I don't remember which floor."

Aristotle rubbed her hand along the tower's wall, feeling its lumpy concrete surface, thinking. She eyed Emiko. The girl had recovered her wits.

"You'll be able to spot the man again faster than I could. Take another peek and describe to me where he is."

Emiko gave a nervous nod, then leaned her head around the corner. She quickly pulled back.

"He's on the fifth floor, three windows from the right."

"Got it. Let me have a look."

Emiko stepped back, clearing the way for Aristotle.

The dormitory was farther away than Aristotle had expected, separated from Moos Tower by a street, a narrow patch of open grass, and a shuttered church. Six floors tall and constructed of drab, coffee brown bricks, the dorm looked more like a low-income housing complex than a place for students. Still, if the map said it was a dormitory, then it was a dormitory. What did Aristotle know of dormitories, anyway? She'd never attended university. She hadn't even finished secondary school. All thanks to the Desolation.

Aristotle counted. Five floors up, three windows in. Squinting, she was able to make out a figure.

She swung back from the corner. "You have good eyes, Emiko. I never would've picked him out if you hadn't told me where to look."

"Thank you." Emiko seemed unsure what else to say. "Did you see the colors he was wearing?"

Aristotle's lips curled into a disbelieving smirk. "Are you saying you did?"

Emiko nodded. "He was wearing *green*."

"Green? What's special about green?"

"All of the General's men wear green."

This was news to Aristotle. The lackey she'd met on Mallard Island, Gallagher, hadn't worn a uniform. Perhaps he'd been an exception. He had been playing a role, after all, slithering his way into Aristotle's good graces before striking unexpectedly.

"So you think this is one of the General's men? One of his soldiers?" Aristotle asked.

"I don't know, but it would make sense, wouldn't it? We did come here looking for the General."

"That we did," Aristotle said. Emiko was probably right. Still, it seemed odd that they'd spotted only one man. Wouldn't the General have men patrolling the area around his headquarters?

"So, what do we do?" Emiko asked.

"I'm not sure yet," Aristotle said, frowning.

"Why don't we sneak over there and have a look?"

Aristotle tugged on one of her brightly colored sweater sleeves. "Do I look like I'm dressed for sneaking?"

"Not at all," Emiko admitted, her cheeks glowing bashfully. "But then what do we do?"

"Well, I think it'd be risky to walk right up there and start asking questions."

"I think so, too."

"And even if I changed into better clothes for sneaking, I'd be afraid of the consequences if we were caught. We could be locked up, beaten, raped, or shot."

"I wouldn't get caught." Emiko flashed a devilish grin, one that suggested she'd done this sort of thing before. Just what kind of wild life had this girl been living?

"Point taken, but I'm afraid I won't be as sneaky as you."

"Then I'll go alone?" Emiko asked, eager to take on the assignment.

Aristotle simply shook her head. There had to be a better way. Maybe they could find a way in from underground, via the sewers? It might've worked, but it sounded complicated. Not to mention stinky.

Aristotle inched her eyes around the corner. She surveyed the surroundings again — the fog-enshrouded trees, the prairie grasses, the other dormitories in the distance, and the church ...

Her pupils lingered on that abandoned house of God. From its roof rose a huge cross, worn and yellowed, like the color of uncooked biscuit batter.

The Desolation had killed man, but the Lord still remained, watching over the world from the heavens. At least that was what some believed. Aristotle didn't count herself among the believers. Still, God was not powerless.

"What are you looking at?" Emiko prodded.

Aristotle turned back to Emiko. She sized the girl up.

"Do you have an idea?" Emiko asked.

"I do," Aristotle said. "We're going to pray."

Chapter 22

June 26th, 2027
Post Status: Public

The rain refuses to fall. Once again the Corn Belt is experiencing drought-like conditions, and there's not nearly enough water remaining in the Ogallala Aquifer to compensate.

President Hernandez has called for the stoppage of all corn ethanol production. All grain will be diverted to the food supply. It's a good move. Frankly, I'm surprised the President didn't enact it sooner.

It's also common knowledge that much of last year's harvest sits in grain silos, uneaten. Prospectors hedged by keeping stores of last year's crop, knowing that another drought would drive the price per bushel sky high.

At first blush it would appear these prospectors got their wish. Fortunately for the rest of us, however, Congress has decided to fix the prices of wheat, corn, and soybeans. Those who try to circumvent these price controls by selling on the black market will be severely punished.

A nationalization of our food resources is prudent. I have no sympathy for these aspiring "corn barons" who are losing out.

It sounds like we'll be able to weather this year's drought by shrewdly managing our current stores of grain. Of course, eventually we'll deplete those too …

Perhaps I should get back to my rain dance.

* * *

CLINGING TO THE WALLS of Moos Tower, Emiko and Aristotle hurried toward the church. When they ran out of wall they ducked into a stretch of plume grass, crawling the final yards on their hands and knees.

They reached the church's back door. Missing flakes of red paint exposed the blond maple beneath. A splintered hole near the base of the door suggested someone had given it a hard kick.

Emiko turned the doorknob, finding it unlocked. It led into a priest's study, furnished with a plain oak desk, a two-door closet, a dusty mirror, and a pair of metal folding chairs.

"We need some robes," Aristotle said.

"Do all churches have robes?" Emiko asked.

"No, but this is a Catholic church. It should have some."

Emiko opened the closet door. Inside were a number of black robes on hangers, along with black veils and white hooded caps.

"I think I found what we're looking for," she said.

"You certainly did." Aristotle fingered the black cloth. "These habits will be perfect."

They took two sets of robes from the closet. After slipping out of their shirts and pants and setting their weapons aside, they donned the holy vestments. On top of the flowing gowns they wore white caps and black veils. Wide, white neckerchiefs covered their necks and upper chests.

"How does it fit?" Aristotle asked after they'd finished changing. The neckerchief and cap closely outlined Aristotle's face, emphasizing her jawline. The veil completely hid her short brown hair. The black gown, though formless, still accentuated Aristotle's femininity.

"Mine's a bit long, but it'll do," Emiko said. The robes felt strange. She typically wore pants and simple tops, and wasn't accustomed to the over-sized, flowing clothes. "Will we be okay without our weapons?" she asked, eyeing the guns they'd set on the desk.

"The Lord will protect us," Aristotle replied cryptically.

With a shrug, Emiko turned to the mirror. She wiped its dust-caked surface with her sleeve, exposing her reflection. The nun's habit had changed her appearance completely. The veil and cap revealed nothing of her long, black hair.

Aristotle appeared behind Emiko in the mirror.

"Did you ever go to church?" Emiko asked, looking at Aristotle's reflected image.

"It's been a long, long time. How about you?"

Emiko shook her head. The motion felt strange without the bobbing of her long hair accompanying it. "My parents never took us to church."

"I see," Aristotle said. "So, do you have a brother or a sister?"

"I have a brother." Emiko craned her head back to look at her inquisitor. "How did you know?"

"You said *us* instead of *me*."

"Did I?" It seemed that no matter how much Emiko wanted to be her own person, to be independent, she would still always be part of a family. When she'd lived together with her brother Nathan in Frontier View, she'd resented the ties that had kept her trapped there. Now that she was on her own she was beginning to realize how important those ties were. They were there to help protect her when she couldn't do so on her own.

"How about you?" Emiko asked. "Do you have any brothers or sisters?"

"I had a sister."

"I see," Emiko said, noting that Aristotle had said *had* and not *have*. "Did the Desolation take her?"

A shade of sadness crossed Aristotle's face. "Something like that. But the past is the past. Now we look to the future."

"I agree," Emiko said eagerly.

Resolve flickered in Aristotle's eyes. She made for the door. "Then let's go do what we set out to do."

"You bet," Emiko replied, following Aristotle outside. Strangely, the more time she spent with Aristotle, the better her injured ankle seemed to feel. Was it just part of the natural healing process, or was there another, more mysterious force at work? Never superstitious, Emiko guessed there had to be a scientific explanation. Maybe her brother or Pierre, that old know-it-all, would have an answer.

The renegade grass in front of the church's door came up to Emiko's waist. Aristotle stood at her side. In her nun's habit, Aristotle looked equal parts bold and tranquil, reserved yet determined.

"If we meet anyone, stay calm and let me do the talking, alright?" Aristotle said.

"Of course."

"What's your last name?"

"Kanno."

"Then you'll be Sister Kanno. I'll be Sister Leon," Aristotle said, pronouncing her name like Lee-own. "As long as we stick to our roles, we'll be safe."

Emiko nodded. Now didn't seem the time to ask Aristotle if she truly believed her own encouraging words.

"Then let's go," Aristotle said.

Was this what having an older sister felt like? Emiko had always wondered what her life would've been like with a sister instead of a brother. Spending time with Aristotle was giving her a taste.

They crossed the road, making for the dormitories like two tvapas plodding forward on a steamy summer's day. They wanted to appear as non-threatening as possible.

As they neared the dormitory, Emiko tilted her head back to look up at its six towering floors of brick. The man they'd seen in the window was no longer there. Notably, most of the windows had their blinds pulled shut.

An overgrown sidewalk encircled the block of dormitories. It led to an intersection that divided the block into four quarters, each containing one dormitory.

"Stay beside me," Aristotle directed as they cut into the block. "And keep your eyes open. We'll want to get a good sense of this area's layout in case we come back later."

"I'll do my best."

"I'm sure your best will be just fine, Sister Kanno," Aristotle said with a half-smile.

They sauntered between the dormitories. While appearing nonchalant, in reality Emiko was hyper-vigilant, absorbing as much as possible. How many men were here? What were they doing? Did they live in all four dormitories? And, most importantly, how could she and Aristotle gain access for a closer look?

Each of the four dormitories was unique. The one Emiko and Aristotle had spotted first, Comstock Hall, was the largest of the four. Next to Comstock Hall was another, older dormitory known as Pioneer Hall. With a snaking design full of oddly angled corners and a sharp roof, Pioneer Hall looked like a school for wizards. The remaining two dormitories were blandly conventional two-story buildings that reminded Emiko of Wal-Mart.

A courtyard occupied the space between the dormitories. Emiko imagined it had once been beautifully landscaped and alive with students not much older than her brother. Now the space was nothing but a tangle of weeds and chipped concrete.

Two aluminum poles rose staunchly from the undergrowth — a volleyball court. Once or twice a year, usually during a village-wide feast, the people of Frontier View gathered for an impromptu volleyball match. Emiko didn't understand the appeal of the sport — she'd rather have been out hunting — but everyone else, young and old, enjoyed it

Emiko was contemplating one of Pioneer Hall's bathroom windows, thinking about how easy it would be to slide the panel open and slip in, when Aristotle spoke.

"Looks like we're not alone." Aristotle gestured ahead with her chin.

Sure enough. Two men in green vests approached. Both men holstered pistols at their hips.

"Just stick to the plan, Sister Kanno," Aristotle said calmly.

"Sure thing, Sister Leon," Emiko replied in the most saintly voice she could muster.

An uneasy feeling welled up in Emiko's stomach. Men just like these two had taken her captive at Sawbill Lake. They had shot at her brother and Beard. They were trouble. Nothing but trouble.

But now wasn't the time for action. Emiko smiled angelically and resolved to let Aristotle take charge.

"Hello there, sisters," called one of the men. He had glacier blue eyes, shortly-buzzed blond hair, and a cleft in his chin wide as the Mississippi.

"Hello there, brothers," Aristotle responded with an air of divinity.

The second man jumped in. "We don't mean to trouble you, sister, but we respectfully advise you to avoid this area." He had a high-pitched, nasally voice, likely the result of his crooked nose. He wore round-framed glasses. All in all, he resembled a cross between a weasel and an owl.

"Why such advice, brother? We merely seek to spread our Father's blessed Gospel. Have we offended your finer sensibilities in doing so?"

"Well, erm, you see, we don't mean any offense, of course ..."

The blue-eyed man thrust a palm into the weasel's chest. "Shove it, Jennings." He regarded Aristotle with an icy stare. "What are you doing here, sister?"

"Our heaven-sent mission is two-fold. We are seeking brothers to join us in spreading the good word, of course. But of particular interest to us is that church across the street. We were examining it to see if it would make a suitable home for the Lord's children."

"I see," the man said. His frosty eyes turned to Emiko. "Does this one talk?"

"This one does, good brother," Emiko said, humbly bowing her head.

"Aren't you a bit young to be joining a nunnery?"

Emiko flushed with frustration. "I'm not too —"

"A sister may receive the call at any age," Aristotle gracefully interjected. She eyed the man's pistol, turning her nose up at it, and cleared her throat. "Just as there are no age restrictions for carrying firearms, a faithful servant of the Lord may join the sisterhood at any age. Sister Kanno here is certainly young, but her faith is strong."

The man twisted his beefy neck towards his crooked-nosed companion. "Is there really a church over there?"

"Why, yes there is, just across the street from Comstock Hall. And I believe it's empty, in —"

The blue-eyed man clamped five fingers around the weasel's shoulder. "Alright, sisters," he said. "You're free to do as you please. But I'll need to pat both of you down for weapons first."

"Weapons? I assure you we have none, brother," Aristotle said.

"Then you won't mind if I check."

Aristotle raised both arms. "I have nothing to hide."

"I don't either," said Emiko, also lifting her arms.

The imposing man stepped behind Emiko. He patted every part of her. She cringed as his hands passed over her chest and touched space between her thighs.

"You're next," he said to Aristotle, stepping behind her.

The man's hands moved leisurely across Aristotle's body. His fingers ran up her legs, tracing her thighs and buttocks. Soon his palms found her breasts. He tightened his hold, massaging the soft mounds of flesh hidden beneath Aristotle's robes.

Aristotle made no move to escape. Fury brewed in her eyes.

"That ... that's quite enough, isn't it?" the crooked-nosed man squeaked.

Glowering at his partner, the blue-eyed man released Aristotle's breasts and shoved her away.

"You're free to go. I suggest you don't stick around long."

Aristotle glared at the man. "Your advice is much appreciated, brother."

"Come on, Jennings. Let's get outta here." The man gestured with his head.

The two men strode past Emiko and Aristotle.

"No weapons. But the older one has a nice rack," the blue-eyed man said with a snicker, glaring menacingly over his shoulder.

The two women looked on, Aristotle's fists clenched into smoldering balls of rage.

Chapter 23

July 2nd, 2027
Post Status: Public

The crop situation is worse than I'd imagined.

Apparently many farmers have given up on the corn. Desperate and with nothing left to lose, they're organizing a march on Washington D.C. The movement is decentralized, powered by message boards, mailing lists, and social media.

Curious, I peeked at an internet forum for Iowa farmers. There I was inundated by references to President Hernandez, maize, and shoving said maize where the sun don't shine.

Graphic to say the least.

The movement is quickly gaining steam. A few resourceful souls have hired buses to carry people (protesters?) to the nation's capital — pay a few bucks and you're on your way to Washington.

I have to be honest. I have no idea what these people want from the President. They will arrive in Washington, and then what? Shake their rainmakers?

* * *

HiNRG HAD ONCE BEEN a promising upstart in the field of alternative energy research. In an age of rising fuel prices and increasing pessimism about the sustainability of running the world on fossil fuels, HiNRG's vision of limitless, pollution-free energy had provided hope for a brighter future. Yet as Nathan tore through the HiNRG offices, it became readily apparent that

HiNRG's promise to investors had been nothing more than a siren's song.

As expected, the offices overflowed with top-of-the-line computers, humongous LCD monitors, and energy-manipulating machines. Yet in addition to these expected discoveries, Nathan also found Caribbean cruise tickets, photos of extravagant lakeside estates, country club membership cards, and a set of golf clubs forged of gold and platinum. By the time he ventured to the company garage he was unsurprised to discover a pair of Lamborghinis parked there, one red as a robin, the other yellow as a #2 pencil.

Among all the overpriced gadgets and expensive perks, Nathan found no evidence to suggest that HiNRG had ever produced a working prototype of their compact power plant. Their promise, their research, and everything else about HiNRG had been nothing but incredibly profitable lies.

As he sifted through the building's contents, Nathan couldn't help but draw comparisons between the promise that had lured investors to HiNRG and the one that had guided John to Minneapolis. Both promises were nebulous and wildly hopeful, appealing to the last-ditch desperation of those who had exhausted all other possibilities.

Reality had long since extinguished the promise of HiNRG. John's beacon of hope was perilously close to suffering a similar fate.

Nathan, John, and Stearns left the HiNRG offices that afternoon just as empty-handed as they'd entered. The blazing sun had burned away all traces of the morning's fog.

John still hobbled along on crutches. Though John was insistent that he'd be rid of the crutches in no time, Nathan harbored doubts. John had at best a week left to find the Northland Core. It seemed unlikely he'd be walking unassisted before that deadline. And that was to say nothing of what would happen if his day of reckoning arrived early ...

Stearns seemed to be in fair spirits. He was every bit as eager as John to find the Northland Core, and he brought a certain levity to the proceedings. He enjoyed bantering with

John about their days in the Marines. And he'd already saved Nathan and John's skin once.

Unfortunately, Stearns' arrival hadn't exactly bolstered their search. Neither MinnePower nor HiNRG, both of which Stearns had vouched for, had panned out. Moreover, Stearns seemed uninterested in further exploring the university, a place which Nathan still felt held potential. Stearns posited that if the core was there, the men in green would've already found it.

Perhaps Nathan needed to suggest a new place to search. In fact, he already had one in mind. He hadn't worked up the gall to share it.

HiNRG had brought the three men to northern Minneapolis. They journeyed towards home along a road that ran parallel to Interstate 94. They passed a Target, a JCPenney, a Home Depot. Each gigantic store had its own expansive parking area. Rusting vehicles, only half-visible above the volunteer sumac and honeysuckle, dotted the lots.

"Do you remember that operation in the Ukraine?" Stearns asked John.

"How could I forget?"

"What was it called again?"

"Operation Free Ukraine."

"I remember that," said Stearns. "But what was everyone on the ground calling it?"

John drew his brow taut. "You mean Operation Saved by a Heart Attack?"

"That was it! Operation Heart Attack."

"You heard about that?"

"A commanding officer hears many things, John. I bet you boys on the ground thought your secret was safe."

John grunted indistinctly.

"Anyway, I remember being in Kharkiv, anxiously awaiting the Russian troops that were approaching the border," Stearns said. "We were all ready to fight the first battle of what we knew would become World War III. But then, when the Russian army was only minutes from the border ..."

" … we were saved by a heart attack," John said, completing Stearns sentence.

"Exactly! That bastard Putin finally croaked, and at the last second the Russian Federal Assembly called the whole thing off."

"We got lucky."

"Sometimes you need to get lucky."

Another war story from Stearns. Nathan knew these stories were comprised of truths, exaggerations, and lies, but had trouble differentiating among the three. This was at least the second time he'd heard Stearns reference the threat of World War III, a war that had never come to pass.

At least Stearns' stories were more entertaining that Pierre's, though perhaps only because Nathan hadn't already suffered through them a thousand times.

The big box stores gradually gave way to more suburbia. The men walked by a dilapidated funeral home. A stately maple cast a shadow across the lawn. The front door had been smashed in, leaving a pair of bronze hinges dangling from the frame.

As the three men emerged from the shade of the maple tree, John suddenly stopped.

"Hold up," he said. "I see someone ahead."

Stearns stepped to the front, cupping his forehead. "Can't say that I see anything."

"Nathan?" John hopped on one leg, adjusting the crutches tucked into his armpits.

Nathan squinted into the distance. "I can just make out someone coming this way," he said with hesitation. He detected a splotch of color in the distance, but couldn't tell if the splotch was moving.

"Just one?" John peered again down the sidewalk. "I thought I saw two people, but you're right. There's only one."

Though Nathan hadn't clearly seen even one figure, much less two, he decided there was no harm in keeping this knowledge to himself.

"I have no idea how you boys see so damned far," Stearns quipped. "I can barely see the next house down."

"Your eyes aren't that old," John said with a wry smile. "Hey, I think our bogey at twelve o'clock is wearing red."

"Red?" Nathan asked. The color brought to mind a certain hoodie-wearing woman. But what would she be doing in Minneapolis? "You don't think it's *her*, do you John?"

"The possibility crossed my mind," John remarked. "Let's hold steady."

The crimson figure progressed steadily closer, past the weed-infested lawns, shattered windows, and houses-turned-tombs. Soon Nathan too could recognize that it was Aristotle. The red sweater, the short-brown hair, and the hip-holstered pistol — all the features he remembered.

She alternated between eyeing the three men before her and scanning the surrounding area. Eventually her wandering attention fixed on John and Nathan.

"Aristotle," John called ahead, once they were within comfortable shouting distance.

Aristotle closed the gap before replying. "I thought we might bump into each other."

"Can't say I thought the same."

"I didn't figure you would. I got a tip to head down this way not long after we parted." Aristotle looked down at John's legs. "So tell me, Osborne — what's the deal with the crutches?"

"I took a shard of glass to the leg."

"Sounds serious."

"I'll survive."

"If you say so." Aristotle flashed a half-hearted smile at Nathan. "And how about you? Holding up alright?"

Nathan nodded. "Same as usual."

"Who's your new friend?" Aristotle tipped her head towards Stearns.

Stearns held out a hand. "The name is Kennedy Stearns. And how may I call you, miss?"

"Aristotle." She and Stearns shook. "A pleasure to meet you, Mr. Stearns."

"Just Kennedy is fine," Stearns said with an exaggerated wink.

"So, how is the search going?" Aristotle asked. "Have you found the Northland Core yet?"

"Not yet. But we will," John replied.

We have no choice but to find it, Nathan thought. Aristotle understood this as well as anyone. She'd been on Mallard Island. She knew what the consequences would be if their search failed. Apparently she agreed that these pessimistic truths were better left unsaid.

"What are you doing here?" Nathan asked. "Do you think the General is in Minneapolis?"

"That's what I heard," Aristotle replied. "I'm here trying to smoke him out."

"The General, you say?" Stearns jumped in.

"That's right. Can you tell me anything about him?" Aristotle asked.

"I've heard a few rumblings here and there. The green-vested men in this city drop his name from time to time."

"Do you have any specifics?"

Stearns pulled his jaw to one side and rubbed his white-flecked beard. "I'm afraid I don't. I myself only got into town a few weeks ago, after all. But I gotta say, he seems a scary fellow. Not the kind of guy I'd want to cross swords with."

Aristotle patted the revolver at her hip. "Then it's a good thing I carry a gun and not a sword."

"Suit yourself." Stearns shrugged. "I'm just an old soul offering friendly advice. No more, no less."

Aristotle's eyes lingered on Stearns for a long second.

"Still working alone?" John asked.

Aristotle considered for a moment, before nodding. "Alone is best."

"I used to think that, too."

John's words were met with silence. A gentle breeze tickled Nathan's arms. Tree branches rustled. An oak leaf tumbled down the sidewalk.

It felt to Nathan as though both sides were withholding information. Aristotle seemed to be in an icy mood. But why?

"How has your search been going?" Nathan asked.

"My search?" Aristotle's head swiveled to face Nathan. "I've been making progress."

"That's good to hear. What kind of progress?"

"Nothing I would want to trouble the three of you with." She swept a hand through her bangs, collecting loose strands of hair and tucking them behind her ear. "I imagine you already have enough on your plate."

"You're right about that," John muttered.

"You could help us search, you know," Nathan suggested, hopeful the offer would be accepted.

Aristotle smiled wanly. "If Osborne says he'll find the Northland Core, I trust that he will. Anyhow, I'd best move along. There's someone I need to find. But who knows? Maybe our paths will cross again."

"I hope they do," Nathan said.

"It's been my pleasure," said Stearns, his mouth open in a gaping, dopey smile.

"Good luck," John added.

"Good luck to you too, Osborne."

Aristotle continued down the sidewalk, her revolver bouncing gently against her hip.

"Wait," John said, just below a shout.

Aristotle looked back over her shoulder. "Yeah?"

"If you find out anything about the Northland Core, come tell us about it. We're at 1013 39th Avenue."

"Got it. I'll do that, Osborne."

Aristotle turned and went on her way. She made a right at the next intersection and vanished behind a brick townhouse, exiting the scene as unceremoniously as she'd entered it.

"Why is she so intent on finding the General?" Nathan asked John as the trio resumed their walk home.

John gave a shrug, barely visible above his crutches.

"Could be a personal vendetta, but I get the impression she just wants to do some good in this world. Searching for the General must be her way of striving to do so."

"Do you think searching for the General is way of doing good?" Nathan asked, realizing how pretentious the question sounded as soon as it left his mouth.

"I think good and bad won't mean much until I find the Northland Core."

Gruff, grizzled, and straight-to-the-point, it was the kind of response Nathan had come to expect from John Osborne. Yet Nathan couldn't help but notice the glimmer in John's eye. Did John respect Aristotle's single-minded determination? Would he have once acted so selflessly for the greater good? Was he contemplating joining Aristotle in her quest after he found the Northland Core?

"Do you think we'll see her again?" Nathan asked.

John stopped and rested on his crutches, staring off into the distance before replying: "Only if she wants to see us."

Chapter 24

July 5th, 2027
Post Status: Public

Now *this* is interesting. Yesterday the squatters in Washington celebrated not Independence Day, but *People's Independence Day*. They hoisted up signs declaring that President Hernandez and the members of Congress are inept, and that "we the people" should throw them out of office.

I wonder if these protesters see their own hypocrisy. They're supplicating the government for help while simultaneously demanding a regime change.

What do they really want?

In my eyes the protests are futile. I honestly believe that the government is doing all it can. I don't see how kicking politicians to the curb could improve the food supply.

Then again, if you're homeless, unemployed, hungry, and have no other avenues to vent your frustration, I suppose you could do worse than camping out on the White House lawn and sending mixed messages.

* * *

EMIKO HAD EXPECTED she would see her brother and Beard again. She had not planned on the reunion happening here.

She crouched behind a fallen cottonwood tree. When she'd recognized Nathan and Beard through her telescopic rifle scope, she'd ducked out of sight without a word to Aristotle. The last thing she needed was Aristotle proposing a family reunion. Emiko hadn't had the stomach to face her brother weeks ago in Duluth, and she didn't have it now.

Would Nathan be angry that she'd left Frontier View? Disappointed? Concerned? She'd considered telling Nathan that Pierre had given her permission to leave, but she knew her brother would never buy that lie.

She wondered if she really owed her brother an explanation. The world was free. She was independent. If she wanted to explore Minneapolis, who had the right to stop her? Though her heart said *no one*, her head knew that Nathan, Beard, and Pierre would see the situation in a very different light.

The reunion would come. Just not yet. Like a wolf stalking its prey, Emiko would reveal herself when the circumstances favored her. Patience was her most important ally.

She remained behind the cottonwood a bit longer before beginning to limp home. Her ankle had grown cold. Gradually her muscles warmed and her pace increased.

What would she tell Aristotle? Fortunately, after years of telling half-truths to Nathan about where she'd gone and what she'd been doing, she was an old hand at concocting short, simple, believable stories.

Whether or not Aristotle was as gullible as her brother remained to be seen.

* * *

Where had that girl gone?

Aristotle gazed out the kitchen window. The sun had fallen below the crowns of the street-side maples. Soft light filtered through the leaves.

Emiko's disappearance had come without warning. One moment she'd been at Aristotle's side; the next moment she'd been gone. Had she injured herself? Been kidnapped? Both possibilities seemed unlikely. Emiko wouldn't have succumbed to injury or kidnapping without audible protest.

This left Aristotle looking at one last possibility: that Emiko had disappeared of her own free will. Maybe the approaching men had given Emiko cause to bolt. But wouldn't the girl have said something?

Aristotle tapped her fingers on the table. Her breasts still ached where the man had violated her. She'd been a fool to lead

Emiko into the dormitory complex unarmed. But what if they had been carrying guns? The encounter could've spiraled out of control. No matter how Aristotle played the events back in her head, the situation looked like a no-win proposition.

She idly cracked her wrists. Days didn't come much worse than this. How could Emiko just up and disappear? As soon as Aristotle found the girl, she wouldn't hesitate to ask. She expected a damn good answer.

Aristotle hadn't felt this personally responsible for another's well-being in a long time; not since she'd lost her sister Isabel to the Desolation. That loss still haunted her. She wouldn't fail again.

The front door creaked open. Aristotle's train of thought flew off the rails. Her heart quickened. How would she deal with Emiko?

Emiko limped into the kitchen, staggering across the room without making eye contact. Aristotle glared at her. Was this Emiko's way of acting like nothing had happened?

If it was she was failing miserably.

After leaning her rifle against the wall, Emiko took the chair farthest from Aristotle. She had a big grin plastered across her face. A big, fake grin.

"Hi," she said, remorseless as the devil himself.

Aristotle crossed her arms, leaned back in her chair, and let her eyes speak her piece.

"I'm sorry about running off like that," Emiko said. "When I saw those men approaching, I thought it'd be a good idea to take up position somewhere out of sight so that I could provide cover fire if you needed it."

Aristotle lifted both eyebrows. Cover fire? She wasn't buying it.

"What?" Emiko asked, her grin drooping.

Aristotle offered a shrug.

"Alright," Emiko said. "The truth is I was scared of those three men. They didn't look like nice people."

She said this with a sniffle. It might have been the phoniest, most insincere sniffle Aristotle had ever heard, but it was unmistakably a sniffle.

"Fair enough." Aristotle leaned forward and braced her hands on the table's lip. "But why didn't you say anything to me?"

"I panicked! My feet carried me away before I knew what I was doing."

"You don't seem like a girl that scares so easily, Emiko."

"Well, usually not, but there was just something about those men that —"

"You know, I just so happened to be acquainted with two of those men, and I could've assured —"

"You know Beard?" Emiko blurted out, a wave of shock crashing over her apologetic veneer.

Aristotle crossed her arms and planted her elbows on the tabletop.

"Beard?"

"I mean ..." Emiko straightened her posture. "You have friends with beards?"

"Sure. Why not?" Though bearded men were still as uncommon as mosquitoes in December, Aristotle wondered if scruffy facial hair was perhaps making a comeback.

"*Really*?" Emiko asked with a tad too much interest. "My brother always told me that only bad, uncivilized men have beards. So when I saw those men, I just ran. I didn't know what else to do."

"Mmmm-hmmm," Aristotle uttered. Something she'd said had given Emiko a jolt. Something about beards, albeit not for the deathly-afraid-of-facial-hair reason Emiko had cooked up. What was the girl hiding?

Aristotle heaved a defeated sigh. How was it that John Osborne, the most lonesome of lone wolves, could work with a pair of partners, while she couldn't manage to trust even one?

But were John's partners truly trustworthy? Though Nathan seemed loyal as a St. Bernard, something about Kennedy Stearns didn't sit right with her. She'd seen a flame in his eyes that belied his friendly old-geezer persona.

Maybe it was just the flame of lust for a woman. Maybe Aristotle was letting Stearns' ogling skew her opinion. The assault she'd experienced not hours before still colored her thoughts.

Aristotle sat back in her chair and smiled tiredly. Though Emiko was hiding something, she didn't seem to be doing so with malicious intent.

"It's getting late. How about we start a fire and cook dinner? We still have plenty of venison."

"That sounds great. I'll go out and build the fire." Emiko gingerly got to her feet and made for the backyard.

Aristotle began preparing a plate of deer cuts. By the time she followed Emiko outside the fire was hot, the water vapor trapped inside the wood sizzling as it escaped. The vestiges of the day's sun hung like an orange murmur over the horizon, bidding farewell before giving way to the dark whisper of the stars.

Aristotle placed a steel grate above the lick of the flames. After searing the steaks, she let them cook gently for several more minutes. When the meat was well-done the two women returned to the kitchen, where they dined under turmeric-colored lamplight. The meal didn't last long. Soon their plates were clean.

"Thanks for the food," Emiko said, belting her arms around her stomach.

"Anytime," Aristotle replied.

Emiko gazed across the table, vacantly transfixed on Aristotle's face.

"Is there something stuck in my teeth?" Aristotle asked.

Emiko's eyes fluttered, as though exiting a trance. She shook her head.

"No, that's not it," she said with a shy smile — a genuine one this time. "I was just wondering if you could help me cut my hair."

"Cut your hair?" Aristotle's head jerked in surprise. Though she cut her own hair, she wasn't much of a stylist. She kept her brown her short because short was functional.

"Yeah," Emiko said. She held up a handful of her long black hair, letting the loose ends dangle. "Let's cut it all off."

"If that's what you want, that's what we'll do. We'll need a scissors. There has to be one in this house somewhere."

"I saw one while I was cleaning up."

"Then take the lantern and lead the way." Aristotle gestured at the source of the room's flickering illumination, hanging from a rusty nail on the wall.

After rounding up a scissors, a bed sheet, and a kitchen chair, they proceeded outside. Emiko had painstakingly reclaimed the home's floors from neglect; there was no sense in sullying them with long, black hairs.

Emiko took a seat. Aristotle swept the bed sheet over Emiko's shoulders to protect the girl's clothes from falling strands of hair.

Aristotle's Backyard Beauty Parlor was open for business.

"What style did you have in mind?" Aristotle asked, standing behind Emiko.

"I want short hair like yours."

"Are you sure?"

"I'm sure!"

"It'll take years to grow back."

"I know." Emiko glanced over her shoulder at Aristotle. "Don't worry. It'll look great!"

Aristotle shrugged. If Emiko wanted short hair, short hair she would get. Aristotle lifted the scissors to Emiko's long, straight locks, chose a point a few inches below the girl's ears, and snipped.

Chapter 25

July 9th, 2027
Post Status: Public

Danielle had an ultrasound today. It's a girl!

We went back and forth about whether to give her a Japanese or English name. In the end we opted to continue the pattern that we started when we named Emiko.

We will name our daughter Yuki. Roughly translated, it means "snow hope" — snow because it was snowing on Valentine's Day, and hope because she's our hope for the future.

It feels wonderful to be welcoming another daughter into our family. Now that we know Yuki's gender we can start planning for her. At some point we'll probably want to move Yuki into Emiko's room … although first we'd have to convince Emiko that her bedroom floor isn't a proper place for storing sharp-edged toys.

Hmmm … so much to think about.

* * *

DARKNESS TIGHTENED its grip on Minneapolis. It amazed John that a place once so bright could now be so vacuous and empty. Yet he supposed the real miracle was that mankind had once managed to fill the night sky with so much artificial light.

John limped away from the living room window and hunkered down in the reclining chair. Nathan sat in another corner, reading by the pale glow of a lamp.

Nathan looked up from his book. "Shouldn't you be using your crutches?"

"I can stumble around just fine, thanks," John grumbled.

"You don't need to prove anything to me, John. Maybe you want to demonstrate your toughness to Stearns, but you don't need to show me what I already know." Nathan returned his nose to his book, some pulp novel about a moon and a mistress. He flipped the page.

Does he think I'm trying to show off? John wondered. *Am I trying to show off?* The addition of Stearns had changed the dynamics of his partnership with Nathan. It was still unclear whether that change was for better or worse.

"What do you make of Stearns?" John asked. Stearns was out taking an evening stroll. John suspected he was searching for a cache of booze to refill his flask.

Nathan set the paperback on his lap. He fingered one of the cover's well-worn corners. Finally he shrugged.

"I'm not sure. He seems like a decent guy, but we haven't seen much in the way of results since he signed on. Then again, he did save our lives. And maybe we wouldn't have found the core yet if it was just you and me, either." Nathan massaged his thigh. "So who knows? There ain't no such thing as a free lunch."

"Huh?" John frowned. "There ain't no free lunch?"

Nathan patted paperback's cover. "A snippet of wisdom from a master of science fiction."

"Meaning?"

"I'm not sure myself. It just sounded like a timely thing to say."

Nathan resumed his reading. It looked like the conversation was over. But then, speaking over the book, he added, "I guess I mean that it's pointless to imagine what the search would be like with or without Stearns' help. We can only have it one way. Hypothesizing about the choice we didn't make is a waste of time."

John nodded contemplatively. Nathan's word rang true. They only had one shot at this. There was no time to stop and smell the roses sprouting from the tvapa dung. What they could do, however, was look back at the path they'd taken thus far to determine if there was a better way forward.

John considered the places they'd searched during the past few days. They'd been targets agreed upon by himself and Stearns with scant input from Nathan. Was Nathan saying, in his opaque way, that he disagreed with their choices?

"Do you have any thoughts about where we should look tomorrow?" John asked.

"Of course I do," Nathan said, eyes still on the pages of his book.

"I'd like to hear."

"Well," Nathan said, tucking his novel between the cushion and armrest of his chair, "I was thinking about where the Pentagon would hide a top-secret energy project. They would hide it someplace big, but in a big place where no one would bother to look."

John nodded. "Go on."

"The problem is that constructing such a facility without drawing unwanted attention would've been pretty hard. China and Russia's orbital cameras would've seen it immediately. Not to mention it would've showed up on Google Maps and Baidu."

"Is this a riddle?" John narrowed his eyes accusingly. "You know how I feel about riddles."

"Everything is a riddle," Nathan said with a sly grin. "And the answer to this one would be to build the Northland Core's research facility in plain sight."

"For example?"

"For example, the Pentagon could've built it underneath another big project."

"Such as?"

"Such as Vikings Stadium."

John ran his fingers down his scruffy jaw. Top-secret Pentagon research, conducted underneath an NFL stadium? As a conspiracy theory it rivaled the grassy knoll.

"It's bold. I like it," John said.

"You do?"

"It sounds better than visiting another investment-embezzling research firm."

Nathan lifted his palms in an aw-shucks pose. "I'm glad you agree."

"Then it's settled. Tomorrow we go to Vikings Stadium."

"Maybe we can find some stale pretzels while we're at it," Nathan said, returning to his book with a contented smile.

John drummed his finger on the armrest of his chair. He would run the idea past Stearns. If the old colonel objected, though it seemed unlikely he would, John would stick up for Nathan's proposal. After everything he and Nathan had been through together, John owed the kid that much — that much and probably more.

"John?" Nathan said.

John looked up. "Yeah?"

"I was thinking. Aristotle said she heard the General's headquarters was here in Minneapolis, right?"

"What about it?"

"Well, this might seem like a bit of a stretch, but ..."

"Go ahead," John said. Nathan had just suggested that the Northland Core was hidden beneath a football stadium. What could he consider a stretch after that?

"Aristotle seems to think the General is here. Those men who assaulted us — the ones Stearns saved us from — also seemed to be working for the General. And then there was that guy we got into a footrace with on campus," Nathan said. "Something is happening here, right under our noses. There must be some part of the picture we're not seeing."

"What do you mean?"

"It just seems to me that, since we've bumped into a handful of people, there should be more. More than we've seen, at least."

"I see what you're saying," John said. Indeed, the city was surprisingly lifeless. But wasn't that what they'd anticipated?

"What if the General and his men are hiding, waiting for us to make a move?"

"Why would they do that?"

"For the same reason Gallagher dropped in on us at Mallard Island ..."

"To find the Northland Core," John said. "But if that's the case what can we do about it?"

"I don't know. Just keep our eyes open, I guess. Speaking of which ..."

"Yeah?"

"There's still been no sign of Emiko. She came down here with those two goons, remember?"

"And we'll find her when the time is right," John said. "Knowing your sister, she's probably doing fine on her own, if she is indeed down here. We'll find her when she wants us to."

"You think so?"

"Of course. She's tough and crafty. Like her brother."

Nathan grimaced bashfully. "You're too kind."

"Give yourself a little credit, kid."

"I'll try," said Nathan.

The walls rumbled as the front door slammed shut. The quiet rustle of laces being untied was followed by a pair of thuds against the floor.

Stearns sauntered into the living room. In his jeans, collared white shirt, and black socks, he looked like an Amish farmer who'd just come in from a long day in the fields. He crossed the room and fell back into an open chair.

"It's been a long one, boys," he said as he produced his hip flask. "Care for a drink, either of you?"

"No thanks," Nathan said.

"John?"

"Not tonight," John replied. "But after we find the core, the drinks are on me."

Stearns wagged an approving finger. "That's the kind of uplifting talk I like to hear."

John grunted an affirmative.

Now they just had to find the damn thing.

Chapter 26

July 11th, 2027
Post Status: Public

What a world we'll be bringing little Yuki into.

Enraptured by the call of the "People's Independence" movement, hundreds of thousands continue to flock to Washington. While I personally don't think they have anything to gain, I do understand the movement's allure. If you've lost your crop to the heat and can't make ends meet, you may as well join the big party in our nation's capital.

The mainstream media has downplayed the story, but bloggers on site report that the encampment of protesters may be a million strong.

Yes. You read that correctly. A million people are camping in and around D.C.

Surprisingly, a number of private benefactors have been contributing food to the cause. Some conspiracy-minded bloggers have suggested that these "private" benefactors are actually government agencies in disguise, endeavoring to suppress dissent while allowing President Hernandez to maintain his firm stance against the protest.

Did I mention that many of the protesters are armed? Is this what the Founding Fathers had in mind when they drafted the second amendment?

* * *

THE GENERAL HAD gone AWOL. He was no longer the only one.

Ramses rode down the streets of Minneapolis on Thunder's back. The sky above was soft like a faded pair of jeans. The warm summer air was as fresh as a maiden's laugh.

It was inhumane to lock a man in a room with only a radio for company. Communications between members of the Restoration Army were sparse, so sparse that no one would notice that Ramses had deserted his post. Besides, the radio could function without his oversight. Ramses' only real responsibility was to monitor transmissions and record notes in the logbook. Surely no lives would be lost over a couple of missing entries in the ledger.

Because of the draconian rules the Prince of Minneapolis' had imposed, this was Ramses' first excursion beyond the dormitories in several days. Thunder, too, had gone weeks without proper exercise, and was overjoyed to bask in the Minnesota sun.

Never had flouting the rules felt so refreshing. Yet Ramses couldn't let the fresh taste of freedom distract him from his objective.

Where had the General gone? Had he gone there of his own free will? Was Prince trying to stage a coup and claim the Restoration Army as his own? These questions had driven Ramses here, into the city. He feared the worst.

Thunder's hooves clopped over the weather-scarred pavement. Drab lifeless homes lined the streets.

Home. The word meant nothing to Ramses anymore.

Long ago his home had been Two Harbors, a small town on the western shore of Lake Superior. The Desolation had destroyed that home when he'd been but a boy of ten. Left with nowhere else to turn, he'd joined a party of settlers that was traveling north. That party had gone on to found the community that would become Frontier View.

Ramses had grudgingly considered Frontier View his home for a time. Yet as the years passed, his disdain for the village and its residents — the wimpy Nathan Kanno, his bratty sister Emiko, and the ever-rambling Pierre among them — had grown unbearable. He'd left Frontier View, vowing never to return.

Now he was here in Minneapolis, a ruined shell of a city that no one in their right mind could call home. Home was no longer a place, then, but rather an organization: the Restoration Army. The army had become his family. Ramses would not rest until he knew that the head of his household was alive and well.

He didn't expect to find the General on campus. Soldiers still patrolled the area, although not as regularly as they had prior to Prince's lockdown. Nonetheless, if the General were on campus, someone would have seen him by now.

Ramses followed the light-rail tracks along Washington Avenue to a bridge across the Mississippi. Calm though its surface appeared, the river was a powerful force, laden with hidden eddies and whirlpools. Testing the Mississippi was like braving a minefield; those who dared enter didn't always return.

On the bridge's far side was the university's West Bank campus. Beyond that awaited downtown Minneapolis. Target Tower reached for the heavens not a mile ahead. Rumor had it that on a recent evening the tower had mysteriously lit up for several minutes. Ramses distrusted this claim. He'd yet to see any hard evidence that supported it.

Ramses grabbed Thunder's reins and directed the horse toward the sky-scraping tower. He didn't get far before he spotted three figures walking down the middle of the street ahead:

A black-haired man with a long-barreled gun and a backpack. Another man on crutches, wearing jeans and a blue shirt, with a pistol at his hip. A third man, dressed similarly to the second, but with graying hair and no crutches.

Ramses quirked an eyebrow. Was this Nathan Kanno and John Osborne, together with a new ally? But why was Osborne on crutches?

Ramses checked his pistol, a CZ 75 semi-automatic. It was ready for action. He rode Thunder around a corner and hastily tied the horse to a fire hydrant. Directly behind the hydrant were the blackened remains of a Japanese restaurant. Charred stalks of bamboo dangled from the ceiling.

The hydrant needed both water pressure and firefighters to do its job. Apparently it had had neither.

"I shall return soon, Thunder," he said, patting the horse's snout. He scurried back to observe the three men.

Where were they headed? Ramses trailed distantly, slipping into building entrances and other nooks whenever possible. He wished to remain unseen.

The trio veered left past a TCF Bank. Around the corner the road came to a T-junction. Beyond the junction a broad expanse of glass protruded from the earth, flanked on either side by gigantic, angular slabs of concrete.

Though Ramses had grown up far north of Minneapolis, he was familiar with the Minnesota Vikings and the contentious arena that they'd constructed, Vikings Stadium.

Ramses grinned smugly, fingering his pistol's steel grip. Football was a violent sport, but there were other games far more deadly.

Chapter 27

August 5th, 2027
Post Status: Public

It's been a slow month here at the Kanno's. If only I could say the same of Washington.

The National Guard has been patrolling the capital for a few weeks now. Though the protests remain peaceful, President Hernandez fears they'll escalate. In fact, today I read that the President is recalling a handful of Army battalions from overseas, ostensibly to bolster the National Guard's ranks.

What does this mean? I'm not sure, but it doesn't bode well.

How scared is the President of this hungry mob before his door? Perhaps he's more afraid than I previously imagined.

* * *

THOUGH OVERSHADOWED BY Target Tower, the geometric frenzy of Vikings Stadium was still a sight to behold. Taking up a quartet of city blocks, the stadium would've attracted the attention of passersby in downtown Minneapolis both day and night.

"You ever watch a game here?" John asked Nathan.

Nathan shook his head. "My dad thought tickets were too expensive. Watching the game at home on a big HD-screen was good enough for him."

Stearns twiddled his beard as he regarded the stadium. The frizzy salt and pepper stubble was growing wilder by the day.

"Didn't the Vikings play the last Super Bowl here?" he asked.

"Don't ask me. I was in a coma," John said.

Nathan looked to Stearns. "The Vikings did host the last Super Bowl. It was the first time a team played the Super Bowl in their own stadium. And the last, of course."

"Did they win?"

"Do you have to ask? The Vikings never won."

"I was always more a fan of the college game, myself," Stearns said. "Anyhow, the field should be open. After we find the Northland Core I reckon we can round up some friends for a game of two-hand touch."

"I got QB," John said. He'd never thrown a football with his bionic arm. He imagined he could've sailed a pigskin straight out of the stadium if not for the glass roof. "Come on. Let's go in."

Two sheer walls of glass converged with the roof to form the stadium's front. A concrete pyramid capped the intersection, jutting forth like a battleship's gunmetal prow. Below the massive protrusion, dozens of transparent doors awaited throngs that would never come. A flock of geese honked overhead, gracefully elevating their V to clear the stadium's roof.

They found one of the front doors unlocked. The corroded hinges groaned as John pried it open.

"If that's not a friendly invitation, I don't know what is," Stearns quipped.

"Everything but the red carpet," John said. "Let's keep moving." He passed through the vestibule and stepped into the building proper.

The stadium's lobby was extravagantly expansive. Summer sunlight flooded in through the high glass dome. The echo of John's footsteps resonated off the distant walls.

"Where to first?" John asked Nathan.

"I'm not exactly sure. How about down?"

"Do you really think the Pentagon would build a research facility here?" Stearns asked.

"We'll find out soon enough," Nathan replied.

Already John doubted the core was here. Hiding a sensitive project in an area bustling with foot traffic would've been inadvisable. He could envision the headline: GOVERNMENT

DEVELOPS VOLATILE POWER SOURCE BENEATH NFL STADIUM. Never mind whether the project was actually volatile. The mere suggestion of danger would've stirred the public into a paroxysm of outrage.

The trio walked through the lobby and began circling the stadium counter-clockwise. Arched openings to their left, leading to the field, brought to mind the Coliseum of Rome. Concession stands lined the corridor. Their signs still boasted of pretzels, hot dogs, brats, and cold, refreshing beer.

Thirty minutes and two loops later the three men had found no evidence of a basement.

"There's got to be a way to get under the field," Nathan said. "The maintenance crew would've needed access."

John looked down one of the arched tunnels, its concrete floor littered with garbage. He imagined a football player leaping heroically to catch a game-winning touchdown pass, only to rip through the field's artificial turf and tumble into a research complex below. The incident would've done wonders for the NFL's not-so-sterling reputation.

"I'm not sure, Nathan," John said. "Maybe we should try looking up instead."

"There might be an administrative office with a blueprint of the place," Stearns offered. "It won't have 'Top Secret Government Research Room' scrawled across it, of course, but it could offer some clues."

"Sounds good to me," Nathan said with a discouraged shrug. Forever his own harshest critic, Nathan's confidence and enthusiasm were dropping in tandem

They backtracked to an elevator. A floor guide was posted beside it: FIFTH FLOOR - TEAM OFFICE.

"Going up?" Stearns said, lifting his eyebrows as he pressed the up button.

No elevator came. John shot Stearns a hard-as-granite stare.

"A guy's gotta try." Stearns raised his hands in defeat.

"The stairs are over here," Nathan said, indicating a door sporting a red emergency exit sign.

They climbed the windowless stairwell, opening the doors on each floor for light. At the fifth floor they exited into a hallway. The team office just a few yards ahead.

John tried the doorknob.

Locked.

"What now?" Nathan pointed to an electronic card reader beside the door. "I doubt we'll have any luck with this."

"I'll handle it," John said. He clutched the doorknob in his left hand. Tapping ever-so-slightly into his bionic strength, he ripped the knob free. He dropped the knob and slammed his fist into the door. It swung open, revealing the office within.

John swooned, staggering forward before quickly regaining his balance.

Stearns snorted. "That'll show the doorknobs who's boss."

"You should save your strength, John," said Nathan, frowning. "We don't know how much charge your battery has left. Stearns or I could've shot out the lock or bashed the door down. It was hardly a military grade."

"I'll keep that in mind," John snarled. He knew Nathan was right, but he was getting impatient.

"So, that's you putting your cyber-strength to good use, huh?" Stearns said.

"You haven't seen the half of it," John replied coolly. He gestured at the open doorway with the rubber tip of his crutch. "Old men first. NFL policy."

"I didn't realize the NFL provided such generous senior benefits," Stearns said, nodding approvingly as he led the group in.

The office looked like the stereotypical nine-to-five hell. Movable panels with taupe fabric and gray plastic edges divided the room into cubicles. Computers, telephones, pencil holders, and pads of yellow post-it notes cluttered the desks.

"Let's get digging," John said. "Remember, we're looking for a blueprint."

Nathan and Stearns headed to different corners of the room. John started with the cubicle closest to the door.

He rifled through the desk drawers. On a shelf he found a touchscreen tablet with a 3D display. It had likely been used to watch game film from multiple angles. John pressed and held the power button with his thumb. Not so much as a 'Low Battery' warning appeared on the screen.

John moved to the next cubicle. The highlight was a rack full of DVDs with labels like "Super Bowl XXI" and "1998 NFC Championship."

"Find anything?" Nathan asked, poking his head into the cubicle.

"Nothing," John said. "You?"

Nathan stepped out from behind the cubicle wall. "I didn't find a blueprint, but I did find this." He held up a flat device about the size of a magazine. Its surface was divided into shiny, matchbox-size panels. "It's a high-efficiency solar panel. On a sunny day it can generate enough power to run a computer."

"What good does that do us?" John asked.

"I was thinking I could fire up my dad's old desktop."

John frowned. He had only a few days before his arm would give out. Now wasn't the time to toy with computers.

"Alright," John replied, his tone chilly. "But save it until after we've found the core."

Nathan hesitated, then nodded. His shoulders slumped as he walked away.

John shuffled out of the cubicle. He found Stearns in another bland-as-American-cheese workstation, examining a map spread out across the desk.

"Find anything?" John asked.

Stearns looked up. "Bad news."

"Hit me."

"According to this map Vikings Stadium has no basement."

John suppressed a curse. "But the basement would be hidden, wouldn't it?"

"Well, yes, but ..." Stearns stood up straight, removing his palms from the desk. "Look, John. I don't think we're going to find anything here. It just doesn't make sense."

"Uh-huh," John said with a nod.

"The Pentagon guys were crazy, but not crazy enough to conduct research under an NFL stadium. The risk involved would've dwarfed any potential benefit. Not that I can see any potential benefit. In fact, to be honest ..." Stearns leaned closer and spoke under his breath. "To be honest, I'm not sure what your boy Nathan was thinking."

"Look, Stearns. This place hasn't panned out, but the places you and I chose didn't fare any better. If we don't find the Northland Core we'll all share the blame."

Stearns raised both palms defensively. "Hey, don't get me wrong! I'm not trying to point fingers. I'm just telling it to you straight."

John lowered his head. "I know," he said, looking up. He patted Stearns on the shoulder. "We'll get out of here soon. But let's show the map to Nathan. Maybe he'll think of something."

"Of course," Stearns said. He turned back to the desk and rolled up the map.

"I'll track down Nathan."

Lost in thought, John left the cubicle without waiting for a response. He'd been short with both Nathan and Stearns. He felt as cranky as an old man who couldn't shit.

He recalled that on Mallard Island his health and spirit had deteriorated as his artificial arm sapped energy from his body. Was he having the same issue now?

He found Nathan and collected Stearns. Together they moved to an open area with two circular fiberboard tables, each surrounded by a half dozen folding chairs. Along the wall stood a water dispenser, tank still half full, and an instant coffee machine. John stared at the coffee machine like a former smoker eyed a carton of Camels. He wasn't ready to kill for a cup of joe, but he was close.

Nathan took a seat, setting his prize on the table.

"What's that?" Stearns asked.

"A solar panel," Nathan said.

Stearns tilted his head and cocked an eyebrow, as though interested in asking more, before deciding to keep his questions to himself. "Take a seat, John. Get off your feet."

John obliged, sitting in a folding chair beside Nathan.

Stearns unrolled the map onto the table. The full-color spread fully detailed the stadium. "So, the bad news is that there's no basement."

"Really?" Nathan asked.

"I'm afraid so, son. That said, it does appear that the players' locker rooms are built on a level slightly below the first floor."

"Should we go check them out?"

"I can't say I see much point. White-coated lab workers passing through a locker room to access a secret research lab seems rather far-fetched."

"I suppose ..." Nathan said.

"Is there anything else of interest?" John asked.

"I don't see anything out of the ordinary. Of course, if there were something fishy, it wouldn't be marked on a map like this."

John tapped his foot as he considered their next move.

"Here's the plan," he said. "Since we're already here, we'll check out the field and the locker rooms. If we don't find anything there we'll leave and decide what to do next."

"That makes sense," Nathan said.

"I can get on board with that," said Stearns.

"We have to kick our search into overdrive. I won't sleep soundly until we've found the Northland Core."

Nathan and Stearns both nodded their agreement.

"Then let's move," John said, energized by his supportive partners. "Down to the field where the last Super Bowl was won."

Chapter 28

August 21st, 2027
Post Status: Public

105 degrees outside.

Air conditioning is intermittent. The power keeps browning out.

This is more than a heat wave.

We have it easy in Minneapolis. In Phoenix it's 125 degrees.

My thoughts are with the elderly and the sick, for whom this heat presents the greatest burden.

My heart also goes out to the encampment in Washington. Though it's a few degrees cooler on the east coast, the protesters there are ill-equipped to deal with the extreme heat. I can only imagine what it must be like to be among those millions of hungry, thirsty people, crowded into a tent with no hope of relief.

* * *

RAMSES' INSTINCTS had been correct, naturally. He had stumbled upon John Osborne and Nathan Kanno.

He crouched in the stairwell's shadows, waiting on the fifth floor for the three men to reappear.

Who was the third man? Ramses, afraid of exposing himself, hadn't gotten a clean look. Perhaps Osborne's new partner was another clodhopping bumpkin from Frontier View? He did dress like a farmer, after all.

Then there was the matter of Osborne's crutches. How had he injured his leg? Osborne was seemingly invincible. To see him nursing a wound was odd indeed.

The door in the hallway clicked open, signaling the three men's return. Would they continue up or go back down? Ramses bet on down. He headed up to the sixth floor to watch and wait, veiled in darkness.

The three men entered the stairwell and clambered down the steps, just as Ramses had anticipated. The rhythmic thump of Osborne's crutches reverberated through the dimly-lit vertical shaft.

The three men neared the ground floor. Ramses tiptoed down the stairs after them. He reached the ground level just in time to glimpse Osborne and company passing under an arched opening.

Ramses followed through the dark tunnel. Six wide-mouthed trash bins lined the passageway, three on either side. Plastic bottles and paper cups overflowed the bins. Whether the mess had been created by untidy football fans or by rummaging Desolation survivors, Ramses couldn't say.

The tunnel led to heart of the stadium. Three tiers of purple and white seats encircled the playing field, each subsequent tier packed with more seats than the one below. A glass dome, supported by a network of steel rafters, capped the stadium. Sunlight pouring down from above illuminated the 100-yard stretch of green turf, the Sunday battlefield.

This was what mankind had once had, what mankind had lost: the ability, the knowledge, and the power to build transcendent spectacles such as this. If all went as planned, mankind would again rise to create such wonders. It would take time, certainly, but time was the common denominator of all things great.

Ramses watched the three men furtively. They progressed through the rows of chairs like archaeologists exploring a Saharan dig site. He was unsure how to approach his quarry. Peacefully? Guns blazing? A compromise between the two?

His eyes narrowed as a suspicious thought occurred to him. What if this trio of rancorous pests had found the General and taken him hostage? Perhaps, then, Thurston Prince, seeing an army suddenly without a leader, had assumed power instead of sending out a search party?

Though Ramses had no proof, the theory was compelling nonetheless.

A confrontation was inevitable. Ramses drew his sleek black CZ 75 from its holster and stepped out from the shadows, squinting in the bright sunlight. Osborne and Nathan were moving down an aisle, just within shouting distance.

Ramses called to them.

* * *

"John Osborne. Nathan Kanno. It's been too long!"

Nathan gritted his teeth. The stadium wasn't as empty as he'd thought. He spun on his heels.

"Ramses!" he exclaimed, glaring at the man who'd once been his neighbor, the man who'd later inexplicably kidnapped his sister.

"I'm pleased that you still recognize me, Nathan." Ramses approached down the aisle, leading with his pistol. His short, silvery blond hair glistened in the sunlight. He wore faded green fatigues over heavy black boots. "Hands up, all three of you."

Nathan obliged with an audible gulp. It felt like he'd swallowed a cherry, pit and all.

"That punk from Sawbill Lake?" John asked. With the crutches under his armpits he could only raise his hands as high as his ears.

"Right," Nathan replied.

"Another man in green," Stearns observed, his brow tight. He eyed a nearby tunnel. "I'll see if I can get a drop on him."

"Wait, Stearns!" John growled. "We don't have any cover!"

But Stearns was already on the move. Showing surprising speed for his age, he made a break for the tunnel.

Ramses' pistol barked. The bullet ricocheted off a seat, narrowly missing Stearns as he vanished into the dark corridor.

That was all the diversion John needed. He gripped his left crutch like a javelin and hurled it forward. The crutch zipped through the air and slammed into Ramses shoulder. With a shriek of pain Ramses stumbled backwards into a row of seats.

"Get down the tunnel!" John ordered.

"But what about your —"

"I'll be fine!"

Nathan jogged ahead. He veered into the tunnel. Stearns was already long gone. Nathan poked his head back out into the stadium.

John, his revolver drawn, hobbled backward on one crutch. "I got a cylinder full of bullets engraved with your name!" he shouted, firing a warning shot.

Ramses struggled to extract himself from the seats.

"Keep going," John urged as he reached the tunnel's mouth.

"Not without you, John."

John groaned his discontent, then nodded. "I can't move fast enough to escape. Let's hunker down behind those trash cans." He pointed at the plastic bins lining the hallway.

Nathan drew his shotgun and took aim at the tunnel entrance. He provided cover until John had staggered behind one of the garbage bins. He then crouched behind a bin along the tunnel's opposite wall.

"How did you heave your crutch like a spear?" Nathan whispered.

"The same way I threw a perfect game of darts."

Footsteps clattered near the tunnel's entrance.

John shouted down the tunnel: "If I were you I'd turn and walk away."

"And why might you suggest that?" Ramses' voice rang back.

"Walk away and you might make it out of here alive," John said. "Step foot into this tunnel and you're a dead man. The choice is yours."

Nathan and John, tucked behind the trash bins, awaited Ramses reply.

"I think he took your advice," Nathan said after a number of seconds had passed.

"I think you're right. Go check the other entrance. I'll cover your back."

Nathan nodded and then dashed to the tunnel's opposite end. He peered out and looked both ways. "It's clear over here," he announced.

John rose to his feet and staggered backwards on one crutch, keeping his revolver trained on the opening into the stadium. He reached Nathan and together they emerged into the outer hall.

"How is your leg?" Nathan asked.

"It'll be fine as long as we take it slow."

"Do you want me to support you?"

John shook his head. "Ramses could be anywhere. Stay alert." His eyes swept the hall. "Where is Stearns?"

"I didn't see him."

"Let's head toward the front entrance and look for him."

"And if he's not there?"

"Walk now. Worry later," John said.

Nathan bit his lip and pressed his shotgun tighter against his shoulder.

* * *

Ramses' back and shoulders ached. Though nothing felt broken, the emergence of a black and purple bruise seemed inevitable.

Apparently Osborne's arm offered not only superior strength, but enhanced precision as well. How else could Osborne have thrown an unwieldy wooden crutch like a hunter's spear?

Ramses circled through the stadium, loping through the aisles. He wasn't safe in the open. Though he didn't expect Osborne and that runt Nathan Kanno to go on the offensive, the third man still posed a threat.

Had confronting Osborne been the correct choice? A thought occurred to Ramses. Perhaps Lieutenant Prince had ordered the army's lockdown to impede Osborne from discovering their headquarters. But why? If John was such a threat, why not just eliminate him? He and his bionic arm were no match for the inimitable force of the Restoration Army.

Ramses peered cautiously into a tunnel. Garbage receptacles surrounded by heaps of excess trash besmirched the corridor. He made his way through, alert to anything suspicious.

Not alert enough.

The shadows moved. A figure lunged from the darkness. An arm smashed into Ramses' throat and pinned him to the wall.

The figure growled: "You have no idea how much trouble you're in."

Chapter 29

August 24th, 2027
Post Status: Public

CNN reports gunfire in the capital.

All eyes are on Washington.

It's unclear who fired first.

The violence spreads.

I don't know what's happening anymore. All I see on TV is madness. Unprecedented madness.

Danielle refuses to watch. She hopes this will blow over. I am not so optimistic.

This furor has been brewing for some time. It'd be easy to blame it all on the heat wave, but to do so would be disingenuous.

I'll sleep restlessly tonight … if I sleep at all.

* * *

THEY COULD GUESS at what the dormitories contained, but they'd have to get inside to know for sure. Last night Aristotle and Emiko had devised a plan to do just that.

The plan was dangerous, but Emiko had agreed to it and it was too late to turn back now. Never mind that Aristotle loathed backing down from a challenge.

They approached the dormitories, wearing the same black and white robes as before. Though their outward appearance remained the same, changes had taken place beneath their robes.

Underneath her cap, Emiko now sported short hair that came just below ear level. She'd also strapped a hunting knife to her calf. Aristotle, meanwhile, was a nun with a gun. Her revolver clung to her hip, hidden by the folds of her flowing skirt.

"Are you ready for this?" Aristotle asked

"Yes! Can you stop asking already?" Emiko groused. Though her gait had improved, she was still a step slow. Could she run if she had to? With any luck she wouldn't be pressed to find out.

The two robed women crossed the weed-stricken road to Comstock Hall. Its windows were all unattended.

"Go ahead, Sister Leon," Emiko said. "I'll be waiting for your signal."

Aristotle was about to give Emiko a final chance to cancel the operation, but she bit her tongue. She already knew what Emiko's answer would be.

"Don't do anything until I give the signal," she said.

"I won't. I know this is risky," Emiko said, with a seriousness that belied her age. "We won't go ahead with the plan unless the situation is right."

Aristotle smiled imperceptibly. Emiko's well of tenacity was inexhaustible. "Then I'm off. Wait for the signal."

The concrete sidewalk cut between the brick-and-mortar expanse of Comstock and the antiquated elegance of Pioneer. Without Emiko by her side Aristotle realized just how quiet the area was. The General's army frightened even the birds.

Aristotle came to the four-way intersection, a vantage point that let her see all four dormitories. Assuming the air of an overwhelmed tourist, Aristotle craned her neck upward and waddled in a circle. Her gaze wandered, lingering here and there, as she examined her surroundings with the aimlessness of a bovine put out to pasture.

The coast was clear. Aristotle clasped her hands together and closed her eyes. She bowed her head in supplication and offered a lengthy prayer, beginning, "Notre Père, qui es au eavenhay ..."

The content was irrelevant; the signal was sent. When Aristotle looked up, Emiko was advancing towards Pioneer Hall.

Casually pivoting on her heels, Aristotle surveyed her surroundings. This time the block wasn't empty. A man approached perpendicularly to the path from which Aristotle had come.

The plan was in motion. Emiko was already deep into the campus block. They couldn't abort now.

As the man drew closer Aristotle recognized his winter-blue eyes, his Clark Kent chin, his broad shoulders.

Glacier Face.

Today he walked alone. Though one man should've posed a lesser threat than two, Glacier Face's demeanor was more ominous without a lackey at his side. He paced steadily towards her, his face frozen in an unfocused stare. To him she was nothing but a troublesome weed, unworthy of his full attention.

If he so much as breathed on her ...

Feigning disinterest in his approach, Aristotle stole another glimpse in Emiko's direction. The girl was fumbling at the simple sash window they'd chosen as her entry point. It should've opened easily. At the moment that assumption looked like a five-dollar cotton hammock fraying under the weight of a bull moose.

"Well look who's back," said Glacier Face.

Aristotle greeted him with surprise, acting as though she hadn't expected him to talk with her. "Oh, what a pleasure to see you again," she said, slathering her words with a godly tone. Beads of sweat formed on her brow, concealed by her cap and hood.

"The pleasure is all mine, sister," Glacier Face said with a trace of malice.

"I wasn't planning to return here," Aristotle said. "During my meditations last night, however, the good Lord spoke to me, and told me that there was work to do here." She gracefully lifted an arm, pressing her eyelids shut as she took a deep, heavenly breath. She raised her chin and turned her head, as though moved by the spirit itself.

This elaborate gesture provided another glimpse at the window — the window, now open, into which Emiko had disappeared.

* * *

Sneaking. Spying. Stalking.

Emiko was in her element. Prying the window open had taken more strength than she'd expected, yet she'd made it inside Pioneer Hall. Hopefully entering would prove the most difficult part.

She pressed against the bathroom wall. A single shower stall was tucked in the corner near the window. On one side of the narrow room were a pair of orange-walled toilet stalls; on the other side hung three white porcelain sinks, each with a mirror above it. Across the middle mirror was a message scrawled in red: FREDDIE WILL DIE TONIGHT. LONG LIVE FREDDIE.

Footsteps approached. Emiko's spine stiffened like a frightened skunk's tail. Her eyes darted left and right, frantically searching for a hiding place. Lacking better options, she bolted into one of the toilet stalls. She latched the door shut and stepped up onto the toilet seat.

A man burst through the bathroom door, hacking uncontrollably. He passed Emiko's hiding spot, summoning a mouthful of phlegm, and then spit into one of the sinks.

The coughing ceased. The man walked by Emiko's toilet stall on his way out, his legs visible in the gap beneath the door. He stopped at the bathroom's exit.

Emiko locked her lips together, afraid to take another breath. Had the man seen her? Was he waiting for her to try to escape?

Her worries were defused when the man cleared his throat with a violent cough and flung open the exit door. Its hinges creaked as it swung back and forth.

Emiko stepped down from the toilet gingerly, one foot at a time. Though her right ankle was becoming stronger, she still needed to treat it with care.

This spy mission brought to mind the time she'd eavesdropped on a recruitment meeting in Duluth. The old cafe she'd snuck into then had been a neutral site; now she was breaking into what was likely the General's headquarters itself. She had to proceed with extreme caution.

Emiko pressed her ear to the bathroom's door. Hearing nothing, she cracked the heavy door open and peered out into the hallway.

Though the building had once been a dormitory, its interior resembled a psych ward. The corridor of white plaster walls and beige floor tiles was barely wide enough for two people. Emiko imagined university students brushing shoulders as they passed one another.

A series of doors lined the hallway. Most were closed. A pair of staircases, inserted between doors, each led both up and down. Emiko visualized herself playing an endless game of cat and mouse with her pursuers, up and down the stairs. She hoped it wouldn't come to that.

Unsure how long Aristotle could stall outside, Emiko moved down the hallway with measured haste, burrowing deeper into the General's den one silent footstep at a time.

Chapter 30

August 24th, 2027
Post Status: Public

My eyes are glued to the television. My fingers hover over the keyboard, unsure of what to write.

The White House is on fire. President Hernandez has been evacuated.

Protesters have ransacked the Capitol. Three representatives are dead and dozens more are MIA.

I remember when the planes hit the towers in New York 26 years ago. I was in high school. One of my classmates ran through the halls shouting, "A plane hit the World Trade Center!"

First came confusion. Later, as the news continued to report on the tragedy, confusion gave way to morbid curiosity and sadness.

I wish I could say I feel that way again now, all these years later. But today, instead of confusion and surprise, I feel only the sorrow of having reached an inevitable, tragic conclusion.

* * *

THE HALLWAYS ZIGGED and zagged like an intestinal tract of plaster and tile. Stairs rose and fell like a wild game of Chutes and Ladders. Open doors were traps to avoid. Shadows were breaths of fresh air.

Emiko flattened against the wall beside an open dormitory door. Hearing nothing from within, she slipped past. Already she'd had too many close calls — the man in the bathroom, the guards patrolling the hallways, and a man she'd escaped by sprinting down into the basement.

The good news was that her ankle was holding up. The bad news was that she needed to leave soon whether she discovered anything useful or not. She feared that Aristotle, standing watch outside, could already be in trouble.

She came to a set of stairs. Longer than the others, the stairway cut through the dormitory like a game trail down a wooded hillside.

Emiko negotiated the stairs carefully. At the bottom she reached a door. She cracked it open to reveal a lobby. The space appeared unoccupied, but then so did all of Minneapolis. If even one soldier was here, reading a book, sharpening a knife, or picking his nose, he could spot her and sound the alarm.

Accepting that risk, Emiko tiptoed in, head swiveling back and forth, eyes peeled.

The room expanded in three directions. Directly ahead was a wide corridor lined with doors. The corridor continued straight for some fifty yards before ending at a stairwell. To Emiko's right was an area full of aging laundry machines, their boxy bodies covered in dust.

The area to Emiko's left, a small library, looked like it saw more frequent use. Books large and small, paperback and hardcover, crowded the shelves. A fireplace sat in the far wall, flanked by two chairs and a couch. Did the General's men stay here late at night, reading by firelight? Though the image clashed with her conception of them, perhaps one or two of the army's members were literate.

Fastened to the wall above the bookshelves was a metal ventilation grate. The duct looked just big enough for her to crawl through. It would let her explore the building while remaining unseen. But where would it lead?

She crept across the room and studied the bookcase. It had five shelves, not counting the top. Would it bear her weight? She placed a leg on the lowest shelf; it held. She tied her robes around her waist and began her ascent, clambering as fast as her sore ankle allowed. The bookcase wobbled threateningly under her feet. Undeterred, Emiko nimbly reached the top.

Four screws held the ventilation grate in place. Emiko unsheathed the knife strapped to her calf and used it to remove the screws. She pulled the grate from the wall, set it atop the shelf, and crawled into the air duct.

The metal corridor was just wide enough for her to scramble through on her hands and knees. A short distance in, she stopped to consider the grate. She hadn't replaced it. If someone noticed it missing, she'd be like a squirrel trapped inside a hollow log — an easy target. That said, she didn't have enough room inside the duct to turn around, and she doubted she'd be able to properly replace the grate from the inside, anyway.

She decided to take her chances. Who would notice a missing grate?

* * *

"That's *very* interesting, Sister Leon," Glacier Face said to Aristotle. "Please, tell me more about your order."

He stood with his arms crossed and his shoulders drawn back, emphasizing his bulk. His iciness had melted into a slush of sarcasm.

He was toying with her, like a coyote pawing a wounded rabbit. He knew he could force his carnal will upon her at any time. What he didn't know was that the revolver at Aristotle's hip would speak up if he tried.

Though the game made Aristotle's stomach churn, she had no choice but to play. She had to stall until Emiko returned.

"What would you like to know?" Aristotle asked, a heavenly smile gracing her face.

"Well, discussing your religious order has put me in a very pious and repentant mood. I was wondering where I could make a confession." Glacier Face narrowed his eyes. "I've done some very bad things that I'd like to get off my chest."

His sins weren't the only thing he hoped to get off in the private quarters of the confessional. Here amid dormitories full of sex-starved men, Aristotle could practically smell the testosterone.

"Well, my brother, we haven't yet been able to extend our services to this area. As I told you yesterday, we are hoping to reclaim the nearby church, but it'll take time."

"But you must have another place I could confess," he said, his neck cracking as he cocked his head. "Doesn't your order have another branch somewhere nearby?"

"Another branch? You speak of our church as though it were nothing but a bank," Aristotle scolded.

"Do you have another steeple in this city, then?"

"We have indeed founded a house of God here, whence we spread the good word. But I'm afraid it's a fair distance away."

"How far?"

"It's in St. Paul, in fact."

"Where in St. Paul?"

"You're a very curious child, aren't you? Our church is near the old state capitol, just a few blocks off University Avenue," Aristotle said. She was thankful she'd read up on the area. Unless Glacier Face knew the name of every street in downtown St. Paul, she could bluff her fake church into existence.

"Come on now, sister." Glacier Face flashed his teeth. "The old capitol isn't that far from here. If I get leave for R&R you can show me the way."

"Perhaps." Aristotle smiled, peppering in a hint of lust. "You do look like you could use some quality time in the confessional," she said, struggling not to gag on her own words.

"I'm glad to hear you agree, sister," Glacier Face said, lifting his brow provocatively.

Aristotle felt like a butcher dangling a leg of beef before a starving wolf. The wolf would exercise patience as long as the beef was offered. Pull the meat away and the wolf would make a meal of both beef and butcher.

Aristotle's only solace was that she was a butcher with a very big cleaver.

Chapter 31

August 25th, 2027
Post Status: Public

Dozens of cities have tumbled into chaos. Arsonists have torched half of Atlanta. Riots have erupted in the Chicago shantytown. Seattle, Houston, New Orleans, and Milwaukee are all in a state of tumult, with people fighting the authorities and raiding government buildings.

Some of these uprisings are more organized than others. It's clear that volumes of pent-up anger have stewed beneath the peaceful veneer of our society for a long time. The anger all bubbled over within the span of a few days, and I'm not sure we can replace the lid.

Though violence hasn't broken out here in Minneapolis, there's a combustible tension in the air. It feels like the smallest spark could plunge the city into brutal madness.

Domestic media softens the truth, claiming that radical extremists are fomenting the crisis. International media has not been quite so shy.

Have you read Al Jazeera recently? Do you know what they're calling this crisis?

They're calling it civil war.

* * *

THE AIR DUCT LED straight ahead. Though Emiko had worried the thin metal might give way, it bent only slightly under her knees. A full-grown adult trying to sneak through the duct wouldn't have been so lucky.

A palpable layer of dust coated the duct, transferring to her vestments as she crawled forward. She sniffled through her stuffy nose. Her allergies were starting to act up.

Ahead, light dithered up through a downward-facing grate, projecting fuzzy yellow stripes onto the duct's ceiling. Hearing voices, Emiko slithered closer. She stopped at the grate and peered through its sharply-angled slits.

She could see horizontal slices of two men engaged in discussion below. One wore a Restoration Army-standard green vest, the other a beige shirt. The former had short black hair, while the latter wore an unusual circular hat.

Afraid a bead of sweat might roll down her forehead and drop through the grate, Emiko retracted her head, closed her eyes, and listened.

"You're closer to the men than I am, Jennings. How is morale these days?"

"Would you like the truth, sir?"

"Of course I want the truth."

"It's not good, Lieutenant Prince," Jennings replied. His sniveling voice brought to mind a rat rubbing its tiny paws together. "Many in our ranks are no longer respecting your order to remain indoors. Men drift through the campus. Some may be wandering off it. That said, we can't keep track of everyone and few men are willing to turn in their fellow soldiers. I'm not sure there's much we can do about it, sir."

"I hear you, Corporal Jennings. Hell, how could the General expect us to keep a rowdy group of young men locked inside for weeks on end?" Lieutenant Prince's voice remained calm, taking the bad news in stride.

"I'm not so sure the General will see things that way, sir."

Emiko heard the sizzling crack of a match catching fire. The warm acrid smell of tobacco wafted into the vent.

"I'm not sure it matters how the General sees things," Lieutenant Prince said.

"And what makes you say that, sir?"

"The General is gone, Corporal Jennings. If he doesn't return soon, someone will have to take his place. That someone will be me."

"But do you think the army would accept that, sir?" Jennings asked, obviously uncomfortable with the conversation's turn.

Pungent cigar smoke drifted up, tickling Emiko's nose. She hastily clamped her nostrils shut with two fingers.

"The men may be willing to reconsider their alliances if I tell them that their great leader deserted them to go on a scavenger hunt."

Corporal Jennings cleared his throat. "While I admire your confidence, sir, I'm not sure I agree."

"And why is that?" Lieutenant Prince asked coolly.

Emiko inched closer to the grate to ensure she could hear every word. She had assumed that the Restoration Army was a singular, unified force. Apparently that wasn't entirely true.

"I'm afraid the men don't regard you as highly as you may believe, sir. I hear rumblings that you're distant, aloof, and something of an ..."

Lieutenant Prince rose from his chair. "And something of a what?"

"And something of an odd character," Jennings squeaked.

"I thought my speeches were received rather well."

"Oh, the speeches are good, sir. Perhaps too good. You tend to come off as a bit too high-and-mighty."

"And?"

"And, well, how to put it ..."

"The hell, Corporal. Just get out with it. Anything you say in this room will stay in this room."

We'll see about that, Emiko mused.

"Well," Corporal Jennings said, fumbling for the right words. "I hear whispers of your ... *peculiarities.*"

"Such as?"

"The beret is a bit much, I hear."

Bur-ay? Bear ray? The word was unfamiliar to Emiko, bringing to mind a black bear with green lasers for eyes. She shook the childish image from her head.

"It sets me apart," Lieutenant Prince replied.

"And then there's the matter of this office's tropical flavor."

"What's wrong with a flamingo and a few miniature palm trees?"

"I don't know, sir. I'm just reporting what I've heard. Personally, I think they're a nice touch."

Lieutenant Prince grumbled under his breath, pacing back and forth across through the room.

"What if I told them the truth about the General's rhetoric? What if I helped them see the lies behind his promises?"

"Truth and lies, sir?"

"You know what I mean, Jennings. The General has sold this army a bill of goods that he'll never deliver. I'm sure half the men here think we'll be driving sports cars, enjoying full water and electrical services, and surfing the internet again within a year."

"But the General never promised any of those things, sir," Corporal Jennings said, confused.

"Not directly. But he does nothing to quash the rumors that spread through the barracks."

"I understand your concern, sir. But, historically speaking, hope for a better future has been a part of every successful military effort."

"If only I could show the men that their General is nothing but a Napoleonic megalomaniac," the lieutenant fumed.

There was a knock at the door.

"Wait a second," Prince said. He sat and stubbed out his cigar; Emiko's allergies thanked him. "Alright, let him in."

Corporal Jennings opened the door. "Yes, private?"

"Requesting permission to enter, sir," said a new, obviously much younger voice.

"Granted," Prince said.

The young man stepped stiffly into the room and stood at attention. He wore Restoration Army green. Scabs on his hairless scalp suggested a recent shave.

Jennings closed the door.

"Yes, Private?" Prince asked.

"Requesting permission to speak, sir," the young private said.

"Go ahead, Private," Prince said with obvious impatience.

"Private Brushnell disappeared this morning, sir. He's been missing for a number of hours. No one is sure where he went, sir, but it looks like he took his horse."

"Private Ramses Brushnell," muttered Lieutenant Prince. "So much promise, yet so little common sense. If only he'd open his eyes a little wider ..."

Emiko's jaw dropped. Ramses was in Minneapolis? He was a member of this rag-tag army? So this was what he'd been doing since leaving the Frontier View all those months ago! The orders to kidnap her must have originated here.

The scabby-scalped private, taken aback by Prince's diatribe against Ramses, coughed awkwardly. "Sir?"

"Never mind, private. Report to me again if he hasn't returned by nightfall. Understood?"

"Yes, sir."

"Dismissed." Prince waved the private away. "Corporal Jennings will show you out."

The corporal had barely grasped the knob when another loud knock came from the door.

"What should I do, sir?" the corporal asked.

"Let the man in, I suppose," Prince said sarcastically.

Corporal Jennings obliged, and another soldier stumbled through the doorway.

"Permission to speak, sir?" he asked, panting for breath.

"Granted," said Prince.

"One of the panels to the ventilation system has been removed, sir."

Emiko's throat constricted. What could she do? No one had heard her crawling through the duct before, but they hadn't been listening. A hasty exit now would surely be noticed.

"What of it, private?" Lieutenant Prince asked the newcomer. "I don't see what a missing panel matters. The AC in this place hasn't worked for years."

"Of course, sir," the newcomer said, exasperated. "But if someone from outside opened the vent, they could crawl through it and ..."

"I understand, private," Prince said, remaining calm. "You're suggesting someone has broken into our headquarters. Indeed, if what you say is true, someone could be listening to us right now."

Prince swung his gaze up towards the ventilation grate. Three more pairs of eyes followed.

Emiko was a kitten stuck in a tree. No fireman was coming to help her down.

Chapter 32

September 7th, 2027
Post Status: Public

What's there to write that hasn't already been written?

This war is stranger than anything I could've imagined. The U.S. government is clearly the party on the defensive. But who exactly is the aggressor? Now that conflict has spread beyond D.C. the answer is less clear than ever. Rebels seem to coalesce out of nowhere.

Though each major city has unique circumstances, they can be categorized into four rough categories:

Rebel-controlled: Cities where fighting has occurred and the rebels have claimed victory. Seattle and San Francisco fall into this category.

Government-controlled: Cities in which fighting has occurred and rebellion has been squashed. Examples include Denver and Boston.

Disputed: Cities where fighting continues. Most of the biggest cities fall into this category, including Chicago, New York, and L.A.

Inactive: There are still many cities where little (no?) violence has developed. While these cities are ostensibly government-controlled, the potential for conflict remains. Minneapolis, St. Louis, and many other mid-sized Midwestern cities exemplify this category.

It's eerie to think that, while Minneapolis remains relatively calm, much of the country is in the throes of war.

P.S. I've had trouble accessing this blog because of DoS (denial-of-service) attacks. Rumor has it that the government is using these attacks to slow communications between the various rebel groups. The government, likewise, blames the rebels. Although I'm not sure which side to believe, I would surmise that the government has more to gain by shutting down the internet than the rebels do …

* * *

IF LIEUTENANT PRINCE hadn't already seen Emiko, he could definitely hear her as she scuttled forward through the duct.

A deafening crack rang out and a spear of light pierced the darkness before her.

"Hold your fire!" Lieutenant Prince shouted. "I want him alive. Spread out and cover the exits."

Why did the General's men assume she was a man? This wasn't the first time. If only they'd known their enemy was a 5-foot-something, thirteen-year-old girl …

She arrived at another grate. The room below, veiled in shadows, was far darker than Prince's office.

Drop into this room or continue forward? Emiko's chest rose and fell with heavy breaths as she paused to consider.

No full-grown male would fit in this ventilation shaft. Prince and his men would have to flush her out. Though this sounded reassuring, in reality Prince's men would soon have every possible exit covered. Then they could just wait her out. Patient as she could be, Emiko would never outlast an army of men in rotating shifts.

She had to escape now. But where? She couldn't go out the way she'd come in. Men were surely already waiting for her there. She could continue forward, but she wasn't sure where the ventilation shaft would lead.

The door below flung open and two men rushed into the room. Emiko inched back from the grate, confident the men hadn't spotted her.

"There's another grate up there. He might try to drop down."

"Then let's wait him out."

That made two men in this room, presumably another by the grate she'd entered, and Lieutenant Prince. But where would Prince be? He didn't seem like a man who would wait patiently in his office while his lackeys smoked her out.

She'd have to make her escape via the one route Prince assumed she wouldn't dare try.

Emiko quietly crawled in reverse. Soon she arrived back at the grate above Prince's office. She cautiously leaned forward to peer below.

The room was empty — at least for now. She could've dropped down into the room and dashed into the winding hallways ... if not for the screws.

Screws held the grate in place. Their heads were on the outer side. Her knife would be of no use.

Emiko's mind raced. The solution came in a blink. She thrust up and down, thrashing like a wild dog trapped in a cage. The duct groaned under her weight.

Back and forth she threw herself. She used every inch of leverage the cramped space had to offer. The duct belched and moaned. Slivers of light poured through the rupturing seams. Finally the metal shrieked like a dying witch as gravity had its way.

Was this what wounded game birds felt like as they tumbled helplessly towards the earth?

Emiko crashed to the floor, the impact knocking the air from her lungs. Her body begged to stay down, but her mind knew better. She peeled her arms free from the carpet, braced her palms against the floor, and willed her reproachful body to its feet.

She gently fingered her right cheek. It was raw from carpet burn. On the bright side, her ankle felt fine. The odds of escaping were looking up. If she could get in, she could get out.

The room offered two options: Through the door or out the window.

Her heart throbbed; her hands shook. Door or window? She had to choose now. Delay would bring death by default.

There were definitely green men inside. She hadn't seen green men outside.

She ran to the window, jammed her fingers beneath the sash, and heaved upward.

Fresh breeze burst into the room, massaging Emiko's rug-burnt cheek. The opening led to a courtyard, deserted and overgrown. From there she could circle around and rejoin Aristotle.

She pulled herself onto the window's ledge. The door to Prince's office flew open just as she leapt outside. A confusion of shouts trailed close behind as she hit the ground and bolted around the corner of the dormitory.

* * *

"I'm afraid I'm not qualified to receive your confession," Aristotle said. "But if you drop by my church, Father Fitzpatrick will surely offer you a chance to ease the burden of your sins."

"Look, sister," Glacier Face said. "You know what I want, and you know Father Fitzpatrick can't give it to me."

The wolf was growing hungrier. Aristotle's dance was twirling to an end. Her hand hovered near her revolver, but she couldn't draw it — not until Emiko returned. Where the Desolation was that girl?

"Fine," Aristotle capitulated, abruptly dropping all holy pretense. "I can see there is no escaping your desire. Where should we go?"

"I thought we were going to the church," Glacier Face said. He seemed unfazed by Aristotle's sudden shift in tack.

"The church? Look, I'll do whatever you want, but I don't want to be taken in the Lord's house."

Already close, Glacier Face stepped closer, nearly knocking Aristotle over with his muscle-bound chest. His breath smelled like a deer carcass decomposing in the sweltering August heat.

"You just said you'll do whatever I want," he hissed. "I want you to march over to that church."

Aristotle retreated a step. She resisted the primal urge to raise her arms in defense, instead keeping her hands at her side, within reach of her revolver.

"Do you have another suggestion?" Aristotle asked.

Glacier Face licked his lips and stretched his arms toward Aristotle. "Right here seems as good a place as any."

The wolf could be held at bay no longer.

Aristotle reached into the thin slit she'd sliced in her robes. She drew her revolver and jabbed the muzzle into the bridge of Glacier Face's nose.

"Don't you dare," she growled.

Glacier Face appeared unconcerned. Either he'd been born without the brain lobe that governed fear, or he did a damned good job of pretending. Still, he was wise enough to recognize that he was an eyebrow twitch away from a high-caliber lobotomy.

Aristotle heard hurried footsteps. A figure appeared behind Glacier Face, dashing around the corner of Pioneer Hall, favoring one leg.

Emiko ran down the sidewalk, giving no sign she intended to slow down.

"Are you alright?" Aristotle asked while keeping her eyes trained on Glacier Face.

"I'm fine," Emiko gasped. "But we need to go now!"

Glacier Face snickered. "No matter where you run, I will find you."

Aristotle narrowed her gaze. "You can look, but all you'll find is a bullet with your name on it."

"You don't even know my name."

Aristotle paced backwards, keeping her sights locked on Glacier Face's skull. Two green-vested men raced into view, spurring her on. She swung around the corner of a building and sprinted after Emiko.

Chapter 33

September 12th, 2027
Post Status: Public

The government has declared martial law in Minneapolis.

9 PM curfew. Light rail shutdown. Food rationing. At the federal government's behest Mayor Brunman has suspended all non-essential services.

If there were dissidents in Minneapolis who wanted to rise up and fight, they could feasibly stage a coup. The military regiment posted here is seriously understaffed and unlikely to receive reinforcements soon.

Desertion is rampant within the military. What was once short-term riot control has now mutated into a morally-ambiguous task. As chaos spreads soldiers are finding it increasingly difficult to justify acts of violence against their fellow citizens.

In any case, the people of Minneapolis have shown little interest in tearing down their own city. For this I'm thankful.

One more note. Phone service to Chicago is out. The situation in the Windy City worsens by the day.

I can only hope my parents are doing well. Mom and Dad, if you read this, please get in touch.

* * *

STILL INSIDE VIKINGS STADIUM, John and Nathan ducked behind a concession counter. They were mere yards away from the main entrance.

The concession stand featured a beverage dispenser and a hot dog warmer. Resting on the hot dog warmer's metal rollers were a dozen beefy frankfurters, still as mold-free as the day they'd left their packaging. How they had remained that way John preferred not to think about.

Ramses had vanished, apparently opting not to give chase. Now John and Nathan just needed to wait for Stearns to show up.

John's eyes barely crested the counter, keeping watch of the sun-filled atrium. His lone remaining crutch lay flat on the floor. His fingers clasped his Colt revolver. Behind him, Nathan guarded the concession stand's rear entrance.

The encounter with Ramses had been unexpected. It told John that he was drawing close to something, even if he couldn't say what that something was.

Ramses was the one who'd directed John to Mallard Island, thereby igniting the fuse that led to the Northland Core. Now the cocky, fatigue-wearing bastard was in Minneapolis, a city no one would visit unless they had a good reason. Even if Vikings Stadium proved fruitless, John had newfound hope that Minneapolis was the right place to be.

But what was Ramses doing here? Had he been following them? John had seen few soldiers in Minneapolis. He had a nagging feeling that he was seeing only the anthill and not the vast network of tunnels beneath.

"Ramses used to live with you in Frontier View, didn't he?" John asked Nathan, keeping his voice down. Though the concession stand afforded a nearly impregnable position, there was no reason to take chances.

"That's right," Nathan said, keeping his eyes on the rear entrance.

"What was he like back then?"

Nathan cocked his head thoughtfully. "He had bad days and good days. Most of the time he was fine, but he could be a bit of a bully. I think life in Frontier View was difficult for him, especially because he came without family."

"No family?" John asked. "He's still young, isn't he?"

"He's about a year older than I am. We found him on our way north, living alone. We invited him to join our group."

"Sounds like he had a rough time."

"Everyone had a rough time," Nathan said, glancing back at John. "Some more than others, I guess. But his past is no excuse for the kind of business he's gotten himself into."

"I'm not saying it is. Why did he leave Frontier View?"

"I think he was just sick of everything. Sick of the life, sick of how everyone treated him. Most of the other villagers felt sorry for him. That was fine while he was young, but when he grew older he'd had enough of being pitied. He left Frontier View to prove that he didn't need anyone's help."

Sick of village life? Tired of being treated like a kid? Nathan's description of Ramses reminded John of Emiko. Given the circumstances, John thought it best to keep this connection to himself.

"So he left Frontier View. Then what?" John asked.

"Then I didn't see him again until he showed up at Sawbill Lake. Everyone in Frontier View assumed he'd just gone off to live in a cave somewhere, but apparently he decided to become a soldier instead."

"Funny how that happens."

"What do you mean?"

"It's hard to live alone in this world. Even I can barely manage it. I can see why a young guy like Ramses would give up and join a militia instead, and why he'd dedicate himself so strongly to the cause."

"So that he can feel like he's joining something greater, rather than just returning to his former life with his tail between his legs?"

"Bingo."

"People are strange," Nathan said.

"You're telling me," John muttered. People were strange. Bionic arms were stranger.

Nathan creased his brow in concentration, tilting his ear towards the open atrium. "Do you hear that?" he whispered, gesturing over the counter with his eyebrows.

John shook his head. He pointed at the rear entrance, silently telling Nathan to keep an eye on it. He took his revolver in both hands and lofted it just above the concession counter's surface. Finally he heard the sound, a chafing noise barely audible above the silence of the vast stadium.

A shadow, stretched to gargantuan proportions by the afternoon sun, materialized on the empty floor.

"Who goes there?" John asked.

"John?" a voice called back.

"Stearns? You alone?"

"Yeah, just me." Stearns drew closer and turned about, scanning the room. "Where are you?"

"I'm back here, behind the concession stand with Nathan."

Stearns spun on his heels and met John's eyes. "Ah, there you are!"

"You alright?" John asked, relaxing his pistol grip.

"Never better."

"Did you see our trigger-happy friend Ramses?"

"Can't say I did. I made a cautious lap around the place, but wasn't able to turn him up." Stearns gritted his teeth. "I did find this, though." He held up John's other crutch.

"My crutch! You went back for it?"

"By the time I circled back through another tunnel, everyone was gone. This was all I found. I figured you might want it back." Stearns approached the counter and handed the crutch to John. "How did you two get away, anyhow?"

"It was slow going without this crutch. I'll tell you more after we get out of here."

John pulled himself over the concession counter. He, Stearns, and Nathan proceeded toward the exit, weapons drawn. Soon they were back outside. The sun hovered below the Minneapolis skyline, its rays diffracted by the desolate towers.

As though by tacit agreement, they drifted in the direction of Nathan's house. John and Stearns took the lead while Nathan guarded the rear.

"It was bold of you to dash off like that," John said.

"Shucks, it was nothing," Stearns said, waving off John's compliment. "It seemed like a risk worth taking. An old guy like me doesn't have much to live for, anyhow."

"You're not that old," John said. Though Stearns was hardly young, John figured the old colonel had a couple decades left — assuming a non-violent end. Given recent events, a non-violent end seemed far from guaranteed.

"You've met that youngster somewhere before?" Stearns asked.

"We did," John said. "He's the one who set us on the path that eventually led here."

"The guy who told you about Muckraker Island?"

"Yeah, Mallard Island," John corrected.

"Do you think it's significant that you spotted him here?" Stearns asked, sweeping the street with his Desert Eagle pistol.

"I'm sure it is, but I'm not sure why." John glanced back at Nathan, who was walking backwards, watching their flank. "You have any ideas, Nathan?"

"Ideas?" Nathan asked, craning his neck to look at John sidelong. "Ideas about what?"

"About why Ramses is here."

"I don't know." Nathan lowered his shotgun and shrugged. "Maybe it means we're closer than we think."

"Mmm," John grunted. If they weren't close he was in trouble. Invoking his arm to hurl crutches and open doors had triggered fatigue. Though the drain hadn't seriously affected him, it was a tangible problem. And it would only get worse.

"Do we have any reckoning about where to search next?" Stearns asked.

"I don't," John said. "How about you, Nathan?"

"Nothing yet."

"Nothing *yet*?" John arched an eyebrow.

Nathan dismissed the question with another shrug as he concentrated on the shimmering skyline.

Chapter 34

September 14th, 2027
Post Status: Public

I just got off the phone with my parents. Actually, the phone didn't work, but I managed to get through to them via Skype.

They told me of the situation in Chicago. It sounds dire — they're afraid to leave their house. And even when they do gather the courage to venture outside, they have difficulty finding food.

Apparently the rebels in Chicago aren't all working in unison. There are two different groups, known as the "Windy City Resistance" and the "Freedom of Illinois." Although they both struggle against the U.S. government, neither group is particularly keen on the other.

So, what happens if the rebels win?

How will their insurgent government create more food? Wizardry, perhaps?

Will a second rebel force overthrow the first batch of revolutionaries?

Will chaos reign?

* * *

ARISTOTLE AND EMIKO didn't stop running until they reached the safety of home. They slipped out of their robes and collapsed on the living room couch.

Unfocused, poorly planned, and lacking a clear, singular objective, the expedition had been a disaster from the start.

Despite this, they had obtained a few vital pieces of information.

Though they hadn't found the General himself — apparently he was MIA — Emiko's espionage work had made it clear that this was his army. It seemed inevitable that, sooner or later, this army would mount an offensive. If forced to bet, Aristotle would've put her loonies on *sooner*.

But what could she do with this information? There was no way she and Emiko could launch a direct assault against an entire army. Even if she tracked down Osborne, Nathan, and Kennedy Stearns, they would still be vastly outgunned.

Five against an army. A dictionary couldn't have defined *suicide* more succinctly.

Another option was to contact Captain Griswold. But what could he do? He barely had enough men to police Toronto. He wouldn't act until the Restoration Army started encroaching on Canada. By then it would be too late.

Minnesota would have to mount a resistance. Resistance would require organization. Though Aristotle and Emiko couldn't organize a counter-force on their own, perhaps they could sow the seeds.

Emiko, much to her credit, had taken the day's events in stride. She sat in an upholstered chair, paging through her mysterious notebook, *World's End.* Though Aristotle was curious, it was better she didn't pry. Emiko would discuss the diary when she was ready.

Emiko set the notebook on her lap. She looked across the couch to Aristotle.

"Have you ever killed a person before?" Emiko asked.

"I have."

"So you were serious about the bullet with his name on it?"

Aristotle rotated, resting her feet on the couch. "Dead serious. People can sense when a threat is empty. If you're not willing to follow through with a threat, you're better off not making it at all. Empty threats only harm their makers."

"I'll remember that," Emiko said.

"And you? Have you ever killed a man?" Aristotle drew her legs closer, wrapping her arms around them.

Emiko shook her head. "No. But I've seen some nasty things."

"I'm sure you have. But if you do ever have to kill — and I hope you don't — just know that the experience will shake you."

"Mmm." Emiko reflected on that nugget for a moment before returning to her father's notebook.

She's a pure soul, Aristotle thought. Emiko clearly had her flaws, as demonstrated by her reluctance to give a straight answer about her vanishing act the day before. Yet she also had the ability to win friends and put hearts at ease, just by being herself. It had been a long, long time since Aristotle had felt so comfortable with someone.

One person that did come to mind was Osborne's partner, Nathan. Aristotle hadn't spent enough time with Nathan to call him a friend, but his unassuming nature quickly earned the trust of those he met. In that way he reminded her of Emiko.

"Hey, Aristotle," Emiko said.

"Yeah?"

"There's something I'd like to show you."

"What's that?"

"We have to wait until dusk, until it's almost dark," Emiko said. She wore a serious expression, as though not yet convinced she should share this secret. "I'd rather show you than tell you."

"As long as you think I'll like it," Aristotle said, playfully cocking an eyebrow.

"You will. I'm sure of it. We can leave in an hour or two."

"Just give the word and lead the way," Aristotle said, eager to see this secret that bloomed only after dark.

Chapter 35

September 20th, 2027
Post Status: Public

San Francisco. Nuclear explosion.

The city gone. Vaporized.

The bomb was set off at ground level.

Culprit unknown. Details forthcoming.

San Francisco was in rebel hands. That would suggest
a strike by the government. But I can't imagine
President Hernandez authorizing such a thing. Perhaps
there were multiple rebel groups, as in Chicago, and
one of them …

Wait … the TV has news of another …

Oh fucking hell

* * *

JOHN RECLINED IN his lawn chair, admiring the western horizon.
The day's sun was in its death throes, bleeding fierce red onto
the silhouetted Minneapolis skyline. Only Target Tower stood
tall enough to rise above the spectacle, concealing its spire in
the dark purple of approaching night like a giraffe stretching its
head into a leafy canopy.

"I gotta say, dead as it may be, this city is still a real beauty
sometimes," Stearns said, taking a pull from his hip flask. The
container's polished chrome surface reflected the dying light.

"You can find beauty in anything if you squint hard enough,"
John said.

"You always were a serious one, weren't you?" Stearns
leaned over and offered his flask to John. "Want a hit? It's

Johnny Walker. The real stuff. I found a couple bottles in a basement a few blocks over."

"Later. After we find the core." On Mallard Island John had learned first-hand that his discharging bionic arm and alcohol didn't play nicely together.

"Suit yourself." Stearns took another hit before replacing the cap and pocketing the flask.

The vivid maroon and orange spill on the horizon gradually ebbed. The night was like a blanket covering a bloody crime scene.

"You remember the sunsets in Egypt?" Stearns ask.

John grunted in reply. Sunsets were near the bottom of his list of memories from Egypt, slotted somewhere between "albino camels" and "loose sand chafing in boots."

"The sun would collide with that vast ocean of sand, and the sky would burn like napalm before petering out for the night. We'd go to sleep thankful that we'd survived another day, knowing that we'd inched closer to achieving political stability in Egypt."

"Maybe your nights were like that. I slept with one eye and both ears open. If a bloodthirsty rebel popped in or a mortar whistled by, I was ready to act."

"Well, I hope you can forgive an old blowhard for romanticizing the past a bit," Stearns said. "Anyhow, we should discuss where our search will take us next, shouldn't we? How about you call Nathan out here?"

"Sounds good." John hopped up on one leg and collected his crutches.

"Ah, I forgot you were still using those things." Stearns grasped his chair's armrests and leaning forward. "I can go get Nathan."

John shook his head. "I got it."

Stearns eased back in his chair. "Then I'll see you back out here in a few winks."

Letting the screen door slam shut, John shuffled through the house and up the stairs. The door to Nathan's room was shut. John knocked. "You in there, Nathan?"

No response. He cracked the door open to peek inside. The room was already dark, the fading sunlight unable to penetrate the closed blinds. Shadows obscured the posters that covered the walls. John could just barely make out the image of Super Mario above Nathan's desk.

He closed the door and proceeded to Nathan's father's office. He rapped on the door with his knuckles.

"Who is it?" Nathan called from inside.

"Mind if I come in?"

"Oh, John. No, go ahead. Come on in."

The door creaked open; its hinges could've used a whole can of WD-40. Inside, Nathan was kneeling by his father's desk, fiddling with something. He'd lit a lantern to complement the fading sunlight.

Nathan looked up from his project. "What's up?"

"Stearns and I want to discuss our next step. Come down and join us."

"Sure. I'll be down in a minute," Nathan said, returning to his work.

John swung into the room for a closer look. Nathan often became completely absorbed in his work; his "minute" could stretch into hours. John peered over Nathan's shoulder. The kid was tinkering with the solar panel from Vikings Stadium, trying to connect it to his father's computer.

"I thought that was going to wait until after we find the Northland Core."

"Oh, right," Nathan said, continuing to fiddle with the contraption. "I guess I forgot."

Why this obsession with fixing his old man's computer? John wondered. He was disappointed that Nathan couldn't put off this personal project. Then again, his chat with Stearns outside hadn't been focused on the task at hand either.

"Come on. We're gonna start the meeting now."

"Alright," Nathan said, still not turning away from his work.

"Now."

"Okay, okay." Nathan gently set down the solar panel. Pressing his palms to the floor for balance, he rose to his feet.

John met Nathan's eyes. "We need your head in this, Nathan. I need you."

"Don't worry, John. You got me."

John nodded. He hoped Nathan's help would be enough. Because if he didn't find the Northland Core soon he would be nothing but a pair of cold dead hands connected to a cold dead brain.

Chapter 36

September 22nd, 2027
Post Status: Public

San Francisco and Chicago two days ago. Philadelphia and Houston yesterday.

Danielle is despondent. Nathan is in his room crying. Emiko is also sad, though I don't think she completely understands.

As for myself? Well …

I've seen many terrible calamities in my life. 9/11. Hurricane Katrina. The Great SoCal Earthquake of 2023.

None of those hit this close to home.

The bomb in Chicago … that destroyed my parents' neighborhood … it changed my perspective of all those tragedies that came before.

I'm sorry I never understood until now.

* * *

ARISTOTLE FOLLOWED EMIKO into downtown Minneapolis, towards a horizon that glowed vermilion like the sand dunes of Mars.

They passed an Apple store with a black Toyota pickup truck driven through its front window. Fragments of glass were strewn across the sidewalk and the store's violet carpeting. A thick covering of yellow-green mold had formed atop the carpet. iPhones littered the truck's hood.

Aristotle pried her eyes away from the storefront biohazard. Emiko was still moving ahead energetically, her limp barely noticeable.

"Are you going to tell me where we're going?" Aristotle asked as she caught up to Emiko.

"You'll see soon enough," Emiko said over her shoulder. "We're almost there."

Aristotle frowned. She wasn't a fan of surprises. In this day and age, surprises were almost always vomit-inducing, life-threatening, or in some other way unwelcome. If anyone other than Emiko had been leading the way, Aristotle would have turned back blocks ago.

They took a left, walked to the end of the block, and then swung back right, due west. Around the corner loomed Target Tower, soaring upward as the sun slowly sank.

"You're taking me to Target Tower?" Aristotle asked.

Emiko spun around. Walking backwards, she flashed a sly grin at Aristotle. "Maybe," she said, twirling to face forward.

They continued ahead. The day's light soon faltered. Emiko extracted a kerosene lamp from Aristotle's compact backpack and lit it.

"We won't need the lamp for long," Emiko said with a mischievous smile.

"What do you mean?"

Aristotle's question went unanswered. Arriving at the base of the tower, Aristotle craned her neck all the way back. The tower's upper stories merged seamlessly with the night.

"Come on." Emiko beckoned with her index finger. "The doors should still be open."

So, this isn't her first visit, thought Aristotle.

A flight of marble stairs led to a row of four revolving doors. Each door had three steel wings inlaid with panels of glass. Only half of the glass panels were intact. A few of them had vanished completely; others were badly shattered.

"Watch your fingers." Emiko stepped to a door, carefully placed her hand on the metal frame, and pushed through. Aristotle followed. Glass shards crunched under the revolving wing.

"Welcome to Target Tower," said Emiko. "Tallest skyscraper in the Midwest, and seventh tallest in the world."

Emiko's lantern light struggled to reach the entryway's far wall. Signs and logos abounded: Louis Vuitton, Prada, and Gucci.

"How do you know it's the seventh tallest? Maybe one or two of the other six have collapsed by now," Aristotle suggested, only half in jest. During her time with the Toronto PD, she'd once narrowly staved off a building's collapse. Perhaps she would recount the story to Emiko when they had some down time ...

Emiko shrugged. "The brochures say it's the seventh tallest, so that's what I stick with. This is my first time showing the tower. I'm still working on the presentation."

"I'm honored to be the first."

"Your guide will now take you to the basement," Emiko intoned. The lantern bobbed in her hand as she led the way.

"Mind if I take a quick peek in here?" Aristotle asked as they passed the Gucci store.

"I don't mind. But it's just a store with a bunch of bags, isn't it?"

Without replying, Aristotle peered inside. Hundreds of authentic Gucci bags glimmered in the faint light. The bags had once sold for thousands of dollars apiece. Now they were worth only the value of their material. No wonder no one had bothered to steal them.

"Why is a bag store called 'Gucky'?" Emiko asked. "It sounds too much like 'yucky.'"

Aristotle chuckled. "It's pronounced 'Goo-chee.' It's Italian."

"I still don't like it."

"I'm not a big fan either. Come on. Let's keep moving."

Continuing past the shops, the two women soon arrived at a stairwell.

"We're going down to the lowest level," Emiko said.

Their soles rang hollow and heavy in the narrow stairwell. They wound back and forth past 1B, 2B, and 3B, all the way down to 4B.

The doorway into 4B was a wreck. Two twisted hinges hung from the door jamb, like the rotted teeth of a dentist-phobic centenarian. The door itself lay on the floor in the next room. A crater in its center suggested a battering ram had clobbered it loose.

"I didn't know you were so strong," Aristotle said.

Emiko rolled her eyes. "It was like this the first time I came."

"So I take it you weren't the first person to come down here?"

"I guess not."

The two women passed through the ravaged doorway into the next room. The lustrous metal walls reflected the soft amber hue of Emiko's lantern. The room reminded Aristotle of the underground lair she'd braved with John Osborne just a few weeks prior. That lair, however, had been equipped with its own lights.

"This way." Emiko led Aristotle to a door on the room's opposite side.

The same color as the wall, the second door was practically undetectable. Without Emiko's guidance Aristotle might not have noticed it. Only a thin, off-color seam where the door met the steel wall divulged its existence.

Emiko tapped a panel beside the door. Leaping to life in vivid, liquid crystal light, the panel revealed a miniature keyboard and a small screen. Leaning closer, Aristotle read the message on the screen: ENTER PASSWORD.

"There's still power down here?" she asked, raising an eyebrow.

"Yep," Emiko chirped.

"And you know the password?"

"Of course." Six-pronged asterisks appeared on the screen as Emiko entered a code. "H-T-R-O-N. 'North' backwards."

Aristotle puzzled over the door. Whoever had bashed down the first door had apparently decided to leave this one intact. Maybe they'd worried about damaging what was inside? Or perhaps they'd feared a trap?

Aristotle started to ask Emiko how she'd obtained the password when a loud, startling whoosh interrupted her. The door had retracted upward into a recess above its frame.

"This is it," Emiko announced. "The control room."

"The tower has a control room?" Aristotle had never considered that a building might have its own control room, but it made sense. Just like a space station or a man-made island, the tower's complexities required sophisticated monitoring and control.

Offering no reply, Emiko proceeded ahead. Her lantern revealed what looked like a super-sized airplane cockpit. The room had two throne-like swivel chairs, surrounded by a console replete with multi-colored buttons and unlit displays.

"What can we do here?" Aristotle asked.

"I don't understand most of the controls ..." Emiko stepped over to a red-handled lever. "But this is pretty neat." She thrust the lever forward.

Aristotle expected to hear the thunk of a generator firing up or the whir of turbines gathering speed. Instead, there was only the barely-there hum of the overhead lights flickering to life.

Chapter 37

September 23rd, 2027
Post Status: Public

This morning President Hernandez emerged from his security shelter. Standing before the Statue of Liberty, he delivered a rousing, heartfelt speech.

He spoke of his failure to resolve the crises that have plagued this nation. While he professed that many problems are beyond his power to fix, he admitted that he could have done better.

He apologized for retreating to a bunker and appearing only via camera when he should have stood with his people as their beacon of hope.

He closed his speech by stating that he is willing to do whatever it will take to bring peace to our great nation, even if it costs him his office. His first order of business is to meet with the various rebel leaders on neutral ground and see what can be done, because he won't stand to see his country tear itself apart any longer.

Tears trickled down his cheeks as he finished his address. Cameras caught him sobbing as he left the podium.

The people cry with him.

* * *

"WE'RE RUNNING OUT of time. The choice we make tonight might be the most important choice of my life."

John wished he were exaggerating. He, Nathan, and Stearns huddled around a campfire in the backyard. Even in the heat of summer, the warmth from the crackling fire soothed John's tired legs.

"So, where's it going to be?" he asked.

Stearns shook his head and took a pull from his flask. Nathan gazed listlessly into the flames.

"If I had a great idea I would've offered it days ago," Stearns said. "We haven't been holding out on you, John."

"I know. But maybe you have a long shot that you've been reluctant to share."

"There's nothing of the sort hiding in this old brain."

"Fair enough," John said.

Nathan remained silent. Was he discouraged because his suggestion hadn't panned out? Though they hadn't found the Northland Core in Vikings Stadium, the same was true of all the places they'd visited. Nathan had no reason to be hard on himself. Surely he realized that?

"Do you have any ideas, Nathan?" John asked.

"I don't think I do, John." Nathan pulled his eyes away from the campfire's hypnotic dance. His mouth opened to say more, but no words came out.

Suddenly animated, he thrust a finger towards the horizon. "Look!"

John twisted around in his chair. "Well I'll be damned."

Three columns of dazzling white lights had materialized in the night sky. At the columns' apex, high above the horizon, a single red light pulsated like an iridescent ruby. Far brighter than stars, the points of light could only have originated from one place.

Target Tower had come alive.

"It does this sometimes," Stearns said.

"It does?" John asked.

"I saw it happen once before, a few days after I arrived here"

John glowered at Stearns. "Don't you think that would've been worth telling us?"

"Maybe. But my guess is the place has already been searched exhaustively." Stearns sighed, shaking his head.

"Why?"

"Last time this happened, about three weeks back, I went to check it out the next day. By the time I got there the place was swarming with men in green. If there was something in that tower they would've found it."

"Where are all these men in green now?" John asked. He took a twig from the ground and tossed it into the campfire.

"Your guess is as good as mine."

Men in green. Stearns had spoken of them. John had seen a few of them for himself. The only surprise was that he hadn't spotted more.

Had these green-vested men already found the Northland Core? If so, John would have to track them down and take it from them. Even outnumbered a hundred to one, it would be better to go out guns blazing than to roll over and die.

"You're thinking that the General's men have the Northland Core, aren't you?" Nathan asked.

"That's what it sounds like" John replied. Usually he was the one who read Nathan's mind. The tables had turned.

"I see two holes in that theory."

"Yeah?"

"First of all, there's no reason to assume that the Northland Core is powering the building."

"I know," John said. "But what else possibly could?"

"Solar? Nuclear? Who knows? But there's more tangible problem. If the General's men found the core in Target Tower and removed it, how could the building light up at night?"

John nodded. "That's a good point."

"Well, then," Stearns interjected, waving a finger in the air. "Where does this leave us?"

The group fell silent. A gentle breeze carried the smoke from the fire towards John. He shifted position to avoid it. All the while the vibrant red light atop Target Tower blinked insistently, warding off airplanes that no longer braved the skies.

"I say we go take a closer look at the tower tomorrow," John said.

"I'm with John," Nathan said.

"Well, I'm of the mind that we won't find anything there," Stearns said. "But it looks like it's two against one."

"You can't win 'em all, Stearns," John said, patting the old colonel on the shoulder.

"Never thought I could," Stearns said with a wily grin. "But a man's gotta try."

Chapter 38

September 27th, 2027
Post Status: Public

The violence wanes. The will to fight subsides.

Peace talks will be held in St. Louis, a site chosen by the President and a few key rebels for its central location and neutral leanings.

While I know these wounds won't heal quickly, it's reassuring to see that treatment has commenced.

Interestingly enough, no party has stepped forward to claim responsibility for the bombings. The term "phantom bombers" is gaining traction in the media. I have mixed feelings about this development.

As for my family, we're doing as well as can be expected given all that we've lost. Nathan in particular is still quite shaken. He feels things more deeply than most. Still, I'm confident he will cheer up in time.

Hope glimmers on the horizon.

* * *

THOUGH IT FELT LIKE the future, Aristotle had stepped into the past.

The elevator doors lurched shut, and Aristotle and Emiko shot up toward the viewing floor. A cel-shaded 3D portrayal of Target Tower appeared on an LCD screen. The display tracked the elevator's position. The journey to the top would take all of thirty eight seconds.

"How did you find out about this?" Aristotle asked.

Emiko hesitated. A timer on the display ticked down. Thirty three, thirty two, thirty one ...

"From my dad's diary," she said.

"*World's End?*"

"That's the one."

"You're very protective of it."

"Wouldn't you be protective of your father's diary?" Emiko asked, as though it were a foregone conclusion.

And it was. If a member of Aristotle's family had left a diary or similar keepsake, she too would've been reluctant to share it. Private reflections were meant to stay within family. On the other hand, most diaries didn't contain secrets about the world's seventh tallest tower.

Eighteen seconds left. Aristotle winced as her ears adjusted to the change in air pressure.

"How did your father come across this information?"

"He came here after the Desolation. Someone had left the control room door open."

"Very convenient."

"Yeah, I guess."

"What was he doing here, though?" Aristotle asked. She could conceive of a few reasons why someone would have visited a skyscraper after the Desolation ...

"I'm not sure. He wrote about it in his diary, but I don't understand some of it."

"Maybe I can take a look."

"Maybe."

Four, three, two, one. The elevator bell chimed and the doors slid open. Aristotle and Emiko stepped out into a wide, roughly circular room. Windows lined the outer wall. Dim overhead lighting helped visitors navigate the room while not impairing the outside view. Furnishings were sparse — a few benches here, a lounge chair there.

Aristotle made her way to a window. Below it was an LCD panel, wide as two canoes set end-to-end. The panel's vivid, high-resolution screen panoramically detailed the sights below, including Vikings Stadium, the Target Center, the University of Minnesota, and the Mississippi River. The display showed the city's dazzling night lights as they would've appeared nine years ago.

"There's an outside observation deck one more floor up," Emiko said. "The view is a lot better from there."

"Lead the way."

The staircase wasn't far. Aristotle clung to the handrail as she ascended. She found the sheer abundance of electricity disconcerting. While a few buildings in Toronto had electricity, they could generate only enough energy to power a few light bulbs here or maybe a stereo system there. The shimmering lights, high-speed elevators, and pixel-packed computer screens of Target Tower were anachronisms.

"Where does all this electricity come from?" Aristotle asked in wonderment, not expecting an answer.

"My dad's diary doesn't say." Emiko reached the top of the staircase and pushed open a door. "Here we are."

Beyond the door, only a short stretch of floor and a parapet separated Aristotle from the unbounded expanse of Minnesota sky. Stars glinted and glowed like particles of pixie dust floating on a lake of tar. Atop the tower's spire a red light pulsated like a beating heart.

"It's beautiful," Aristotle said.

"That's why I brought you here." Emiko stood on her tiptoes for a better look over the parapet. "I came up here during the day once, but the view just made me sad."

"I can see why. You would look down at all those buildings and think about all the dead inside them."

"Mmm," Emiko murmured.

Aristotle could discern faint outlines of the buildings below. Before the Desolation, the night view here would've been a spectacle of neon, halogen, and liquid crystal. Now nature provided the only show, the stars brighter than ever thanks to the absence of light pollution.

"Did you ever come up here before the Desolation?" Aristotle asked.

"I did, but I don't remember it well," Emiko said, playing with a handful of her short black hair. "My dad and mom brought me here in winter. This viewing platform was closed."

"Do you miss your family?"

"Doesn't everyone?"

A gust of wind buffeted the observation platform. Though cool and refreshing at ground level, here the summer breeze summoned up primal fears of being blown off the tower.

"You said you have a brother, right?" Aristotle asked.

"Yeah. Somewhere," Emiko said, letting the strands of hair fall from her hand.

Aristotle stared at the night sky, waiting for Emiko to continue.

Somewhere? Was that all Emiko had to say? Aristotle wanted to hear more about this brother.

Perhaps the burden of sharing first was Aristotle's to bear. She hung her elbows over the parapet and admired the stars.

"My real name is Sylvia Leon. I became Aristotle only recently, after I left the Toronto police force. A new name for a new start."

"You were a police officer?"

"I was, but not for long. I joined the police to help people; I left because I thought I could do more good on my own."

"Sounds difficult."

"Very difficult. 'Doing good' isn't as straightforward as it sounds." Aristotle leaned her back against parapet and looked to the throbbing glow of the tower's highest point. "Do you know what else this tower makes me think of?"

"What?"

"My sister."

"Your sister?" Emiko cocked her head. "Why?"

Aristotle let her shoulders sag. Some conversations never got easier.

"After the virus took my mom, my sister went to the top of a tall building and jumped. Suicide. At the time my sister didn't know that she'd had a chance to survive, like I ultimately did. If I had been able to help her endure those terrible first days, maybe she would still be here now."

"I'm sorry to hear that," Emiko said.

Carried by the wind, Aristotle's words of regret rose onward and upward. Was her sister Isabel somewhere up there listening?

"So, you must've gotten viral immunity from your father," Emiko said. "And your sister might have gotten the immunity gene from him, too."

"Right. She had a fifty-percent chance."

"But what about your father? Didn't he survive?"

Aristotle shook her head. "He died long before the Desolation. He was caught in a violent squall on Lake Superior. The wreckage of his sailboat was never found."

"Oh," was all Emiko managed. Her face expressed the sympathy that her words couldn't.

Aristotle pushed off from the parapet with her elbows. Her eyes lingered on the tower's shining red spire.

"The tower's external lights are on," she said, agape.

"So?"

"So everyone in the whole city knows something strange is going on here."

Emiko grinned sheepishly. "I guess so."

"We need to get out of here."

They retreated down the staircase and returned to the elevator. The LCD screen announced their thirty-eight second descent. The air pressure again irritated Aristotle's ears.

"You know ..." Emiko said, her voice trailing off.

"Yeah?"

Emiko nibbled at the corner of her lip. "Never mind. It's nothing."

The elevator came to rest at the first floor. The bell chimed and the steel doors parted.

"We should go turn off the power," Emiko said.

"Any reason not to just leave it on? I don't want to stick around longer than necessary."

"My dad turned it off. We should, too."

"Point taken," Aristotle said. "But let's make it quick."

Together they revisited the basement. A few minutes later Minneapolis returned to its natural, starlit state.

Chapter 39

October 1st, 2027
Post Status: Public

The peace talks appear to be going well. Though there are still many disagreements that need resolving, there is an overwhelming sentiment to put these horrific events behind us and move forward.

There are objectors to peace, of course. Yet the more these objectors speak, the more they undermine their own viewpoints. Whatever perceived value their ideas once had has vanished.

Transportation networks are reopening, as are schools and businesses. The university is set to reopen next week. I'll probably drop by and make sure my affairs are in order for the new semester.

Perhaps lecturing eager young minds will lighten my heavy heart.

* * *

RAMSES LINGERED IN Vikings Stadium until all was dark before setting off. On Thunder's back, he rode aimlessly down the unlit streets of Minneapolis.

Ramses loathed the hours between dawn and dusk. Night was a sinister time, a time of assassins, psychopaths, and thieves. A time of evil, evil of which he wanted no part.

Ramses championed justice. He endeavored for a Minnesotan revival. He strove to further the General's grand mission. He stood with the forces of light!

His housing block appeared in the distance. The complex was mostly dark, save for faint traces of light escaping from a few windows.

Soon the General's army would no longer need to hide.

Ramses led Thunder into the army's stable. After securing the faithful steed in his stall and replenishing his hay and water, Ramses headed for Pioneer Hall.

He had orders. Orders that were to be executed immediately.

Ramses strode into the dormitory's main corridor. In a large alcove to one side, a group of soldiers huddled in chairs, reading by firelight. Ramses wondered if any were tackling the visionary wisdom of *Taking the Power Back* by Howard Armstrong Steel. Ramses had left his copy in the army's library in hope that others would discover its inspired teachings. He feared none had. Was there any way he could further promulgate the book's message? Surely the entire Restoration Army would benefit if every soldier versed themselves in Steel's Laws of Power.

He arrived at his destination, Lieutenant Prince's office. A diffuse golden light glimmered from the gap beneath the door. With any luck the Prince of Minneapolis would still be willing to accept a visit at this hour.

Ramses knocked.

"Yes?" Prince called through the door.

"It's Private Ramses Brushnell, sir. I'd like a word with you if you have time."

"Certainly. Come in."

Ramses twisted the doorknob and stepped into Prince's office. The lieutenant was at his desk, his face tinted pale orange by the lantern light. He had removed his beret, revealing a buzzed head of hair. A thin wisp of smoke spiraled up from the ashtray on his desk, carrying with it the pungent scent of a freshly snubbed cigar.

"Private Brushnell," he said, straightening his posture and resting his elbow on the desk. "Your visit comes as a pleasant surprise."

"The pleasure is all mine, sir."

"It's been a long day, Private. I hope you have something important to tell me."

"A long day, sir?"

Lieutenant Prince frowned. "Indeed. I'm afraid we had a breach in security today."

"I hadn't heard, sir."

"Naturally. It's difficult to know the goings-on here when you aren't present yourself."

"Naturally," Ramses replied, keeping his voice steady. So, Prince was aware that he'd left the army's grounds? Ramses didn't find this surprising. Nor did it change what he'd come here to accomplish. "May I inquire about the nature of this breach, sir?"

"There's not much to say. Two women posing as nuns infiltrated our complex. Although it appears they didn't take anything, we're still investigating the incident."

"I hope you're able to find and apprehend them in due course, sir."

"It's a big city out there, but we'll do our best." Lieutenant Prince retrieved the blue beret from his desk and replaced it on his head. "You said you had something to tell me."

"Yes, sir." Ramses folded his hands behind his back. "First, I'd like to apologize for my transgression today. Our force is currently on lockdown, and it was foolish of me to leave the premises."

"I understand, private. While I don't condone your actions, I know it's not easy for a young man such as yourself to be cooped for weeks on end. The General and I have asked much of you." Prince's eyes drifted toward the lantern hanging from his wall, as though seeking advice from its dancing flames, before returning to Ramses. "Given your exceptional record, and given that today's slip was not a major failing, I am willing to accept your apology."

"Thank you, sir," Ramses said, nodding curtly. He remained frozen in place.

"Is there anything else, Private?"

Ramses cleared his throat. "Sir, I thought I might explain why I left the housing complex today."

"Oh?" Lieutenant Prince lifted his chin slightly, a sign he expected Ramses to proceed.

"I needed time to think, sir. Time to think in solitude, away from the barracks. As you yourself just said, recent events have strained our organization, and I am not above feeling the effects of this strain."

"Indeed. We've already discussed as much. Is there anything else?"

"While I was off thinking, I came to realize something important, sir."

"Go on."

"My thoughts were related to our earlier discussion, sir. Today I realized that my loyalties lie not with the General, but with the Restoration Army itself. For though a great man he may be, the General is not the Restoration Army. The army and its goals — to spread peace, prosperity, and justice across Minnesota, and hopefully across the world — are ideals that live apart from the General."

Lieutenant Prince nodded appreciatively.

Ramses continued. "Indeed, the General has made great efforts to sow the seeds of restoration. But watching over this restoration is a responsibility that falls to all of us, and I've come to realize that perhaps the General is not the best man to lead us in this pursuit."

The statement was wordier than Ramses had intended. Indeed, it was worthy of a pretentious windbag. Still, he had played his hand. How would Prince counter?

The truth, of course, was that no matter how Lieutenant Prince responded, Ramses would win. Only the method of victory would change.

Prince rose from his desk and peered out his window into the moonlit night. He was thinking, Ramses could see. Deciding how much to trust this newly professed ally. Finally he pulled away from the moon's mesmerizing light. He paced around his desk and stood face-to-face with Ramses.

The two men locked eyes.

"Thank you for sharing your thoughts, Private Brushnell. We will talk on this subject again soon. Perhaps very soon. You are dismissed."

Prince spun on his heels, circled his desk, and reclaimed his chair.

Ramses stood dumbly as he deliberated over how to react. Fortunately, standing dumbly was likely an acceptable choice.

Lieutenant Prince sorted papers on his desk, paying Ramses no mind.

"Thank you, sir. Have a good night," Ramses said. He saluted before leaving the room.

He snickered under his breath as the door latched shut.

PART THREE

Chapter 40

October 3rd, 2027
Post Status: Private

You will never believe what I saw at the University today. "You" being only myself … and perhaps one other.

I don't dare post this publicly.

I knew the university, like many schools in the nation, had been turning to the military-industrial complex to keep its budget in the black. But I never imagined I'd see what I saw today.

The afternoon began unassumingly enough. The campus was nearly empty. Workers were repairing the walks outside. After leaving my office in Smith Hall, I decided to see if my friend Professor Stevens was in. To avoid the noisy construction on the campus mall, I swung underground through the Gopher Way towards Tate.

I've walked the Gopher Way hundreds of times. I know every twist and turn, every exit and entrance. So you can imagine my surprise when, near the tunnel branch that leads up to Tate proper, I spotted a door, set about a foot into the concrete.

As I was trying to make sense of this unexpected sight, I heard the loud clack of boots, precise and rhythmic, approaching from the other direction. Frightened by the ominous sound, I swung into an opening on the opposite wall.

Soon a squad of armed men in U.S. army green marched past my hiding spot. They escorted a forklift that carried a single crate. Only the words "Northland

Core" stamped on the crate's wooden panels alluded to its contents.

Somehow I doubt this "Northland Core" is the core of a new apple cultivar.

To my great fortune, the shadows hid me well. None of the soldiers noticed me. After they all disappeared through the door, I slipped out of the opening and bolted through the tunnel and up the stairs to Tate.

Professor Stevens wasn't in. I hurried home and now here I am, at my computer.

I always knew the university had ties to the military, but I never expected to see soldiers marching through campus.

Is this a recent development, or has it been going on for a long time?

* * *

JOHN SLEPT FITFULLY. When he awoke the next morning, his brain felt as though the sandman had buried it in a few tons of fracking grade.

Shaking off the unwelcome brain fog, he rolled out of bed, grabbed his crutches, and swung his way to the window. The sun was a sliver of fire above the trees, painting the houses and sidewalks burnt orange.

Target Tower awaited.

It was early. Stearns' loud, nasal snores carried upstairs from the living room. Nathan was probably still curled up under his sheets. If they didn't rouse soon John would wake them.

John shuffled down the hallway, eager to get outside and start a cooking fire. As he passed Nathan's father's office, he noticed the door was cracked open. Nudging the door open with a crutch, he found Nathan sitting at the desk, staring at the computer monitor. Nathan had placed the solar panel on the windowsill and wired it to the computer. The pale glow of the LCD monitor reflected from Nathan's face.

"I thought this project was going to wait until after we found the Northland Core."

"It was. But I couldn't wait," Nathan said, his eyes bound to the computer display. "And then I found the Northland Core."

John stared at Nathan. He blinked repeatedly, shaking his head to clear out the cobwebs.

"Could you repeat that?"

"You heard me correctly, John. I found the Northland Core."

John gaped at Nathan and the computer. His brain understood the words, but was slow to accept their significance. Only the sharp yapping of a feral dog outside stirred him from his stupor.

"Well then where is it?"

"It's all right here." Nathan pointed at the monitor as his eyes met John's. "Right here in my father's blog." He proceeded to explain his findings.

The kid had come through once again.

* * *

Nathan now understood his urge to repair the computer. Years ago he'd regularly hacked into his father's blog, *Ryota in the Minneapple.* Back then many of his father's musing had flown miles above his nine-year-old comprehension level. Though Nathan hadn't understood all the ideas, many of the words had stuck. Like a wad of bubble gum pressed to a desk bottom, "Northland Core" had remained firmly rooted in his mind.

Invigorated by their breakthrough, Nathan and John roasted a feral chicken and fresh yams over the fire. When breakfast was ready they roused Stearns and the discussion began in earnest.

"Let me get this straight," Stearns said after Nathan had explained his findings. "What you're telling me is that your father mentioned the Northland Core on his blog, which was archived on his computer, which you managed to repair?"

"That's what I'm telling you," Nathan said. In his excitement to share the good news he'd barely touched his food.

"And his blog states that the Northland Core is hidden beneath the University of Minnesota, in tunnels built to protect college students from frostbitten toes?"

"That's right."

Stearns shoveled his last forkful of chicken into his mouth. "But you also said that your father, Ryota ... Ryota, is that Japanese?"

Nathan nodded. "My grandparents were immigrants from Japan."

"You say he wasn't involved in developing the Northland Core?" Stearns asked, resting his fork on his empty plate.

"Right. He bumped into a contingent of soldiers who were transporting it."

Stearns scratched his graying beard. Before long it would compare favorably to John's jawful of scruff.

"Then I suppose it's off to the tunnels instead of Target Tower."

"That's the plan," Nathan said.

Stearns' mouth cracked into a smile. "I knew I was onto something when I voted against Target Tower yesterday. I could feel it in my bones."

"Why didn't your bones speak up yesterday?" John retorted.

"Well, that's because they're old bones," Stearns quipped. "They don't give answers on demand. They need time to ruminate."

"Undoubtedly," John said, clearly unimpressed.

"When will we set out?" Nathan asked.

"How about right now?" John replied. Though the biggest eater of the group, he still hadn't cleaned his plate.

"Hey, hey, now. Let's hold up a moment." Stearns rose from his chair and leaned over the table. "Nathan, you still have a half a plate of good food there in front of you. John has a few bites left too. If the Northland Core is in these tunnels now, it'll still be there in an hour. Let's finish eating, get these dishes washed, and go from there."

"Fair enough," John said. "But since when did you care about doing the dishes?"

"Old Ma Stearns was a stickler for clean dishes. They had to be absolutely spotless."

John cocked an eyebrow. "Seriously?"

Stearns sauntered towards the rear door. "No. It just sounded better than telling you that I have to go see a man about a horse. An old man's bowel movements are like a president's mistresses. They visit a few times a week and are never spoken of."

"Spare us the details," John said.

"Rest assured I will." Stearns disappeared from the dining room.

Chapter 41

October 6th, 2027
Post Status: Public

Everything seems to be settling down.

Many still go hungry, and many still shed tears in the wake of all the destruction, but we shall carry on.

The new semester started at the U today. Better late than never, I suppose. Even now many of the school's departments are in disarray, and student turnout is far below expectations.

But at least we're back in business. Many schools on the east coast won't be reopening for another few days. Apparently a highly contagious virus, a variant of the swine flu, is spreading across the eastern seaboard. Schools are remaining closed until it passes.

I'm glad the schools are playing it safe and not hurrying to open their doors. This country has already suffered enough.

* * *

JOHN AND NATHAN had scoured the university before. Unlike those uncertainty-plagued visits in the early days of the search, this time they came with fresh hope and clear purpose.

"Which building did you say we should go to?" John asked. Though still on crutches, he felt confident he'd be able to rid himself of the walking supports any day now. Perhaps an energy boost from the Northland Core would alleviate the nagging soreness in his leg.

Nathan took another look at his notebook. In it he'd jotted the information pertaining to the core.

"It looks like we should start at the Tate Lab of Physics. Once we go underground there we should be able to retrace my father's tracks."

"Sounds like as good a plan as any," Stearns said.

"Agreed," John said.

They proceeded to the campus mall. Nothing had changed. Arbor vitae and cherry trees formed a rectangular barrier around a field of weedy grasses. A steady wind tugged at the wild greenery, bending the pliant stalks towards the east. Soon the three men stood before the Tate Lab of Physics' classic facade.

"In here?" Stearns pointed at the lab's doors with his thumb.

"This is the place," Nathan said.

"Let's keep moving," John said, beginning up the stone steps. He had to give Nathan credit. The kid's instincts had told him that the core was in the university. The hunch was proving correct.

He looked back over his shoulder. Stearns was on his way up, a couple steps behind, but Nathan hadn't budged from the sidewalk. Something in the distance had caught his eye.

"See something?" John called down the stairs.

Nathan's focused expression softened. "No. I'm just thinking about that rainy day, when we got into a footrace with that guy."

"I remember. That was before I had these." John lifted a crutch above his head. "What about it?"

"Nothing in particular. I'm just thinking. Wondering."

"There will be time for reflection after we get the Northland Core."

Nathan nodded. "I know." He sprang up the staircase like a chipmunk bounding up a tree. "Let's go get it."

"Let's."

Nathan opened one of the twin lab doors for John. Though brighter than it had been during their previous visit, Tate's interior was still dappled in shadows. Stearns was already inside.

"Special relativity was Einstein's thing, right?" Stearns asked, squinting at the cryptic graffiti on the wall.

"John and I couldn't figure out what that meant, either," Nathan said.

Stearns twiddled a strand of his hair. "You two have been here before?"

"Yeah, a few weeks ago," Nathan said as he lit a lantern, banishing the shadows to the corners of the room. "The Gopher Way is over here." He pointed to a dark corridor that branched off from the entry hall.

The three men navigated the halls and descended into the basement, leaving a trail of footprints in the dust. Soon they arrived at a familiar purple and yellow sign that read "The Gopher Way."

"Down this path?" Stearns nodded his head at the dark tunnel.

"That's the one," Nathan said. "Could you take the lantern? I want to take another look at my notebook."

"Anything you ask, son," Stearns said, taking the lantern.

Nathan briefly scanned his notes. "I think I know the way," he said, clapping the notebook shut with both hands. "Let's go."

Stearns, lantern in hand, led the group down the corridor. The walls, floor, and ceiling were cast of heavy-duty concrete.

"Have you been down here before?" Stearns asked Nathan.

"Maybe a long, long time ago. My dad might've taken me down here, but I'm not sure. The entire campus was an overwhelming blur to me back then."

"Funny how growing up changes your perspective, isn't it?"

"His perspective isn't the only thing that's changed," John offered. Over the past decade the world itself had undergone change enough for a dozen lifetimes.

"A very good point you have there, John," Stearns replied.

They came to a T-intersection. Nathan directed them to make a left. They took only a few steps before Nathan stopped abruptly.

"Over here." Nathan indicated an opening in the wall, just large enough for a man to squeeze into. "My dad mentioned this nook on his blog. He hid here while the men carrying the Northland Core marched past."

"Wasn't your father concerned about what he wrote on his blog?" Stearns asked.

"Of course. This post was set to private. Only people with the password could read it."

"I'm not sure a password would've stopped the Pentagon from reading it."

"I doubt the Pentagon had the resources to track millions of blogs."

"Oh, you'd be surprised, son." Stearns grinned. "But I see what you're saying. If your father wasn't already a person of interest, the Pentagon wouldn't have searched his private posts."

"I think the Pentagon had greater concerns at the time."

"You don't know the half of it."

Nathan stepped past the opening. "Anyway, after passing my father's hiding spot, the Northland Core was taken into another room. The entrance should be on the opposite wall, not far beyond here."

"There?" John said. He saw only a wall.

"The journal says that the men disappeared into a door my father had never seen before. It should be along this wall somewhere."

"A magic disappearing door, huh?" Stearns held the lantern up to the wall, exposing the tiny bumps, divots, and ripples in the bare concrete. "Was your father into hallucinogens or psychotropics, perchance?"

Nathan turned to John. "Can I just pretend I didn't hear that?"

"Hear what?" John said. He scowled at Stearns and loudly cleared his throat.

"Heavy air down here. I'm just trying to keep things light," Stearns said with a shrug.

John grunted in reply.

Nathan ran his fingers across the concrete. "We should check the wall for irregularities."

The men spread out and inspected the wall. They scanned the concrete's bumps and dimples with their hands, like three blind winos looking for a bottle of Chardonnay.

"Hey, Stearns," Nathan said. "Could you bring the lantern this way? I think I found something."

Stearns walked over and returned the lantern to Nathan.

"Here." Nathan traced a line on the wall with his index finger. "The pattern of bumps looks suspicious. Some of them are half-formed."

"The bumps have a pattern?" Stearns asked incredulously.

Nathan nodded. "Roughly speaking."

John put his nose to the wall and squinted. The bumps did look slightly misshapen, as though they'd been melted and reformed.

"You think the door is here?" he asked.

"Yes, I do."

John crossed his arms, grinding his molars as he thought. Was their eagerness to find the core making them see things that weren't there? Then again, they were dealing with a Pentagon-sponsored project — the same Pentagon that had designed SPEAR, a dead ringer for John's original limb.

John unfolded his arms and squeezed his left shoulder. "Step back, you two. This could get ugly."

Stearns arched one of his bushy gray eyebrows. "Ugly?"

"I think I know what John has in mind," Nathan said. He put a hand on John's shoulder. "Are you sure you want to do this? We don't know how much charge your arm has left."

"Sure as I've ever been," John replied with a grim smile. He was overstating his level of confidence, but he'd made up his mind. Lingering doubts could do no good.

"Hold these for me," he said, handing his crutches to Nathan. "Get back a few yards and be ready to cover your eyes."

"Come on, Stearns." Nathan waved the old colonel away from the wall. "Let's give John space to do his thing."

Though Stearns didn't seem to completely understand what was about to ensue, he dutifully retreated to stand by Nathan.

Back straight and head high, John stepped up to the concrete wall. He regarded the inanimate slab as a boxer would regard a rival in the ring.

He slid one foot back, assuming a power stance, and focused on a single concrete bump. The world around him fell away. Only he and the wall remained.

With a primal scream he threw his fist forward.

His knuckles pulverized the concrete. Cracks rippled outward from the crater beneath his fist. The wall rumbled and groaned like an expanse of blacktop above a quaking fault line.

Piece by piece the wall crumbled to the ground. The freshly dislodged chunks threw up chalky white dust as they hit the floor.

John's heart raced. Bile threatened to gush up his throat. His knees quivered and shook. It took all his will not to collapse in a heap.

The dust gradually settled, revealing a rectangular steel panel. Though it lacked a handle, it was obviously a door. It bore a knuckle-shaped imprint near its center.

"Now, I could be mistaken, but I think this here is what, back in my day, we would've called a door," Stearns said. He gingerly tiptoed forward over the concrete shards.

"But how do we open it?" John asked. He gagged, forcing his breakfast to stay in his stomach.

"Maybe a skeleton key?"

John gave Stearns a stone-faced stare. "I hope you brought one. I forgot mine at home."

"Well, when you put it that way ..." Stearns trailed of, scratching the back of his head.

Nathan stepped before the steel door and held up his lantern.

"What do you think?" John asked.

"Do you see the hinges on the left side?" Nathan asked.

John shook his head. "Can't say that I do."

"They're in bad shape," Nathan said, peering at the door as though it were a science project. "Maybe ..."

"Maybe?" asked John.

"Maybe ..." Nathan laid his palm flat against the door, just beside where John's fist had left a crater. He pushed.

The door groaned like a drunken banshee. John winced as the steel panel wobbled and fell with a deafening clang.

The doorway opened into a corridor lined with orange bricks. The newly-revealed passage was shorter and narrower than the Gopher Way, and every bit as dark.

Nathan removed his fingers from his ears. "If you'd punched a tad bit harder, you would've knocked it off its hinges yourself."

"I wanted to save some fun for you," John said dryly.

"What about me?" Stearns asked.

"There's an age limit on fun." John patted Stearns on the shoulder. "Now let's head in."

Chapter 42

October 8th, 2027
Post Status: Public

That flu I mentioned previously … it's more serious than I imagined.

Maybe the media is sensationalizing the story? If reports are to be believed, people on the east coast are dying at an alarming rate. The flu isn't just affecting the old and the feeble. Anyone who contracts the virus becomes violently ill. The mortality rate is unclear.

The virus is no longer limited to just the eastern seaboard. Cases have been reported in other cities, including Portland and Orlando. If the spread continues I suspect Minneapolis will be shut down again soon.

This is precisely, absolutely, exactly, just what we need right now.

(That was sarcasm, by the way. In case you couldn't tell.)

* * *

ARISTOTLE LAZED ON the living room sofa, stretching her arms and legs across its plush expanse. She stared listlessly at a patch of mold on the ceiling.

She'd found the General's base. But what kind of response could she muster?

Radioing Captain Griswold in Toronto was an option. Though Aristotle hadn't found the General himself, she'd seen and heard enough to know that the General was here, and that he posed a threat to regional stability. Griswold would want to know.

On the other hand, Aristotle didn't see what preventative measures Griswold could take. Griswold's resources were already stretched thin. He would wait until the General was standing on the shores of Lake Ontario. By then it would be too late.

Aristotle pounded the back of her head against the couch's cushioned armrest, shaking her brain like a magic eight ball. What could she do, here and now? The answer remained the same: Try again. Try again. Try again.

"Are you okay?" Emiko asked from her chair across the room.

Aristotle closed her eyes and let out an exasperated sigh.

"I'm fine."

"It looked like you were having a seizure. My neighbor's son used to have them sometimes. They always went away —"

"Emiko, I'm fine."

Emiko fell silent. Aristotle rolled onto her side and opened her eyes to find the girl sitting peacefully, paging through her father's journal, *World's End*.

"Weren't you planning to share that with me?" Aristotle asked. Though she did hope to help Emiko interpret the journal's more difficult passages, her interest wasn't purely altruistic. The journal would tell her more about Emiko's father, which would in turn help her better understand Emiko. And with a title like *World's End*, the journal probably contained eye-opening anecdotes about the Desolation, as well.

"Yeah. Soon," Emiko said, her concentration remaining on the page.

Aristotle, in no mood to prod further, left it at that. Emiko would share when she was ready.

What else was there to do?

The previous night's journey up Target Tower had given Aristotle an idea. The source of the tower's electricity was unclear. Could it have come from the Northland Core? Though Aristotle couldn't say, she did know a certain bearded individual who would want to investigate further.

It was time to pay Osborne and Nathan a visit. Aristotle could tell them about the tower. And maybe the laconic John Osborne could offer sage advice about how to deal with the General.

"There's a place I want to go. Would you like to come along?" Aristotle asked.

"Sure," Emiko said, glancing up from the journal. "Where?"

"Another house. I don't think it's far from here." Aristotle swung her legs off the couch, hopped to her feet, and stretched her arms toward the ceiling. "Why don't you bring the journal? We might have some time to kill after we arrive."

* * *

Where was Aristotle taking her?

The answer became clearer with each street corner Emiko passed. A reunion with her brother and Beard was imminent. The question from days earlier arose again: Meet her brother now or save the confrontation for another day?

The situation had changed slightly. With Aristotle's help, Emiko had confirmed that the General was in Minneapolis. That accomplishment was surely worthy of Nathan's praise. But would it be enough to soften the sharp edges of her brother's wrath?

Though she hated to admit it, Emiko knew there would be no perfect time to reveal herself to Nathan and Beard. Was this the best she could do? Maybe Aristotle could provide some inspiration. Emiko tucked her father's journal into her armpit and asked away.

"How far away are we?"

"Just a few more blocks now."

"Are we going to a house?"

"Yeah, a friend's house."

"What for?" Emiko asked, perhaps a tad too quickly.

Aristotle cocked her head. "Feeling a bit hyper-kinetic today?"

Emiko shrugged. She didn't know what "hyper-kinetic" meant.

"I was thinking about Target Tower," Aristotle said. "The lights obviously require an energy source. A friend of mine might be interested in hearing about it." Aristotle hesitated a moment, as though unsure how much to share. "My friend is looking for something called the Northland Core. It could be in Target Tower."

Emiko listened intently and replied with a slow, wide-eyed nod, pretending that the explanation had gone over her head. She'd known that Beard was looking for something. She hadn't known it was called the Northland Core.

"So, we're gonna go to this house and tell your friend about Target Tower?" Emiko asked.

"Exactly," Aristotle said.

Emiko mulled this over. Beard and Nathan would be excited to hear about Target Tower. Maybe, just maybe, that would be enough to distract Nathan and stave off a scolding. A better opportunity was unlikely to appear.

Butterflies fluttered in Emiko's stomach as they continued toward the house. This reunion would be awkward even if all went well. Beard and Nathan would find out that Emiko wasn't in Frontier View. Aristotle would realize that Emiko had been withholding important personal details.

They reached Emiko's old city block. Emiko had skipped up and down this stretch of sidewalk hundreds of times. She'd drawn rabbits, cats, dogs, and other animals on it in colorful chalk. She'd even helped her father shovel it in winter. Recalling those cold snowy days now, she realized that burrowing tunnels through snow drifts probably hadn't been particularly helpful.

Soon they were at the walk that led to Emiko's front door. The oak tree in the front yard towered over Emiko just as it always had. Just beyond the tree was the familiar two-story house with light blue siding and inviting windows.

1013 39th Avenue. The place where Emiko had spent her first years. A place that held memories, joyful and terrible.

Aristotle studied the neighboring houses before looking back to Emiko's. "One of the digits is missing, but I'm pretty sure this is 1013. Let's see if anyone is home." She headed up the weed-ridden walkway.

Emiko froze. Her heart thumped. A frigid chill ran up her arms and spine. The moment of reckoning was only steps away.

Halfway to the house, Aristotle glanced back over her shoulder. "You coming?"

"Yeah, yeah, I'm coming," Emiko said. Taking that first step felt like pulling her foot free from a block of concrete, but the steps got easier and soon she caught up with Aristotle.

Aristotle was right. The "3" from 1013 had vanished — a detail Emiko hadn't noticed on her previous visit, nearly a month ago.

"I suppose we'd better knock." Aristotle rapped her knuckles on the door.

No one stirred inside. A Baltimore oriole sang from the top branches of the oak, perhaps trying to inform them that no one was home.

"I think we can just let ourselves in," Aristotle said. "Etiquette between friends is more casual than it used to be."

"If you say so," Emiko said. She hoped Beard wouldn't shoot the intruders on his couch before he recognized them.

Aristotle knocked again. When no one replied she invited herself inside. The unlocked door opened without a creak.

The entryway looked like it hadn't been cleaned in nine years. Apparently Nathan and Beard didn't care about keeping their home tidy. Had Nathan turned into a slob during his time away from Frontier View?

"Looks like no one will mind if we keep our boots on." Aristotle cautiously advanced through the entryway. To her this was unknown territory.

Emiko could've offered a guided tour of the home's best-kept secrets, but she bit her tongue. She wasn't ready to reveal that this was her house.

Aristotle turned into the living room. "I think we can sit here and wait," she called.

"Whatever you think is best," Emiko said. She slunk into the living room after Aristotle, like an intruder breaking into her own home.

Aristotle took a seat on the couch, facing the television screen that had once provided cartoons for Emiko's enjoyment. Emiko plopped herself into one of the chairs nearby.

Where had Beard and Nathan gone, and when would they return? There was no way to say.

Perhaps it was time to make her secret known. Revealing the truth first to Aristotle, then to Nathan, would be best.

How could Emiko bring up the topic? She couldn't just say, "Hey, you know that Nathan guy? He's my older brother!" There had to be a subtler way.

Emiko squirmed nervously in her chair. It took all her willpower not to wring her father's journal like a wet towel.

That was it — the journal! Emiko would put the information in Aristotle's hands. Aristotle was smart. She would figure it out.

Trying to act casually, Emiko slipped out of her chair and cleared her throat.

"You can look at this now," she said, presenting the journal to Aristotle.

"You're sure?"

Emiko nodded. "I'm sure. Just let me find a good page for you to start with." She flipped through the pages until she found an entry that would make everything clear. "Here," she said, placing the notebook in Aristotle's hands.

"Thanks for letting me have a look."

"Um, yeah. You're welcome," Emiko mumbled before scurrying back to her chair. She fidgeted, rocking back and forth as she watched Aristotle absorb her father's words.

Aristotle's expression remained impassive. Emiko's chest tightened. *How long can she study the journal and not figure it out?*

Aristotle pulled the journal closer. A deep crease formed along her brow. A moment later her lips curled into a gaping, silent, "Oooooh."

She slowly looked up from the page and stared blankly at Emiko.

"Nathan," she said, as though the word was the final number of a combination lock clicking into place.

"Nathan," Emiko repeated. "My older brother."

"But why are you ... why doesn't he ... how did you come to ..." Even if she'd had three mouths, Aristotle would've agonized over which question to ask first.

Emiko grinned sheepishly. She had a lot of explaining to do. Where to begin?

Chapter 43

October 10th, 2027
Post Status: Public

Bioterrorism?

You mean to tell me that just as the situation looked like it was improving, some idiot decided to unleash an untested, incurable virus unto the world?

Why would anybody do such a thing? What kind of madman would *invent* such a thing?

The media has dubbed it the "killer flu." It's laying waste to people all over the country. Cases have also been reported in Perth, London, and Jakarta.

This flu is spreading fast. My family is not leaving the house until it passes.

Someone please pinch me. Tell me I'm dreaming.

* * *

NATHAN LED THE WAY through the unlit tunnel. The narrow corridor brought to mind a bomb shelter in London circa World War II.

"How do you think the military guys removed and replaced that concrete wall?" Nathan asked John.

John coughed loudly. "Hard to say. They might have used a laser to make a razor-thin incision. A similar laser could've fused the concrete back together when they left. That would explain the subtle outline in the wall."

"That sounds about right," added Stearns. "The Pentagon had technology like that."

"I had no idea," said Nathan. To him, the pinnacle of technology had been the Samsung Æther in his living room. He imagined most of the Pentagon's cutting-edge tech was now collecting rust in locations unknown.

The tunnel was surprisingly short. One by one, Nathan, John, and Stearns emerged into a room the size of a basketball court.

The room was divided into two levels. The tunnel exited onto the lower of the two. Straight ahead was a raised metal platform, about waist height. The rectangular platform ran the length of the room, abutting the side and rear walls. Stairs led up it from either end.

Six wooden crates sat on the platform. They'd been meticulously placed so that the distance between any two adjacent crates was equal.

"Six crates!" Nathan exclaimed. "Does this mean there are *six* Northland Cores?"

"Let's find out," John replied.

Six Northland Cores. Nathan had assumed there was only one. What would John do with the extras?

"Looks like we've got company," Stearns announced.

"The crates?" Nathan asked.

"No. Take a look over here."

Stearns pointed to a decomposing body slumped against the wall. Tattered remains of a shirt and pants clung to the bones. The skull had fallen from the neck like an acorn from a tree and lay sideways on the floor. The arms and hands had also detached. Two jumbled piles of finger bones had formed beside the legs.

"What do you think he was doing here?" Nathan asked.

"Standing guard, probably," John surmised.

"Do you think he died of the Desolation virus?"

"It's possible. But his corpse won't tell us much. Let's go take a look at the important stuff." John coughed. Phlegm from his throat splattered on the cement floor.

"You holding up alright?" Nathan asked.

"I'm fine. But I'll be even better soon."

Let's hope so, Nathan thought.

The three men mounted the platform's left-hand stairs. Their feet clanged on the metal surface. The crates, each about two feet wide, three feet long, and three feet tall, drew near.

Nathan had expected to find the Northland Core stored in a high-tech, heavily fortified vault. Even a treasure chest would've been an improvement over these nailed-together collections of pallet boards. Yet this was definitely the right place: the crates all bore the words NORTHLAND CORE, stamped on their sides in bold, black letters.

They approached the nearest crate. A wooden cover, nailed in place, protected its contents.

"Well, what are we waiting for?" Stearns asked. "Let's rip her open."

"Do we have any tools?" Nathan asked.

"Tools?" John scoffed. He knelt before the crate and set his crutches to one side.

Nathan raised an eyebrow. "Are you sure you should exert yourself more than you already have?"

"We're this close," John said as he fingered the crate's lid for a place to grip. "There's no reason to hold back now."

Dissatisfied with this response, Nathan scanned the platform for tools. He noticed that one of the middle crates was already open, its lid lying on the floor. He started towards it.

"Where are you going with that lantern, son?" Stearns asked accusingly.

Nathan shuddered in surprise and spun around. "I was going to look at another crate."

"Can't it wait? We have a perfectly good crate right here. Says 'Northland Core' and everything. John is gonna pry it open now." Stearns nodded at John.

John grunted. He was still searching for a handhold. Nathan suspected John would punch through the lid if he didn't find one soon.

Nathan shrugged. "Well, now that you mention it ..."

Stearns' eyes darted about the room. He smacked his lips thoughtfully.

"You know, on second thought, why don't you go ahead? There's no reason not to spread out. Just don't wander too far, you hear? We gotta share the light."

"Uh, okay," Nathan stuttered. "I'll be on my way then." He shook his head, exasperated.

He stepped up to the open crate and peered down into it. Save for a layer of faded indigo padding it was empty.

Nathan dropped to his knees, set down the lantern, and clawed around the crate's interior, checking every crease in the fabric. Finding nothing, he proceeded to rip out the cloth lining. Underneath he discovered only pallet boards. Empty!

No. There were still five sealed crates. At least one of them had to contain a Northland Core.

Nathan collected the lantern. Rising to his feet, he looked over to check on John. His brain struggled to process what he saw:

John, kneeling on the floor, his hands above his head; Stearns, standing behind, his pistol jabbed into John's skull.

Nathan blinked. This was no dream.

"I think we're in trouble," John said.

Nathan couldn't find the words to disagree.

Chapter 44

October 12th, 2027
Post Status: Public

It's everywhere now. Asia. Europe. Africa.

It spreads through the atmosphere, highly contagious, infecting anyone and everyone. It hangs in the air, invisible, waiting to claim its victims.

There is no cure. Vomiting. Loss of appetite. Dehydration. Death. Worse than the black plague.

This can't be real. This is only a dream.

Who invented this? How could someone set it loose? Somewhere, a sadistic lunatic took a vial labeled "magic airborne viral death powder" and dropped it in a subway car. He set this madness in motion and then — poof — he disappeared!

If you brought the world to its knees, wouldn't you want to claim credit for it?

We've survived drought. We've survived war — nuclear war. We've been through hell. And now the inexplicable action of one unknown man has reversed all the progress we've made towards peace.

This can't be real. This is only a dream.

News reporters are dropping like flies. Live TV broadcasts will soon cease completely. There's plenty to report, but there will be no one left to report it.

It's coming to Minneapolis. It's in Minneapolis.

The virus is everywhere. If I open my door for even a minute it will find its way inside. Even with all the doors and windows shut, I still fear it will breach the walls of my home.

If we stay inside, we die of starvation. If we go outside, we catch the virus. I don't know what to do. Maybe if we hide long enough it will pass.

What can we do?

Wait. We can wait.

This can't be real. This is only a dream.

Yes. Yes. It's a dream.

A goddamn nightmare.

* * *

JOHN HAD DODGED volleys of bullets. He had nearly been blown into camel feed by land mines. He'd even had his arm torn from his body. Yet in all his years as a marine, never once had he felt the cold muzzle of a gun on the back of his skull.

Betrayal was new to John. He didn't like the taste.

His body weakening, he coughed up mucus. It spattered onto the Northland Core.

The core was a black wafer the size of thin billfold. Its humble appearance belied its supposed power. If only John could've grabbed it ...

"Reach for that shotgun and I put a bullet in Osborne's brain," Stearns warned Nathan. The folksy twang had left his voice, giving way to the hard-edged intensity that John remembered.

Stearns 2.0, the Good Samaritan drifter who gunned down bad guys like it was his Sunday afternoon hobby, had been an act. It didn't take a performing arts degree to deduce what he was after.

Nathan's lamplight flickered in the corner of John's eye. John trusted that Nathan, cautious by nature, wouldn't give Stearns cause to follow through on his threat — a threat enforced by the kiss of a muzzle.

"What now?" John asked.

"Now we wait. Keep calm. You could get out of this alive," Stearns replied.

Get out of this alive? Even if John left this room alive, he wouldn't make it far without a Northland Core. Evidently there were six.

Beads of sweat trickled from John's brow and rolled down his cheeks. Questions raged: *Why do you want the Northland Core? Who are you, really? What have you been doing since the Desolation? How could you do this to me?* Though the questions burned like red-hot coals on his tongue, he refused to give Stearns the pleasure of answering.

Nathan, however, had no such compunctions.

"Why are you doing this?" he asked.

"Haven't you already figured it out, Nathan?"

"You're one of the General's men, aren't you?"

Stearns chuckled haughtily. "Is that the best you can do?"

A tense silence festered in the room. John's shrapnel wound throbbed.

"You are the General," Nathan said, his voice self-assured.

"So I am. My reputation precedes me."

That was all John needed to hear. He could deduce the rest by following the trail of blood.

Stearns was forming an army. Stearns had killed two of his own men to buy John's trust. Stearns had conversed with Ramses in Vikings Stadium just yesterday. Stearns had ...

"What did you do with my sister?" Nathan growled.

"Your sister?" Stearns asked.

"Ramses Brushnell kidnapped her from my hometown. And those two thugs from the Dinkytown bar brought her down here from Duluth."

"So that was your sister at Sawbill Lake? That explains how you came to be John's sidekick."

"Where is she?" Nathan demanded.

"I don't know, Nathan."

"How can you not know? She came here with your men!"

"Smith and Redding never mentioned her."

John throat tightened. Was Stearns speaking truthfully or adding to the mountain of lies? Though he sounded sincere, recent events provided reason to doubt.

"You really know nothing about my sister?" Nathan asked.

"Not a thing."

"She could've been beaten. Raped. Killed!"

"You're jumping to conclusions, Nathan."

"How can you hurt people you don't even know?" Nathan shook the lantern in his hand.

"Believe it or not, Nathan, death and pain are the building blocks of peace and prosperity."

"I already know peace and prosperity!"

"Peace, perhaps. But prosperity, definitely not. This country ceased to be prosperous long before you were born. Play nice today and I might show you the way forward."

"You wouldn't know the way forward if it hammered you in the face."

"Are you so sure?"

"I am," Nathan said. He extended his free hand towards the lantern's base. "Because no one can find the way forward in the dark."

Nathan turned a knob, retracting the lamp's wick and plunging the room into utter blackness.

Chapter 45

October 15th, 2027
Post Status: Public

I went out for food.

We had nothing to eat. I saw no other choice. I stepped outside.

Everything was quiet and peaceful.

Then I noticed the dead man slumped against the side of our neighbor's house. Death hangs in the air, invisible.

I think most people must be hiding inside, as my family is, because I only saw a few other souls as I drove to the grocery store.

A car had smashed into a fire hydrant not far from our house. A woman was running frantically through the streets for god knows what reason. A white-haired man was puking his guts out into a storm drain.

He's probably already dead.

I entered the grocery store and grabbed some non-perishables. Judging from the half-empty shelves, many others had done the same.

Only a handful of people were in the store, hurrying through the aisles. None of us made eye contact. I took my food and left without paying. There were no cashiers to pay.

Now I'm back home. We have food. But we may also have death.

Most centralized media has gone offline. I get all of my news from internet forums now. There are a few individuals who claim they've gone outside without contracting the virus.

Perhaps they're telling the truth. Perhaps they're mistaken or lying.

My instincts tell me it's the latter. Internet dwellers are always full of shit.

Nathan and Emiko are watching Japanese anime on TV. I probably infected them, Danielle, and even our unborn baby girl, but what other choice did I have?

We're all going to die, vomiting to death in the living room.

This is the end. We wait. I'll keep blogging until the end.

* * *

THE DARKNESS WAS ABSOLUTE. Nathan felt like a bottom-feeder braving Lake Superior's depths. He knew Stearns wouldn't dare try to shoot him. Stearns wouldn't give John an opportunity to act.

Stearns' disembodied voice pierced the darkness. "And what was that supposed to accomplish, Nathan?"

Nathan was improvising. Stearns' sudden shift from ally to enemy had shocked him. It had clearly surprised John, too. As recent events flashed through Nathan's mind, he saw the antecedents of betrayal. Stearns had set them up in that bar. He'd remorselessly used his underlings as cannon fodder.

Taking great care to remain steady-handed and silent, Nathan reached over his shoulder for his shotgun. His next step was unclear. Even if the room were lit, the spread pattern of his Remington 870 wouldn't afford him a clean shot at Stearns. Vengeance for his sister would have to wait.

"Where are you hiding, Nathan?" Stearns asked.

Nathan wasn't hiding. His feet hadn't moved since the light went out. Was there need to hide?

Perhaps there was.

* * *

Stearns' pistol remained firmly entrenched in John's hair. Neither John nor the pistol possessed the will to act first.

"Think, Nathan," Stearns called out. "You aren't making things better for yourself or John by slinking around in the dark. Why don't we talk this out like men?"

Nathan remained silent, not rising to Stearns' bait.

They were at a stalemate. Stearns wouldn't dare move his pistol and give John a chance to act. Nathan wouldn't shoot at Stearns for fear of accidentally hitting John. And Stearns wouldn't shoot John, his sole defense against a salvo of buckshot from Nathan.

"Lose your tongue, John?" Stearns whispered from behind.

"I have nothing to say," John growled.

"You could still join me. The Restoration Army needs officers. I would even grant you a Northland Core in exchange for your services."

"It's too late for that," John sputtered, coughing.

"Is it?"

"Why didn't you make the offer sooner? Before Sawbill Lake. Before Mallard Island."

"Because I knew you would never accept."

John grunted his agreement. The world was free now. There was no need for armies, just as there was no need for dictators.

The silent seconds stretched into minutes. John's thoughts drifted. What was Nathan doing? John hoped the kid would sneak up behind Stearns and wallop him in the head, but that was probably hoping for too much. Or perhaps Mumford would heroically plod in to save the day.

A luminous haze appeared in the tunnel from which they'd entered. The source of light became more distinct and then divided. Four figures strode into the room, each holding a lantern. Three of the men wore the familiar green vests of the General's army — Stearns' army. The other was dressed in neatly pressed military fatigues and sported a blue beret.

The beret-wearing man carried a pistol. He looked like a career soldier, the kind John had once imagined himself becoming, though John would've forgone the tacky headgear.

Two of the green-vested men set their lanterns on the ground and shouldered long-barreled firearms. The third man in green held a pistol and a lantern. As John's eyes adjusted to the light, he recognized this last man as none other than Ramses Brushnell.

Ramses grinned smugly. Had Stearns told Ramses of the Gopher Way when they'd met in Vikings Stadium?

No, John thought. The timeline didn't fit. They'd encountered Ramses yesterday. Nathan hadn't discovered Ryota's blog until this morning.

Speaking of Nathan, he was still nowhere to be seen.

"Lieutenant Prince. It's good to see you," Stearns called down from the raised platform.

"It's a pleasure to see you as well, sir," Lieutenant Prince responded.

"The Northland Core is ours. There are six of them, in fact." Stearns prodded John's skull with the pistol. "Let's handcuff Osborne and transport the cores back to HQ."

Handcuff was an upgrade over *shoot in the head*. Not that John trusted a word that came out of Stearns' mouth.

"I'm afraid that's not how this showdown will transpire, General Stearns," Lieutenant Prince said. "You see, the Restoration Army has changed during your absence. Faith in your leadership has withered. Many in the army wouldn't be disappointed if you never returned at all. I see no reason why your abdication shouldn't be made permanent."

Lieutenant Prince snapped his fingers. His three lackeys raised their guns at Stearns.

"No one will miss you, Stearns," the lieutenant continued. "The army will be stronger without your delusions of grandeur. Minnesota, and by extension the entire world, will be a better and more peaceful place for having avoided your vainglorious conquest."

"I find that hard to believe, Prince," Stearns said. "I've assembled an army. That army is eager for a fight."

"Do not think me a fool, Stearns! The Restoration Army will remain intact, and it will apply violence as necessary. But to plunge the entire continent into war, as you intend, would be to go too far. Surely, a strong vision and proper stewardship are what will bring this world back from the brink — not further destruction by your hand."

John rolled his eyes. Prince clearly overestimated the worth of his ten-cent monologues.

"You can't rule the world by speeches alone, Prince," Stearns said. "Or should I call you the Prince of Minneapolis?"

Prince glared at Stearns. "Where did you hear that moniker?"

"Did you think you were my only contact within my own army?"

"And what if you had other contacts, Stearns? They'll do you no good in death." Prince stretched his pistol as far forward as his arm allowed.

Prince's eyes unexpectedly fell to John. "You must be John Osborne. I've heard much about you. After this situation is resolved, would you consider lending your talents to the Restoration Army?"

"We can talk when there isn't a pistol to my neck," John said.

"Of course. Now is no time for me to make such requests of you." Prince's eyes returned to Stearns. "So, General Stearns, I believe this is the end. Do you have any last words?"

Stearns responded calmly. "Do you know what your biggest problem is, Prince?"

"I'm afraid I don't. Would you care to enlighten me?"

"You overestimate your powers of persuasion. My men aren't turned so easily."

"What do you ..."

The question went unfinished as Ramses Brushnell thrust his pistol into the lieutenant's spine.

Chapter 46

October 17th, 2027
Post Status: Public

Danielle has developed the fever. The rest of us will follow soon.

I really shouldn't be here writing this now.

Danielle is vomiting. The infected don't last long once the vomiting starts.

I wanted to be with her. And I was with her. But then I left the bathroom for a moment and she locked herself inside.

I don't know what to do.

The kids and I are fine. We should be dying. But we're fine.

I told Danielle we'd all die together. TOGETHER!

THIS IS NOT TOGETHER!

I'm going to go break down the goddamn bathroom door.

* * *

SOME CHOICES WERE not choices at all.

Ramses' allegiance to the General was an oath etched in steel. The pontificating sack of traitorous pretense known as Lieutenant Prince had never stood a chance.

"That's you behind me, isn't it Private Brushnell?" Prince asked, his voice quavering slightly.

"A most astute deduction, Lieutenant Prince. Did you really believe I could be so easily won over?"

"I thought you might recognize the truth, Ramses."

"Truth?" Ramses snickered as he prodded Prince's spine with his pistol. "You are the last person I'd expect to hear the truth from."

The scenario was playing out as Ramses had anticipated. Prince and his two cowardly goons still had their guns trained on the General, who in turn had his sights on John. The only unexpected twist was the absence of John's insufferable lapdog, Nathan Kanno. Ramses awaited the signal to act.

"What if I told you that your precious General would've sacrificed you like a lamb to get in Osborne's good graces?" Prince offered.

"Hogwash," Ramses declared. "Your desperate lies can't win me over now."

"Where have Smith and Redding disappeared to, Private Brushnell? They were the only other men who'd encountered Osborne. If they had failed their mission — a suicide mission — *you* would've been sent next," Prince said, his voice growing more impassioned.

"Poppycock. If those two buffoons indeed met their ends, it was surely the consequence of their own idiocy."

"The General does not have your best interests in mind, Ramses," Prince pleaded. "Trust your instincts!"

Ramses chortled. "Trust my instincts, Lieutenant? I'm doing exactly that."

"Enough," the General said. "It's time."

That was Ramses' cue.

He squeezed the trigger. A bullet sliced into Prince's back. Prince screamed as he fell to the floor like a gelatinous mass.

Ramses swung his pistol towards one of the lieutenant's goons. The goon spun away from the General and leveled his rifle at Ramses.

Ramses was faster. A bottle-cap-sized hole appeared in the goon's forehead.

A third gunshot rang out. Turning on his heels, Ramses saw the last of the villainous traitors hit the floor.

"Ramses ... you ... fool ..." Lieutenant Prince gasped.

A final shot from the General silenced him forever.

Two kills for the General. One for Ramses.

"Losing your edge, Osborne?" the General asked.

Up on the raised platform the General still towered over John Osborne. Osborne clutched his revolver but hadn't managed to withdraw it from its holster.

"You didn't give me much of an opening," Osborne replied, his words giving way to a bout of coughing.

"I know you all too well, Osborne," the General said. His attention turned to Ramses. "You've done well, Sergeant Brushnell."

"Sergeant, sir?" Ramses replied.

"That's right. You've shown yourself worthy of promotion."

"Thank you, sir. I'll never forget that you had my back today."

"As you had mine," Stearns said. "Did Prince carry out all of the orders I gave him over the radio?"

"I believe so, sir. He sent a ..."

"I remember what I asked for, Sergeant. It's enough to know that it's been done."

"Very well, sir. So, what do we do next? How will we deal with Osborne?"

"I'm afraid you're getting ahead of yourself, Sergeant Brushnell," the General replied, clearing his throat. "We have one more complication to deal with."

"Sir?" Ramses asked, seeking clarification.

"Look, Sergeant." The General tilted his head to one side. Following the gesture, Ramses glimpsed none other than Nathan Kanno.

Nathan was kneeling in one of the crates. The sights of his jet-black Remington shotgun were dead-set on Ramses' head.

Chapter 47

October 18th, 2027
Post Status: Public

i smashed a hole through the door reached in and unlocked it. blood red vomit stains on the floor. danielle hunched over the toilet in the grips of death. our baby inside her.

i went to her side. she looked at me. her eyes were empty. her head went limp.

my wife. gone. my world. gone.

hope is dead.

why continue.

* * *

"So THAT'S WHERE you disappeared to," Stearns said. "You've done well, Nathan, but the odds are still against you. You shoot Sergeant Brushnell, I shoot John, I shoot you."

Stearns spoke the truth. Even if Nathan managed to shoot Ramses and Stearns in quick succession, he would still lose John.

Bullets weren't the answer. Nathan had to find another way.

"My proposal? John gets one of the Northland Cores, you take the other five, and we all walk out of here alive," he said. "Final offer."

Stearns grinned smugly. "I take all of the Northland Cores. I let you and Osborne walk. Final offer."

"Sounds like we have a disagreement to resolve," Nathan replied.

"Indeed. As I've already told our friend Osborne here, I'm willing to give him a core in exchange for his services."

"Somehow I don't think John will agree to that. Right, John?"

"Yeah," John grunted. His grunt snowballed into a coughing fit. He was in rough shape. No wonder he'd been slow to draw his revolver.

Nathan had a hunch about the missing core's location. His plan would require a pinch of time and a cupful of luck. He hoped Stearns hadn't noticed that the open crate was empty.

"And what's stopping me from shooting Ramses, shooting you, and walking out of here?" Nathan asked, keeping his barrel leveled at Ramses.

"I know you, Nathan. You wouldn't do that to your dear friend John," Stearns said.

"Are you willing to stake Ramses' life on it?"

"If that's the price I have to pay, then yes. Even Sergeant Brushnell would admit that his death for the death of John Osborne would be a fair trade."

Ramses, the lone living soul on the ground floor, grimaced. He nodded unconvincingly.

Nathan pretended to consider his options. He had to convince Stearns that this decision weighed heavily on his conscience. He hoped John would play along.

"Alright," Nathan replied after a long pause. "You take the cores. John and I walk out that door."

"Are you sure we should leave here without the core?" John cut in.

"I'm as sure as Mumford is slow," Nathan said. Looking Stearns in the eye, he repeated his offer. "You take the cores. John and I walk out of here. And we get a lantern."

"And a lantern?" Stearns chuckled. "You drive a hard bargain. It's a deal." Stearns retracted the pistol from John's head. "Stand up, Osborne. Don't reach for your weapon."

Like a mountain slowly coming into view on the horizon, John collected his crutches and struggled to his feet.

"Now hobble over to the stairs," Stearns ordered.

John obeyed without protest, coming to a halt at the edge of the platform's staircase. The barrel of Stearns' gun traced his path.

Nathan stepped out of the wooden crate. Keeping his gun trained on Ramses, he moved to John's side.

"Come on, John," he said. "Let's go."

"I hope you know what you're doing, Nathan."

"I do," Nathan said, though he wasn't entirely sure he did.

Nathan and John shuffled down the staircase. Nathan crouched to pick up a lantern left by Lieutenant Prince's men. Fresh blood dripped from the lantern's underside.

"My offer still stands, John" Stearns said. "If you'll work with me, I'll offer you one of the Northland Cores."

"No chance, Stearns. I'm already planning to find your base, annihilate your army, and take the cores back."

"Good luck to you then," Stearns said.

With a dismissive grunt John headed for the exit. Nathan followed a step behind.

* * *

Ramses eyes didn't stray from the tunnel until the last rays of Nathan's lamplight disappeared. He looked to the General, who had trotted down from the platform and was kneeling beside the traitorous remains of Lieutenant Prince.

"May I ask a question, sir?"

"Go ahead, Sergeant."

"Would you really let Osborne join the Restoration Army, sir?"

The General stroked his bearded chin. Ramses still hadn't grown used to the unsightly collection of facial hair, having only seen it twice.

"Long ago, perhaps. The John Osborne of old would have been a superb addition to the Restoration Army. But he no longer shares our view of the future."

"I see. But then why make the offer, sir?"

"For the same reason Nathan offered me six cores when there are clearly only five in this room — gamesmanship."

"One of the crates is empty, sir?"

The General nodded. "Nathan thinks he and John can unearth the final core." He slid his Desert Eagle into its holster and fixed Ramses with a hard stare. "You're certain Prince carried out all of my orders?"

"Yes, sir. Four of our best men were dispatched to 1013 39th Avenue. They should be in position now."

"Then our Osborne problem should be resolved shortly. Come, Sergeant. Let's return to HQ. I'm long overdue for a haircut and a shave." The General strode towards the exit tunnel. His lantern swung gently on its handle.

Ramses' feet remained glued to the floor. "What of these bodies, sir?"

"Let them rot," the General said without glancing back. "They're getting the burial they deserve."

It was a fitting end, Ramses supposed, and a grisly reminder of the fate that awaited those who crossed the General. With an involuntary shudder, he left the cold-blooded scene and hurried down the tunnel.

"One more question, sir?" Ramses asked, trailing the General.

"Yes, Sergeant?"

Ramses fell silent. The rhythmic scuff of boots echoed in the tunnel. He wasn't certain his next question was appropriate.

"Sergeant?" the General said.

Ramses chose his words carefully. "Lieutenant Prince mentioned that you had considered ... sacrificing me."

"And what of it?"

"Is that true, sir?"

The General's pace did not waver. The pale yellow glow of his lamp bounced fitfully along the claustrophobic walls.

"I don't lie to my own, Sergeant. Not everyone in the Restoration Army shares my honesty."

"I see, sir."

Ramses contemplated this response. The conclusions he drew were less than reassuring.

Chapter 48

October 20th, 2027
Post Status: Public

Hello world.

This is Nathan.

My dad left the house yesterday. He hasn't come back yet, but he left his blog open. Really!

Is it okay if I write something?

I should feel bad for writing here, but I don't because I don't think anyone reads this anymore.

First, about my dad. He's been trying really hard to tell us that everything is OK. Maybe it helps my sister, but I know what's happening. Everyone is gone.

My dad is gone now too. I hope he comes back soon.

Sometimes I sit in my bedroom and cry. But I'm trying not to. I don't want to be a crybaby.

I don't know why we didn't get sick. I don't think my dad knows either.

My dad nailed a board over the hole in the bathroom door. He locked the door before he left the house. He didn't tell me when he would come back.

I know what's in there. I don't want to think about it, but if I try not to think about it, I only think about it more.

It's good we have a bathroom downstairs, too.

I'm going back to my bedroom now. I miss my mom.

If you see my dad, tell him to come home. I miss him, too.

P.S. The internet is very slow today. And the electricity is flashing on and off. I think the internet might die. I'm copying this blog to the hard drive.

* * *

ARISTOTLE SAT ALONE in the living room, paging through Ryota's journal, *World's End.* A gentle wind whistled across the front lawn. Chatty birds punctuated the natural serenity.

Emiko was visiting Mumford in the backyard. Until a few minutes ago Aristotle's understanding of the girl had been like a map with no streets. There'd been a house here, a school there, and a store on the other side of town, but nothing connecting them.

Her talk with Emiko had sketched in those streets. Aristotle now saw the paths connecting Emiko's history, hopes, fears, and motivations. It was no wonder Emiko had vanished when faced with the prospect of confronting John and Nathan. The awkwardness of the reunion would've been difficult to bear.

That wasn't to say Aristotle approved of everything Emiko had done. In running away from home, Emiko had shirked her responsibilities to her friends and family. John and Nathan were certain to upbraid her for that.

Aristotle wondered when the two men would arrive. Would they still be traveling with Kennedy Stearns? Aristotle couldn't put her finger on what it was about Stearns that bothered her. Maybe he'd been overly eager to make her acquaintance?

Outside, voices mingled with the bird songs and rustling prairie grass. Were John and Nathan back? Aristotle set Ryota's journal on the sofa cushions and went to peek out the window.

She recoiled at what she saw. Four men in green vests were advancing towards the door. They didn't look like guests of John and Nathan.

Aristotle darted to the front door. She quietly locked it and slid the deadbolt into place. She pressed her ear to the wood. The men outside spoke in deep, guttural voices.

"You sure this is the place?"

"This is the one."

"The house number says 101. Aren't we supposed to be at 1013?"

"Did you drink yourself blind again last night, Robby? Obviously the three is just missing."

"Hell, Robby, I can see the outline where it used to be."

"Alright, alright already. I see it now."

"Numbskull."

The doorknob rattled.

"It's locked."

"Locked?"

They tried the knob again.

"Sure is. What do we do?"

"Well, we can't break the door down. We might scare away our targets."

"A bearded guy and an Asian kid, right?"

"That's right, Robby. Hell, I'm surprised you remember."

"Screw you, Fordham."

"Come on. We'll try the back door. If that's locked we'll slip in through a window."

"Tread lightly, now. We can't leave any trace that we're here."

Imaginary hands tightened around Aristotle's throat. Emiko was still out back.

Aristotle flew through the house, her soles barely touching the floor. She silently nudged the back door open. Emiko was outside, scratching Mumford between his antlers.

"Emiko," Aristotle called softly, her voice three parts mouse's squeak and one part coyote's howl.

Emiko cocked her head and looked toward the door. Aristotle beckoned wildly for her to come inside.

"Quick! Hurry!" Aristotle mouthed.

Emiko didn't hesitate. Leaving Mumford, she hurried silently inside.

"The General's men are here," Aristotle whispered as she closed the door behind Emiko.

"What!" Emiko exclaimed, thankfully keeping her voice low.

Aristotle locked the door. "Four of them. They must be here for Nathan and John."

"What do we do?"

"You go upstairs. Take your rifle and lock yourself in a room. Shoot anyone who comes in and don't come out until I tell you it's safe."

"But what about you?"

"I'll make sure these men never have a chance to meet you."

"But I can help you!" Emiko insisted. "I know I can!"

"I know you can too. But there's a difference between can and should," Aristotle said. Emiko was minutes away from a reunion with her brother. If something happened to her now ...

"But —"

"There's no time. Go!"

With a frustrated groan, Emiko fled for the staircase.

Aristotle bit her lip. She could've used the extra firepower, but this was how it had to be. Emiko had barely escaped Pioneer Hall. Aristotle wouldn't thrust her into harm's way again.

Aristotle unholstered her pistol and checked its four chambers. They were loaded with three standard rounds and one shotshell. Her fingers discovered three more rounds in her pocket.

Four men. Seven bullets. She'd faced worse odds.

Aristotle pressed her back against the rear door and set the revolver to Snipe. She heard a murmur of approaching voices. Her adversaries expected to find the house empty. That expectation was an advantage Aristotle would squeeze until it bled.

The door handle shook.

"This door is locked, too."

"Should we try the windows, then?"

"Couldn't we just bash this door down? I mean, come on, the guys are gonna come in through the front. They aren't gonna come back here to check first."

"You're probably right, Jessie. But I don't want to take unnecessary risks. Let's check the windows first."

"Fair enough."

Aristotle gritted her teeth. One way or another these men would breach the house's walls. Keeping low, she crept away from the door and into the kitchen. She crouched beside the counter, just below a window.

In all the pages of pulp fiction Aristotle had read, the hero never struck first. Tradition dictated that the hero wait for the enemy's attack. Only then could the hero return fire.

Aristotle peered above the counter. One of the men was fumbling with the window, trying to pry it open.

What was a hero?

There were no more heroes.

Rising to her feet, Aristotle leveled her revolver at the man. He was a hulking brute with a hideous scar running across his forehead.

His eyes grew wide as Aristotle pulled the trigger. Gunpowder exploded. A bullet pierced the kitchen window and nailed the man in forehead. He slumped to the ground without so much as a grunt.

One down. Three to go.

Blood trickled down the window pane. A jagged web of cracks emanated from the bullet hole.

"What the hell?" a voice outside cried. "Man down! Jessie is down!"

"I thought there wasn't anyone here!"

"Shut up and keep low!"

Aristotle removed the spent round from her revolver and slid in a live one. There would be no more free shots. She scrambled out of the kitchen and returned to the rear door.

The Kanno house had a linear design. Only one path led from the rear door to the front. If the men entered through a window in one of the middle rooms, they would cut Aristotle off from Emiko. Aristotle couldn't let that happen.

Just as she broke towards the front of the house, the bathroom door swung open. Two men stood inside. A third was pulling himself through the open window.

"Peek-a-boo," said the man in the door frame. He had harsh black eyes and skin that looked soft as red clay after a torrential downpour.

He shouldered his rifle. Aristotle ducked and rolled just as the crack of gunfire rang out. She sprang to her feet and ran for the staircase near the front entryway.

"After her!"

Heavy boots pounded on the floor. The house rumbled as though a pack of wild horses was galloping through.

Aristotle flew up the stairs two at a time. At the top she screeched to a halt, spun, and dropped onto her belly. Clutching her revolver with both hands, she lay prone and watched the landing.

One of the men popped around the corner and scaled the first step. Aristotle's revolver snarled, delivering a bullet to his chest. The man stumbled backwards and splayed out across the landing, his arms spread as though nailed to a cross.

Aristotle fired again. The man's head bobbed. His eyes rolled back.

Two down. Two to go.

Aristotle let the spent rounds slide from the revolver's cylinder. They clattered down the staircase.

"Robby! Robby! That blood-sucking bitch!"

"Shut the hell up!"

Remaining out of sight, the two men spoke in faint whispers. Aristotle used the downtime to chamber the final two rounds in her pocket. Once again her revolver held three standard bullets and a shotshell.

One man, careful to expose only his arms, reached out and tugged his fallen comrade away from the landing. The body left two narrow streams of blood in its wake. A second later three men materialized at the base of the stairs.

One was already dead.

The two living soldiers hoisted the dead body between themselves, using it as a human shield. Aristotle cursed under her breath. She didn't have bullets to waste on low-percentage shots. She pulled back from the ledge and sprang to her feet.

This was her first time upstairs. Only one of the hallway's doors, a dark hardwood door with a board haphazardly nailed beside its knob, was shut. Aristotle hoped Emiko was safely locked behind it.

Aristotle bolted down the hallway and veered into the first open door. Inside were a desk and a computer, the makings of a home office. She left the door ajar and pressed her back to the wall beside it.

A thump reverberated from the hallway. The two men had dumped their human shield. Aristotle's pulse drummed in her ears like a mallet beating a leathery hide.

Something rattled. Aristotle cocked an ear. It was the locked doorknob.

Emiko's hiding place.

Pivoting on one foot, Aristotle twirled through the door frame. She pointed her pistol down the hallway. The man twisting the doorknob was exactly where she'd expected.

Her index finger yanked the trigger and a bullet screamed out, splitting the man's skull just above the ear. Dark splotches spattered onto the walls as the man flopped to the floor, lifeless.

Aristotle swung back into the office. Her hands trembled from adrenaline overdose. She had killed before, but never like this, one corpse after another.

Only one soldier remained. It was time to go on the offensive. Aristotle clicked her revolver to Spread and rotated her lone shotshell into firing position.

Before she could act, a hulking blur of black hair and ruddy flesh sprang into the office. The man bowled into her with enough force to knock a bull moose off its feet.

Aristotle crashed to the floor. Her revolver discharged as it slipped from her hand and clattered across the floorboards.

The man mounted her and clasped his hands around her throat. Aristotle thrashed wildly on the floor, beating his arms with her fists.

"You know, my dad used to toss me in a burlap sack and beat me with a Louisville Slugger," he said, opening his fierce black eyes wide. "Said I deserved it. Never said why."

He slammed Aristotle's skull against the floor and jammed his thumbs into her windpipe.

"When the old sack of shit was dying from the virus, he begged for mercy. For painkillers. For anything to end the suffering. So you know what I did? I took a huge-ass bowie knife and stabbed him in both lungs. I'll never forget the look on his face as he choked on his own blood."

Aristotle gagged and gasped. Fuzziness swept over her. If only she'd had a knife, a shard of glass, or even a rusty nail. She frantically slapped the floor, searching for a weapon.

"The old bastard deserved it. He'd gotten drunk as a skunk, freaking out about the Desolation, and beaten my mom into a blood-flavored slushie."

Does he tell this story to everyone he strangles to death? Aristotle wondered. *Is it how he justifies himself?*

"He killed my mom. If he hadn't, she would've survived the virus. Just like me."

Aristotle's hands desperately searched for a weapon, but there was nothing. Through the office's entrance she could see the locked door in the hallway. Behind it was Emiko.

"My old man killed my mom. I killed him. Violence never ends."

Emiko will have to fight. She'll have to succeed where I failed.

"I'll give you credit. You're one tough bitch. Most people would've passed out by now."

A smoky black haze encroached upon the edges of Aristotle's vision. It crept inward, engulfing her surroundings. Were her eyes still open? She could no longer tell.

A tunnel of white materialized from the black haze. At the shimmering tunnel's far end she saw her father, mother, and sister, their arms outstretched, waiting for her.

The tunnel only went one way. There was no choice but to follow. This was it.

Somewhere far and away an explosion sounded. A cannonball flew over Aristotle's head and hurtled towards her family like a meteorite. Her family vanished just before the speeding black sphere made impact.

A heavy presence bore down on Aristotle. She coughed and sputtered, choking on her own spit. Her lungs had reopened for business.

She forced her eyes open. Her assailant lay atop her. Though his fingers still loosely clasped her throat, he was no longer choking her.

Oxygen flooded to her brain as she wriggled out from under the lifeless body. Absolutely spent, she had no desire to rise from the floor.

Already she knew who'd saved her. A raspy whisper emerged from her throat:

"Emiko?"

There was no reply.

"Emiko?" she repeated. The muscles in her neck burned as she searched frantically for her friend.

Her eyes fell upon the doorway. There stood Emiko, her rifle tight against her shoulder.

"You shot him," Aristotle croaked, hoarse as a ninety-year-old chain smoker.

Emiko nodded weakly. She then doubled over and vomited at the dead man's feet.

Chapter 49

10/21/2027

The internet is down. I'm writing my thoughts in a journal instead. If the internet comes back up, maybe I'll post this entry to my blog. If not, well ...

A few days ago I left the house in a flight of madness. I couldn't handle everything that was happening. Who in their right mind could?

I roamed the desolate streets. I even wandered into a house or ten. The dead are scattered along roads and inside of buildings. Many victims didn't wait for the virus to run its course, instead killing themselves before the vomiting began.

The image of one particular bullet-riddled family still haunts me. The father must have shot his wife and children before turning the sawed-off shotgun on himself.

Perhaps that was where my death wish originated.

I continued through the city in a daze, sleeping and eating wherever I pleased, like a vulture picking through the remains of a war zone. The aura of death over the city won't dissipate anytime soon.

Eventually I found myself at the foot of Target Tower. I craned back my neck and contemplated the ninety floors of steel and concrete. Just a few years ago I couldn't have imagined that such a monstrosity would one day dominate the Minneapolis skyline.

I went in. My feet carried me to the elevator. I ascended to the viewing level.

At the time I didn't understand the impulse that drove me so high. Now I understand that I was testing myself.

I exited the elevator and ascended a staircase to the outside observation deck. A cold gust of wind riffled my hair as I stepped outside. I approached the safety rail and looked down to the ground, hundreds of meters below.

No fear.

I climbed onto the safety rail, stood up straight, and closed my eyes. I thought of Danielle. Of our unborn child. Of my parents.

I could've joined them. They were just a short step and a long fall away. Maybe my wife was waiting for me at the tower's base.

Maybe wasn't enough.

Swaying in the wind, I thought of Nathan and Emiko. Of how I couldn't abandon them. Of how I wouldn't abandon them, no matter what.

They are my hope. My reason to live.

I carefully stepped down from the parapet and started for home. As I was about to leave the tower, however, a notion struck me.

Surely others felt as I had, felt like abandoning hope. Someone had to stop them from making the mistake I'd almost made. That someone was me.

I descended into the tower's basement. The door to the control room was open. Considering the tower's price tag, I half-expected to meet armed guards. But no one was there.

On a scrap of ruled-paper tucked beneath a keyboard, I discovered the system password scrawled in blood ... or maybe it was just red ink.

I changed the password to HTRON. The password is universal. I tested it on the door on my way out. But I'm getting ahead of myself.

I shut down the tower's power systems and locked the control room door behind me. Now no one can use the elevator. Eighty-

something floors of stairs should deter even the most despairing souls.

My work was finished. I hurried home to see my children.

The world is dead. But hope lives on in us — in me, in my children, and in the other survivors that surely exist.

Yes. There are other survivors.

I must find them.

* * *

RETREATING HASTILY, Nathan soon reached the university's north gate. John followed behind, struggling to keep up. Demolishing the wall into the secret passage had left him totally enervated.

"John, I left the Northland Cores behind for a good reason," Nathan said.

"Yeah?" John grunted.

"There were six crates in that room, but only five cores. The open crate was empty. I think I know where the last core is."

"Target Tower?"

Nathan nodded. "Right. We'll stop by the house, gather our things, and then hurry to the tower."

"Fine," John huffed. "Let's go."

They proceeded north to Nathan's house. John pulled up every few blocks to catch his breath. He was running on fumes.

Finally they turned onto Nathan's street. The house at 1013 39th Avenue looked exactly as they'd left it.

Nathan twisted the doorknob. To his surprise it was locked.

He always left the door unsecured. Had Stearns locked it? Nathan's heart pumped harder at the mere thought of Stearns.

Seeing no other recourse, Nathan did the obvious thing. He knocked.

After a long pause, the door clicked. Nathan braced himself as the door swung inward, unsure who to expect.

A woman in red stood in the door frame.

"Aristotle!" Nathan exclaimed. Her pleasing features and genuine smile were a soothing sight.

"Come in. It's not safe outside," Aristotle croaked, her voice weak and raspy. Her eyes lingered on John, her concern evident. "Bring him into the living room."

"Come on, John," Nathan said. "You can lay out on the couch."

John nodded weakly.

Nathan led the way in. His heart skipped three beats when he saw the streaks of blood on the stairs. A dead man dangled limply from the upstairs landing.

"Loons over the moon," he uttered under his breath.

"That son of a bitch," John growled, shaking his head.

"Stearns?"

"Who else?"

"So, Stearns never intended to uphold his end of the bargain?"

"Are you surprised?" John scoffed, hobbling past Nathan and into the living room.

Apparently Nathan hadn't been the only one bluffing. Stearns had also been negotiating in bad faith. Already he'd laid one trap. Did he have more surprises in store?

Nathan sat beside John on the couch. Aristotle appeared in the doorway.

"What's Osborne's status?" she asked Nathan.

"Honestly?" Nathan eyed John sidelong. "Not good. I think he could use some food."

"You two are talking about me like I'm already dead," John grumbled.

"No we aren't," Nathan replied. "Dead men don't need food."

John muttered a profanity under his breath.

"What happened, anyway?" Aristotle asked. "Where did Kennedy go?"

"Kennedy?" Nathan arched an eyebrow. "Oh, you mean Stearns! It's a long story. Long story short, we need to get to Target Tower. We think the Northland Core is there."

"Funny," Aristotle said. "I was thinking exactly the same thing."

"You were?" Nathan asked.

"Yes. In fact, my companion and I came here to tell you just that."

"I thought you were alone," Nathan said. "What happened here, anyway? Why is there a dead guy by the stairs?"

"Well, about that ..." Aristotle cleared her throat. Her voice seemed to be recovering its vitality. "My partner and I were waiting for you here, and then these green men came to break into the house."

"How many?" John asked.

"Four."

"And you and your companion fought them off," John said. "Impressive."

"I couldn't have done it without her help."

Nathan was curious. "Who is this companion, anyway?"

"That's the thing. Wait here." Aristotle disappeared into the next room.

Do we really have time for chitchat? Nathan wondered. Though this chance meeting with Aristotle had seemingly lifted John's spirits, the reality of the matter remained unchanged. John needed the Northland Core and he needed it now.

What if the sixth core wasn't in Target Tower? They would have to launch an assault on Stearns' base to obtain one of the other five. It would be a suicide mission, but Nathan didn't care. He had his own score to settle with Stearns ...

Aristotle stepped back into the door frame. "Are you both comfortably seated?"

"Yes," Nathan said, knitting his brow. "Why wouldn't we be?"

Aristotle smirked awkwardly. She looked aside and waved her companion closer.

"Well, gentlemen, the truth is that you're already well acquainted with my partner."

"We are?" Nathan asked, suddenly nervous.

Aristotle's partner remained in the hallway. Frowning her disapproval, Aristotle dragged the mystery person into the living room.

Nathan blinked. It couldn't be. But it was. The pressure in his chest erupted in a single word.

"Emiko!"

He sprang from the couch and rushed to embrace his sister.

"Jeez, Nathan!" Emiko protested. "You're crushing me!"

Though reluctant to let go, Nathan relented. He took a step back.

His sister had thinned out and perhaps sprung up an inch. Her long, flowing black locks were gone. In their place was a shorter, more mature haircut that hung just below her ears. The style looked conspicuously similar to Aristotle's.

"Where have you been?" Nathan asked.

"How did you know I was gone?"

"We stopped back in Duluth on our way down here. The clerk at the hotel told us about you."

"Oh! Well ... here I am!" Emiko smiled sheepishly. "You're not angry?"

"Angry? Why would I be angry?" Nathan asked, before realizing that he had more reasons to be furious than Minnesota had lakes. "You have a lot of explaining to do, Emiko, but now isn't the time. Let's get John some food and head for the tower."

Chapter 50

10/22/2027

Today we laid Danielle to rest in the community graveyard. After removing her body from the bathroom, I locked the door and threw the key into the sewer drain. I never want to go into that room again.

Within a day of catching fever, Danielle was dead. Absurdly high body temperature, exacerbated by a complete inability to retain fluids, appears to be the cause of death. Essentially, she burned up.

The people who invented this bioweapon were a sick and twisted bunch, indeed. Was triggering the apocalypse their intention?

To keep Nathan and Emiko's minds off everything that's happened, I've been giving them chores to do in and around the house. I see no reason to keep them cooped up inside. I don't know what protected us from infection, but I suspect it's an immunity of some sort. Hopefully further exposure to the virus won't have any effect.

I can't say for sure how many days it took for the virus to sweep through Minneapolis. People could be hiding in their homes, living off stockpiles of food, waiting for the virus to pass. Whether they can outlast the contagious period or not remains to be seen. The virus could still be lurking in the atmosphere. Perhaps I'm even carrying it.

Going forward, I intend to gather other survivors. It's time to see what we can make of this new world.

* * *

NATHAN BADE HIS HOUSE farewell knowing he was unlikely to return. Once a safe and familiar place, the home was no longer secure.

Target Tower loomed in the distance. Nathan walked alongside Aristotle, Emiko, and John. Behind them Mumford pulled a cart full of gear.

Their weapons were loaded. Ammunition spilled from their pockets. Whatever they encountered, they would be ready.

Nathan carried a USB thumb drive in the tiny coin pocket of his jeans. He'd saved a copy of his father's blog, *Ryota in the Minneapple*, on the drive. Although he couldn't access the files without a computer, the drive was a comforting memento.

Emiko, meanwhile, cradled *World's End* in her arms. Inside was the secret to Target Tower.

Nine years ago Nathan's father had scaled the tower with the darkest of intentions. He had teetered on the edge before stepping away. Recognizing that others harbored similar thoughts, Ryota had disabled the tower's electrical systems on his way out.

Nathan wasn't sure Emiko fully understood the significance of their father's words. Perhaps one day he would explain them to her.

"Alright, Emiko. There's one thing I haven't figured out," Aristotle said, breaking the bubble of silence.

"What's that?"

"I thought you were hiding behind that locked door. How did you come save me in the office?"

Emiko grinned mischievously. "Maybe I wasn't behind the door."

"You thought she was hiding in the bathroom?" Nathan asked.

"Could be," Aristotle said. "I'm not very familiar with your house."

"That door has been locked for nine years now." Nathan glared at his sister. "Emiko must've been hiding elsewhere."

"Well it all worked out for the best, didn't it?" Emiko protested.

Aristotle ruffled Emiko's black mop of hair. "I suppose it did."

They approached the maw of downtown Minneapolis. Target Tower only grew more prominent. Nathan thought back to his notion that the core was hidden in plain sight. Maybe he'd had the right idea but hadn't run far enough with it. Following the notion to its logical extreme would've led to Target Tower, a marvel of engineering visible from every house, office, park, and alleyway in the city.

A monstrous cough racked John's body. He pressed ahead in spite of his weakness, fueled by the hope found within the margins of *World's End*.

But what if they were wrong? What if the final Northland Core wasn't in Target Tower? These unspoken questions weighed on the group's collective psyche like a truckload of iron ore.

"Do you need to take a break?" Nathan asked John.

John shook his head. "No. We need to keep going. And it looks like we have company,"

Nathan lifted his brow. "We do?"

John gestured over his shoulder. "Six o'clock."

Everyone turned to look.

"Well I'll be damned," Aristotle said.

Five soldiers approached. They marched down the center of the street, confident they would encounter no opposition.

"Our original plan for today was to visit Target Tower. Stearns knows that," John said.

"What's his hurry? Doesn't he think we're dead?" Nathan asked.

"Probably. But he has enough men at his disposal to make doubly sure."

Nathan gritted his teeth. "What do we do?"

"You three go," Aristotle said, drawing her revolver. "I'll slow them down."

"One of us should stay and help you," Nathan suggested.

"I'll stay!" Emiko volunteered.

"No." Aristotle shook her head. "Go. All of you. Nathan, you might have to help John if he starts feeling weak. And Emiko, you're the only one who's been to Target Tower before. John needs both of you."

"She's right," John said, waving ahead with his crutch. "Let's keep moving." He gave Mumford a dirty look. "You too, Frankenmoose."

A shot rang out. Chips of pavement burst into the air before Aristotle's feet.

"Go!" Aristotle barked.

Emiko protested. "But —"

"Now!"

There was no changing Aristotle's mind. The tower was only minutes away. Nathan and Emiko hurried after John and Mumford.

Nathan chanced a parting glance over his shoulder. Aristotle had already disappeared into the urban landscape.

"Will she be okay?" Emiko asked.

"She said she could handle it. I'm sure she'll be fine," Nathan replied, though the truth was he didn't know.

Chapter 51

10/30/2027

Life isn't difficult, but I can't say it's not bleak.

Nathan, Emiko, and I drive around the city every few days, stopping at grocery stores to gather food. Though the shelves have more than enough to get us through winter, eventually they'll run empty. Come spring we'll need to start growing our own food.

We've found a handful of survivors. Many of us who remain are meeting downtown every day to exchange information and discuss the future.

Not all survivors are friendly. Even though the danger has seemingly passed, some survivors still treat everyone and everything as a threat. While this reaction is understandable, it seems ill-advised.

The truth is that now more than ever we live in a world of abundance. We have abundant food, abundant water, and abundant shelter.

We also have abundant death.

The virus wiped out some ninety percent of humanity. Unfortunately, I think most of the bodies scattered about the city will simply be left to rot. The few of us that remain can't be expected to provide proper burials for the multitude of dead.

Gas is also abundant, although I'm not sure how long this will remain the case. Unlike food, gas doesn't grow on trees. And the gasoline sitting in parked cars will go bad within a year or two at best.

It's getting cold. Winter is coming. But as I wrote above, shelter is not an issue. I don't foresee the bite of winter causing us any unseen difficulties.

* * *

FIVE AGAINST ONE.

Aristotle ducked into the entryway of a movie theater. Faded posters advertising *Batman Reborn* adorned the windows. Large portions of the doors' glazing had been smashed and were missing.

Aristotle peered around the corner. She cursed at what she saw.

The men were dispersing. Aristotle recognized their strategy at once. They would take separate routes to the tower before regrouping in front and entering together.

Aristotle couldn't stop them all. She twisted her revolver to Snipe and sighted a fleeing soldier.

She fired once. Twice.

The second round did the job. The soldier stumbled to the ground, dead or disabled. It didn't matter which.

Aristotle seethed. The soldier's sacrifice had paid for the other four men's escape.

No, Aristotle realized. The man's death had only bought three tickets. One soldier yet approached, striding down the block like a retiree enjoying an afternoon stroll, fearless.

Fearless like Glacier Face.

Her heart racing, Aristotle retreated into the concave entryway. Surely Glacier Face couldn't have known that she would be here? His appearance was a coincidence.

Somehow Aristotle didn't find that reassuring.

She took a deep breath and poked her nose around the corner. Glacier Face was a block away. His fingers clenched his pistol.

"Long time no see, Sister Leon," he called out. "It's been what, twenty-four hours now?"

Aristotle steeled herself. She couldn't protect her friends from all five men, but she could stop this one. She swung out from the entryway to take the shot that would end this.

She was too slow. Before she could shoot, a bullet blasted the ground by her feet. Concrete grit splashed into her eyes as she retreated to cover.

"Hold tight," Glacier Face called. "I'll be there soon. Then we can finish what we started."

Aristotle gulped. Her neck still burned where her last opponent's thumbs had wrung her throat. Glacier Face was even more formidable. To fight him in close quarters would be like inviting herself to death's house and beating down the door.

Another shot rang out. A chunk of concrete exploded from the wall near Aristotle's shoulder.

Aristotle was out of options. She fled into the shadows of the theater's lobby.

Her thoughts were with Nathan and Emiko. She hoped the Kanno siblings were up for a firefight.

Chapter 52

11/09/2027

Today I bumped into a fellow university professor named Pierre. He was a member of the history department. I'd seen him in passing on campus but we'd never spoken.

He's a friendly fellow, if a little long-winded. I invited him to the next survivor meetup. He sounded quite eager to attend. Hopefully he can offer some fresh perspective.

* * *

JOHN, NATHAN, AND EMIKO hurried into Target Tower as fast as John's crutches allowed.

"Do you think Mumford will be okay out there?" Emiko asked, lantern in hand, as she led the group past the Louis Vuitton and Gucci storefronts.

"I don't see why not. He's harmless," Nathan replied.

"Harmless?" John said. "I beg to disagree."

"Really?" Emiko asked.

"John still hasn't overcome his irrational fear of tvapas," Nathan explained.

"He can be such a baby sometimes," Emiko said.

John growled his displeasure.

Emiko's lantern illuminated a flight of stairs. "Down this way."

"You and Aristotle made the tower light up last night?" Nathan asked, descending the stairs behind Emiko. John brought up the rear.

"Yup. That was us."

Nathan shook his head. "Only you would be audacious enough to power up this tower after you'd confirmed that the General's base was nearby. This place is like a giant neon advertisement for free electricity."

"Jeez, Nathan. Could you stop complaining?" Emiko said. "The blinking lights are what gave us the idea that the Northland Core could be down here. Wasn't the reward worth the risk?"

Though John agreed with Emiko, he kept his mouth shut. He already had a splitting headache and was in no mood to insert himself into an argument between siblings.

They reached the bottom of the staircase. The basement was littered with the telltale signs of a struggle — a struggle between the door and whoever had beaten it from its hinges.

"Did you do that?" John asked, gesturing at the open doorway.

"Are you serious, Beard?" Emiko replied.

John scowled. "Beard?"

"Yeah. Remember?"

John grumbled unintelligibly. He'd forgotten the nickname. He wished Emiko had, too. "It was like this when you came here?" he asked.

Emiko nodded. "Someone had broken through this door, but not through the next one that leads to the control room."

"Smart move on their part," John said. He'd seen firsthand how these government researchers defended the fruits of their labor. If the self-destruct mechanism on Mallard Island hadn't incinerated Professor Singh's documentation, John would've found the core weeks ago.

Emiko led them into the next room and tapped on the far wall. An LCD display came to life and demanded a password. Emiko keyed in H-T-R-O-N, and the door drew open like a castle's portcullis.

"Here we are. It's my third time here. This place is like my second home."

"Speaking of home, where have you been living?" Nathan asked.

"I found a nice place and cleaned it up."

"Why not live in our old place?"

"It just ..." Emiko hesitated. "It just didn't feel right living there alone."

They stepped into a control room replete with keyboards, buttons, and monitors. Emiko rested her hand on a lever.

"Are you ready?" she asked.

John nodded.

"Sure thing," Nathan said.

Emiko threw the switch. Halogen bulbs powered on overhead, burning brighter than the noontime sun. Blinking lights, colorful buttons, flashing screens, and rows of switches came to life. Intricate and mostly unlabeled, the control console would've been right at home in a space station.

"Power's on," Emiko announced.

"Now what?" John asked.

"We look for the Northland Core!" Emiko said. "What does it look like?"

Nathan rubbed the back of his neck. "You know, I didn't actually see it. But you saw one, didn't you John?"

"I did." John spread his thumb and index finger a couple inches apart. "It was a square, about this long on either side." He drew his fingers closer. "And about this thick. Less than an inch."

"What color was it?" Nathan asked.

"Black, I think."

"You think?"

John grunted. What else was there to say? Stearns had stuck him with a gun as soon as he'd opened the crate. His focus hadn't been on the core's cosmetic details.

"So where does this leave us?" Nathan asked. "The core might not even be in this room. It could be anywhere in the tower. And we don't know what it looks like."

"It was your idea to come here," John replied, massaging his aching forehead.

Nathan raised his hands in frustration. Silence befell the group. Yet the silence was incomplete.

"Did you hear that?" John whispered.

"Hear what?" Nathan squawked.

"Sshhh." John raised a finger to his lips. "Emiko?"

"I heard it," Emiko whispered. "Footsteps."

"Someone's coming," John said. "And I don't think it's Aristotle."

Chapter 53

11/30/2027

Lack of resources is not an immediate concern. Survival is a non-issue. But should we strive to do more than survive?

A dead city isn't conducive to a fresh start. Maybe twenty or thirty years from now Minneapolis will be ready.

What to do until then?

Pierre has suggested that we leave the city. We'd be setting out for the unknown. But rebuilding in a part of the world that doesn't feel so dead and lonely could be exactly what we need.

In any case, we have months to consider. No one is going anywhere in the middle of a Minnesota winter.

* * *

ARISTOTLE DASHED THROUGH the theater's ticketing gate and swerved towards the concession counter. Atop the counter was a glass case with jumbo pretzels dangling inside. Plastic signage advertised popcorn for seven dollars and Pepsi for five.

Aristotle planted her hands and swung over the counter. She landed on her feet. Keeping low, she flipped open her revolver's cylinder. The spent rounds hit the floor. She fed three shotgun rounds and one standard round into the cylinder and clicked the barrel to Spread.

A gunshot erupted nearby. A storm of glass exploded in Aristotle's face — the remains of a popcorn tank.

She rolled backwards. Shards of glass clawed at her sweatshirt and jeans as she scrambled. She had to find a better place to hide.

Rising above the counter, she unleashed a single blast from her revolver. The volley of buckshot flew far to Glacier Face's right, but it was distraction enough. Aristotle dove over the counter's far end. She landed with a forward roll and sprang to her feet.

She whipped her gun arm back and fired another shot. Though hopelessly off target, the shot bought her time to escape the lobby. She sprinted down a hall lined with cinema auditoriums on either side. Magenta carpeting covered the floors and walls.

"Would you prefer an action flick or a romantic comedy?" Glacier Face taunted, his voice booming from the lobby.

Ignoring him, Aristotle spotted an emergency exit between two auditoriums. Racing silently across the carpet, she pushed through the door and began to plot the next scene.

Chapter 54

12/11/2027

Yesterday we celebrated Nathan's birthday. We found a pound cake at Target, lathered it with chocolate frosting, lit nine candles, and sang Happy Birthday.

I must admit that Emiko seemed to enjoy the festivities more than Nathan. My son is still preoccupied with recent events. Danielle's passing has left an emptiness that we will likely never fill.

Be strong, Nathan. The world may be dark, but I see bright things in your future.

* * *

"HERE'S THE PLAN," John said. "I'll guard the door. Nathan will man the console to figure out where the Northland Core is."

Nathan nodded. "I'll do my best."

"And what about me?" Emiko asked.

"You'll ..." John hesitated. "You, the Great Huntress of Frontier View, will take that long-barreled dragon slayer and help me cover the door."

"You got it, Beard."

John eyed Nathan, who nodded in consent. If Nathan had reservations about putting Emiko in danger, he was keeping them to himself.

Nathan sat at the control console and started hammering at the keys. Emiko stood at attention with her World War I sniper rifle in hand.

"That rifle isn't meant for close quarters, but you can still provide cover fire," John said. "No matter what, keep your body behind this door frame. Understood?"

"Yes, sir!"

Feet clattered down the staircase. John took position beside the door, crutches under his armpits, gun in hand.

"Can you close this door?" John asked Nathan.

"No," Nathan said distractedly. A computer geek in a world bereft of electronics, he was completely engrossed in his task.

The basement had three sections — the stairwell, the middle room, and the control room. John intended to convert the middle room into a no-fly zone.

"Stand behind me, Emiko," he said. "My revolver has six rounds. If I pull back to reload you can swing out and fire a shot. It's okay if you don't hit anything. Just make them think twice about charging in here."

"Got it." Emiko pressed up against the wall at John's side.

The footsteps grew louder. John leaned out the door. A kaleidoscope of arms and legs was flying down the staircase. John hoped the threat of a .45 caliber colonoscopy would keep his attackers at bay.

His thumb cocked his revolver, his index trigger pulled the trigger, and a bullet wailed through the middle room. It thudded to a halt against the staircase.

He immediately fired a second round. The bullet kicked up a shower of sparks as it skidded across the floor.

"You sure you can't close this door?" John asked.

The only response was the frantic clack of computer keys.

John let two more rounds fly. The soldiers had stopped their forward rush. They knew John, Nathan, and Emiko were trapped like three gophers in a hole.

"Any progress, Nathan?" John asked.

"Not yet." No longer fingering the keyboard, Nathan was now inspecting the colorful rows of buttons and switches.

John fired the last two rounds from his cylinder. Neither scored a hit.

"Your turn, Emiko. Don't expose your head," John whispered as his spent rounds clattered to the floor. He took six fresh bullets from his pocket and fed them into his cylinder.

Heeding John's warning, Emiko awkwardly jabbed her rifle's muzzle into the doorway and pulled the trigger. Booming with a thunderous crack that put John's Colt to shame, the rifle slipped free of Emiko's haphazard grip and clattered to the floor.

Shrieks of pain rang out from the middle room.

"I hit one?" Emiko asked.

"You hit one," John replied. The soldiers must have known he employed a six-shooter. They'd waited for him to empty his cylinder before charging forward.

Talented and lucky, Emiko apparently had it all. She collected her rifle from the floor, discharged her spent round, and locked another into firing position.

John peeked around the corner. The wounded soldier had fallen in the middle room's far doorway. A dark pool spread across his green vest. Hopefully his mistake would make his pals think twice about rushing in.

John fired a round before retreating behind the wall. Nathan had abandoned his chair and was now on his hands and knees examining the console's underside.

"John, there's a panel here that says 'Do not open.' I'm going to open it," Nathan said.

"You sure that's a good idea?"

"As good as any."

Nathan extended an arm to touch the panel. The instant his fingers made contact his body jerked and slumped to the floor.

"Nathan!" John shouted.

The kid didn't stir.

Emiko gazed at her brother. "What happened?"

"I'm not sure. Maybe he got hit by a high-voltage shock." John bit his lip. "Emiko, do you know how to fire a single-action revolver?"

"No, but I'm a quick learner."

It wasn't the answer John had hoped to hear, but it would have to do.

"Take this." John set his Colt in Emiko's open palm. "You gotta cock and fire. You have five rounds. When you run out, slide it to me and switch back to your rifle."

"And what about you?"

John didn't reply. Abandoning his crutches, he hobbled to Nathan's side, dropped to his knees, and put two fingers to the kid's neck.

Nathan had a pulse. A strong pulse. His chest expanded and contracted with regular breaths. Like a sheep at pasture unaware of the circling wolves, he was at peace.

A shot rang out. Glancing over his shoulder, John saw Emiko waving his precious Colt Single Action Army at their enemies.

John eyed the panel. It bore the words do not open in bright yellow.

The warning begged to be ignored. John curled his bionic fingers into a fist and thrust his arm forward. His knuckles easily punctured the metal. He ripped the panel off its hinges and tossed it aside.

Now, he just had to dig through —

Bile surged up John's throat and splattered onto the floor. He flopped onto his chest, his heart racing, his lungs struggling for air.

SPEAR had protected him from the high-voltage trap that had felled Nathan. But using SPEAR without the Northland Core incurred a heavy cost.

John knew pain. He'd broken bones. He'd taken bullets. He'd had his arm severed from his body.

Now his own body betrayed him. He'd reached the apex of suffering. A voice in his head screamed: *Just let me die!*

He struggled to pull himself together. His head throbbed. Bloody vomit spewed from his mouth. His eyes lurched up to where the metal panel had been.

Inside he saw it.

The Northland Core. It was tucked within a morass of wires, connected to the console by two thick strands of black.

John's legs wobbled as he struggled to his knees. He reached forward, only to collapse into a puddle of his own vomit. So close but so far.

This isn't just for me, he reminded himself. It was for Nathan and for Emiko. For Aristotle. Maybe even for Mumford.

He would not let Stearns win.

John lunged forward and ripped the Northland Core free. A tingling sensation swept through his left arm. Something snapped up from his shoulder, puncturing a hole in his shirtsleeve.

Before John could examine his shoulder, the overhead lights suddenly lost power, pitching the room into complete darkness.

Chapter 55

01/29/2028

We keep track of the days even though they no longer matter.

We eat. Though we tire of subsisting on Oreos and Campbell's soup, there is no shortage of food.

We scavenge. We scour Wal-Marts, food shelters, and Burger Kings for fresh treats.

We sleep. Long hours are spent curled up in the warmth of blankets.

We read. The electrical grid has been out for months now. Nathan has read three full novels this week. Emiko enjoys paging through picture books.

We stargaze. It's strange and wonderful to realize how much of the night sky is visible when the city isn't perpetually aglow.

We chat. No longer connected to each other through wires and waves, we treasure human contact all the more.

We hope. For we know a new beginning lies just beyond the choppy waves of desolation's wake.

* * *

HOW MANY FLOORS did this theater have?

Aristotle sprinted up the stairs. Light filtered in from windows along the wall. On the second floor landing she found the back entrance to a salon, Eva's Beauty Shop.

She tried the knob and cursed. Locked.

The door on the ground floor swooshed open and slammed shut. The stairwell's railings rumbled and shook. Glacier Face was on his way.

How high could she run? Aristotle resumed her flight up the stairs. She regretted not paying more attention to the building's exterior.

On the third floor she arrived at a door marked EMPLOYEES ONLY — also locked. She continued to the fourth floor. The pounding of Glacier Face's boots reverberated up the stairwell.

Approaching the fourth floor, Aristotle raised an arm to shield her eyes. Bright, waning light streamed through the open door ahead.

There were only three floors. The fourth was the roof.

Aristotle burst out onto the rooftop. The sun was a succulent Florida peach steeping in a vat of fiery blood.

The rooftop had few places to take cover. On the far side was a water tank. Behind her was the stairwell she'd come up. Aristotle spun and fired a warning shot down the stairs, hoping to make Glacier Face reconsider his approach.

Only a single .55 caliber round remained in her cylinder. She needed to reload. Twisting the revolver's barrel to Snipe, she hurried to duck behind the water tank.

She didn't make it.

"Don't worry, Sister Leon," Glacier Face said. "I wouldn't shoot a nun in the back. Not even a fake nun."

Aristotle gazed out at the Minneapolis skyline. Stark vanities of steel and concrete stood between her and the scarlet-tinged sky. Those lifeless buildings, tombstones of a fallen civilization, spoke of what this world had become.

Target Tower's shadow extended all the way to the Mississippi. Beneath the tower John, Nathan, and Emiko, that little girl who was now like a sister to Aristotle, were locked in mortal struggle.

Aristotle had already lost one sister. She would not lose another.

"Saying your final prayers?" Glacier Face asked, still behind her. "Take all the time you need. I'm not going anywhere."

This is it, Aristotle thought. *I have one shot.*

Turn. Shoot. Win.

She lunged to one side, throwing her body into a half-turn. The report of Glacier Face's pistol exploded in her ears — one shot, two shots, three shots.

No hits.

Her shoulder struck the rooftop. Lying on her side, she gripped her revolver with both hands, instinctively chose her target, and fired. Her last bullet shattered the Minneapolis calm, slamming into Glacier Face's wrist. His pistol hurtled into the air.

Glacier Face clutched his hand, roaring ferociously. His eyes seethed with unbridled rage.

He charged across the rooftop. Aristotle knew he wouldn't stop until he'd pummeled her into a lifeless mash.

She leapt to her feet and inched backwards. Her heels teetered on the ledge.

Revolver empty. No time to reload. Only one way out.

Down.

Glacier Face rushed at her, oblivious to danger. As his arms reached to grab her, Aristotle dropped her revolver from the ledge and grasped the collar of his vest. With a forceful jerk, she sent their bodies tumbling together over the edge.

Clenching each other's clothing, they accelerated towards the earth. Broken windows and unlit signs spun around them as they shot down.

Just before impact, Aristotle shoved Glacier Face's chest, gaining separation and ensuring he would hit the ground first.

Glacier Face crashed into the asphalt. Aristotle's body slammed into his, cushioning her fall. A chorus of cracking bones and painful groans resounded through the empty streets.

Then silence.

Aristotle lay atop Glacier Face. Maybe his neck had snapped. Maybe his heart had given out. In any case he wasn't breathing.

Her spine aching, her muscles protesting, Aristotle rolled off the dead body. She grunted in anguish as she settled onto the street.

There was no time for rest. Emiko, John, and Nathan were waiting. Aristotle struggled to her feet, brushing the dust from her jeans and hoodie.

Her revolver had landed a few feet away. Though the impact had scuffed its body, the barrel remained straight and true. The cylinder spun with well-oiled ease.

Aristotle slipped the weapon into its holster and staggered towards Target Tower.

Chapter 56

02/21/2028

Without road salt and snowplows, winter in Minneapolis is dicey indeed. Thanks to heavy snowfall, we can't even back the car out of the driveway. Fortunately we've stockpiled enough food to last us a few weeks.

That said, this experience is just another sign that continuing to live in this city is untenable. Come good weather, I'll follow Pierre wherever he wants to go.

Spring can't arrive soon enough!

* * *

IF ONLY SHE'D had night vision.

Men with guns lurked in the impenetrable darkness around her.

Darkness was fear. Fear demanded submission. Emiko's brave face was cracking like brittle skin on a winter's day. Microscopic at first, the cracks expanded with her every breath.

"Beard?" she murmured.

Her hands clung to Beard's revolver. Did it have any bullets left? If one of the General's men attacked, could her fingers find the trigger?

Something crackled nearby. Dancing orange lantern light spread across the wall of the middle room, where the green men were.

"Beard? Nathan?" Emiko whispered. When the overhead lights had cut out, Beard had been retching his guts out; Nathan had lay unconscious.

Footsteps approached. Emiko readied Beard's revolver. The darkness tripled the gun's weight. It shook in her hands, pulsating to the rhythm of her heart.

A sudden, blinding flash lit up the room, accompanied by a deafening bang.

Panic raced up Emiko's spine. The revolver slipped from her hands and clattered to the floor. Who had fired? What had he fired at?

Falling to her knees, Emiko scoured the floor. Instead of Beard's revolver, her fingers discovered her M1903 rifle. She fumbled with it, trying to determine which end was which.

The footsteps drew nearer. The lamp reached the threshold of the control room. Emiko found the rifle's stock and shouldered it.

The lamp hovered in the doorway, held aloft by a soldier's arm.

Emiko fingered her rifle's trigger. She swore to herself she wouldn't hesitate to pull it.

Her right ear twitched. A primal growl emanated from the darkness nearby.

"John? Is that you?" she asked meekly.

The growl swelled into a roar as a formless shadow flitted past the wall. The soldier's muzzle flashed; gunpowder boomed.

The roar became more savage still. The lamp trembled in the soldier's hand.

Suddenly Beard burst from the darkness, slamming his fist into the soldier's chest. The soldier shrieked, dropping the lamp as he flew backward.

The soldier's screams abruptly ceased. Beard stood in the doorway, admiring his handiwork, before bending over to snatch the lamp.

"That felt good."

A gunshot erupted from the middle room. The bullet clanged into the door frame.

"Hammersnap," Beard growled, taking cover beside Emiko.

"Did you get it?" Emiko asked.

"Get what?"

"The Northland Core."

"Oh, I got it alright." John patted his left shoulder.

"What about Nathan?"

"He'll pull through."

"Are you —"

"We'll talk after we take care of the bad guys. Where is my revolver?"

"I dropped it. It's somewhere around here."

Beard set the lamp on the floor to search for his most prized possession.

A salvo of three shots rang out, flaring white from the far room. Then silence.

Emiko leaned closer to the door. "Do you think that's ..."

"It has to be," John replied. He'd recovered his revolver from the floor.

They waited anxiously for a sign that all was clear.

"Osborne?" Aristotle's voice called.

"Glad you could make it," John replied, struggling to his feet.

"How many of them did you take out?" Aristotle asked.

"Two dead or damn near it."

"That makes five. We should be clear."

Aristotle shuddered audibly as she passed the dead soldiers in the middle room. She entered the control room with a lantern in hand. Blood trickled from gashes and scrapes on her face. Loose threads dangled from her sweatshirt.

She was in rough shape. But she was here.

Everyone was here.

"Did *you* mangle that guy?" Aristotle pointed back at the middle room.

"I did," John replied. "How does he look?"

"He looks like you sledgehammered his ribcage."

"Sounds about right."

Aristotle's eyes gaped. She quickly collected herself. "Where's Nathan?"

John nodded towards the room's corner. Nathan was sprawled across the floor. "His system took a high-voltage jolt but his vitals are stable. He should recover soon."

Aristotle knelt by Nathan's side. After checking his pulse, she looked to John.

"Judging from Mister Ribs-Jutting-From-His-Back in the next room, I'm guessing you found the Northland Core."

John nodded. "It was beneath this computer terminal. As soon as I touched it, a slot in my shoulder opened up. The Northland Core slipped in and I was good to go."

"Glad to hear that. Now you can get on with your life."

"Yeah," John muttered. He looked to Emiko. "Was that the first man you've killed?"

Emiko shook her head. She held two fingers up in the air. "The second. The first was this morning."

"I'm surprised you held your lunch in. Most lose it the first few times."

"Thanks." Emiko laughed sheepishly. Aristotle eyed her knowingly.

Nathan groaned, stirring from his slumber.

"Nathan?" Aristotle said.

"That's me," Nathan mumbled.

"How are you feeling?"

"Like a million bucks." He yawned. "Maybe a billion, depending on inflation."

Aristotle's lips curved into a crooked smirk. "Sounds like he's gonna be fine."

John rubbed his shoulder where his shirt was torn.

"Everything's gonna be fine now," he said. "Let's get out of here before reinforcements arrive."

Everything's gonna be fine. Emiko wanted to believe those words. The army of men at the General's command gave reason for doubt.

John's quest for the Northland Core was over. A greater battle was already brewing.

Chapter 57

03/13/2028

Finally the last of the snow has melted. While there's a chance more of the white stuff will fall, I'd like to think that winter is over and spring is here to stay.

Our plans for leaving the city are taking shape. Our group of two dozen will pack our things, top off our gas tanks, and venture north to a new frontier.

We haven't decided whether we'll try to settle in an existing community or build our own little village. I'm open to either possibility. We will see what opportunities present themselves as we head north; away from the city, away from the stifling heat of summer, and away from the pain and suffering that has long dogged us.

Our departure is still a few weeks away. We won't set out until we're confident no more snow will come.

* * *

AND NOW THEY were four.

The group hurried to Emiko's home.

Aristotle looked like she'd fallen from a fifteen-story building. Emiko's cheeks and forehead were smeared with streaks of blood. John had abandoned his crutches; he walked with a noticeable limp. Mumford steadily pulled their cart, none the wiser.

As for Nathan? Life was good. His sister had returned to him and his friend had resolved a life-threatening problem.

Bright as today was, however, tomorrow's forecast was not sunny. An army was literally forming in their backyard.

Upon arriving at Emiko's house, Nathan and John herded Mumford into the backyard.

"You're sure he won't make any noise?" John asked.

Nathan tied Mumford to a willow tree. "Have you ever heard him make any noise?"

John shook his head. "But these brutes must be coordinating their uprising somehow."

Nathan rolled his eyes. "Have you ever seen Mumford chatting with another tvapa?"

"No." John leveled his index finger at Nathan. "But he could be using you to carry messages for him."

"So now I'm complicit in the tvapa revolution?"

"Guilty until proven innocent."

"Is that a tenet of the tvapan constitution?"

"Don't ask me." John shrugged. "I don't read frankenmoose."

After getting Mumford settled, Nathan and John went inside to meet Emiko and Aristotle. The four weary souls gathered in the living room. They closed the blinds and spoke softly. Stearns was still hunting for them. They needed this house to look as uninhabited as its neighbors.

"It's time to put Minneapolis behind us," John said. "Nathan, we accomplished what we set out to do. What's next for you?"

"I'm heading back to Frontier View with Emiko," Nathan said.

"Who said I'm going back to Frontier View?" Emiko protested.

"Who gave you a choice? Besides, what else would you do?"

"I would ... I would ..." Emiko fumbled for words.

"Exactly. You have no idea. And I'm sure Pierre has a fresh batch of stories waiting for you," Nathan said, though he knew full well that he and Emiko would be the ones telling stories upon their return.

"Fine. But what about the General and his army?" Emiko asked.

Nathan shrugged. "John?"

"You know," John said contemplatively, "there's a part of me — a damn big part — that wants to break down Stearns' door and punch a hole through his chest."

"But?" Nathan said.

"If it were just Stearns and a handful of men, I would already be at his gate. But Stearns and a whole army, maybe thousands strong?" John shook his head. "Too much for me."

"Even the four of us together couldn't handle the Restoration Army," Nathan said.

"Right. So, for the time being at least, I'll head north with you."

Hearing these words, Nathan could only smile.

"You'll come with us, Beard?" Emiko asked.

"Keep your voice down, Emiko," Nathan said.

Emiko harrumphed scornfully.

"I'll stick with you for now," John said. "We'll see what the future holds."

Emiko cheered quietly, pumping both fists. Nathan shared her sentiments. As long as John was around the adventure wasn't over.

"Don't get too excited, huntress," John warned. "Our paths might diverge yet."

"Also, I was thinking that we should warn the government in Duluth about the General," Nathan said.

"We could try," John said. "Although I'm not sure they'd take us seriously."

Nathan nodded solemnly. "Maybe if you shaved your beard ..."

John shook his head. "Beard or no beard, our claim would sound outrageous."

"Well, it could be worth ..."

"Shaving my beard? Not gonna happen."

Nathan threw up his arms in defeat. He looked to Aristotle. She had yet to say a word.

"And how about you? What's your plan?" he asked.

"That's a very good question," she said with an understated grin. "I think I've accomplished all I can in Minneapolis for the time being."

"So come with us," Nathan said.

"Yeah, come with us!" Emiko chimed in.

Nathan hushed Emiko. Emiko directed an eyeful of daggers at his heart. It was good to have his sister back.

"I'll tell you two what," Aristotle said. "I owe my old police captain a call. Let me make it, and then I'll decide what's next for me."

Aristotle slipped out of the room, returning a moment later with a walkie-talkie.

"Captain Griswold will want to hear about the situation here," she said, reclaiming her chair. "I'll see if he has any advice for us."

Nathan watched impatiently as Aristotle fiddled with the radio's buttons. Her frustration apparent, Aristotle popped off the back panel. She removed the battery and shook it violently before replacing it. Frowning, she tried the buttons again.

"Battery's dead," she said.

"Is it rechargeable?" Nathan asked.

"Probably. Looks like a lithium-ion battery."

"Well, I do have a solar panel in my ..." Nathan trailed off, running a hand through his hair.

Aristotle lifted an eyebrow. "In your what?"

"In my father's bedroom, which is probably under heavy surveillance," Nathan said with an awkward grin.

"Point taken," Aristotle said. "Do you know what this means?"

No one replied. Emiko's eyes nearly popped out of their sockets as they waited for Aristotle to announce her decision.

"It means I'm coming with you."

Emiko pumped her fists again. "Yes!"

Nathan tried to glare at Emiko, to remind her to keep her voice down, but all he could manage was a smile. He too was heartened by the prospect of Aristotle joining them on their trek home.

"Then it's settled. We'll sleep here tonight and set out tomorrow," John said. He looked haggard, hungry, and in need of a long slumber. But for the first time since Nathan had met him, the bearded man seemed at peace.

Chapter 58

03/25/2028

Tomorrow we head north into the great unknown.

We've packed our belongings into the Subaru. I made sure to include a handful of mementos — photos, a few pieces of jewelry, and a couple of Emiko and Nathan's childhood art projects. Nathan is also bringing a collection of books, and I've allowed Emiko to bring a few toys.

It's hard to say what we'll find in the north. Currently the plan is to drive to Duluth, see what the situation is like there, and continue on if necessary.

How will we know when to stop?

We'll stop once we're far enough from the painful memory of Minneapolis to lay down new roots and begin anew. How long we must travel before this fog of desolation no longer hangs over us remains to be seen.

This entry marks the conclusion of World's End. From this day onward I'll concern myself not with the end of the last world, but with the beginning of a new one.

As such, I'm leaving this journal here on my desk. Maybe one day Nathan, Emiko, or someone else will rediscover it.

To the north we go. May the future see us well!

P.S. Nathan, if you ever read this, I hope you don't still feel guilty for hacking into my blog. "Nahtan!Okime!" was a weak password. If I'd wanted to bar your access I would've changed it.

*Maybe one day we'll again read all those harrowing words I wrote.
I hope we can do it together.*

* * *

HAMMERS POUNDED and solar-powered speakers blared as men
erected a stage on the banks of the Mississippi.

The General had hand-picked this location to reintroduce
himself. The river symbolized power. The stage faced an open
field that abutted a grove of majestic sugar maples. Within that
grove lurked the ultimate spectacle. Carefully hidden beneath a
mound of dirt and leaves, the spectacle awaited the General's
cue.

The army assembled before the stage that afternoon. They
applauded thunderously as the General stepped onto the
podium. A flurry of golden leaves swirled past, carried west by
the early autumn breeze.

The General stood at the lectern and leaned towards the
microphone.

"Attention!"

His amplified voice boomed through the speakers. The
crowd fell silent. Even the wind seemed to wane at his
command.

The General scanned the sea of men before him, over a
thousand strong. Though he couldn't lock eyes with every one
of them, he could make it seem that he was. After impressing
himself upon his followers he began.

"I have heard the rumors; the whispers that I had
abandoned this army, that I had been overthrown, that I was
dead. As you can see, reports of my desertion, deposition, and
death were premature. Rest assured that I would never go so
quietly into the night.

"Yet rumors often carry hints of truth. These were no
exception. A faction within our ranks did try to oust me during
my absence. This faction's leader thought he could assassinate
me and claim this army as his own. Needless to say, he is no
longer with us. May his fate serve as a warning to those who
would cross me."

The General raised a fist to his mouth and cleared his throat. No longer did stiff bristles tickle his hand. How Osborne endured such an unkempt chin, he couldn't understand.

"Now look around you. Look not just at your fellow man, but at everything. Look to the rivers and the trees, to the grass beneath your feet. This is a beautiful country. It has always been and will always be. And, by right, it is already yours.

"Yet this beautiful land was once so much more. The men who lived here drove cars and flew planes. They sent information through wires and over the air. Not a decade ago, men were harnessing this planet's resources and molding them into a world more fantastic than the ancients could've imagined.

"The reminders of this world are everywhere. All around us are towers, arenas, factories, and machines — the artifacts of this lost age. The memories of this age still live on within us, never to be forgotten."

The General paused to survey the crowd, meeting eyes and seeing faces drunk on recollections of the world that was.

"We will revive these memories. We will bridge the gap between our past and our future. History will come alive. We will have cars and trains, trucks and tractors. We will have airplanes. We will have tanks!"

The General slammed his fist on the lectern. The earth trembled right on cue. The surly growl of an engine coming to life filled the air.

The General swept his arm towards the grove of maples. The eyes of his army followed.

An enormous, forest green vehicle rumbled out of the trees. Propelled by two soil-churning treads, the heavily armored behemoth clambered forward and circled around, coming to a halt at the army's flank.

"Behold, a tank!" the General announced. His engineers had converted it to run on the inexhaustible power of the Northland Core. Letting his men admire it in dumbfounded awe, he continued:

"This is the first of many. We will have more machines. We will generate more power. We will bring a new age to dawn. Do you hear me?" the General shouted.

"Yes, sir!" the crowd roared.

"I said do you hear me!"

"Yes, sir!" was the reply, twice as loud as the last.

"Then we will fight, and arrive in this new age together!"

The General stepped away from the lectern to an explosion of cheers. As he approached the edge of the stage, he spotted Sergeant Ramses Brushnell near the stairs. Solemn and unimpressed, Brushnell stood apart from his hollering and chanting comrades.

The General could read Brushnell like a two-year-old read a pop-up picture book. The story wasn't new: Brushnell was realizing that he was nothing but a pawn. Soon he would come to terms with the fact that some pawns were sacrificed while others were promoted, and that the line between those two fates was as thin as a land mine's tripwire.

Brushnell was pouting, but he would come around.

If not there would be consequences.

Join the Mailing List!

Would you like to:

- Hear about Henry's new releases first?
- See cover art before it's unveiled publicly?
- Learn about exclusive contests?
- Receive occasional updates from Henry?

Sign up for Henry's **free** mailing list today:
http://simplyunbound.com/mailing-list/

Acknowledgements

The Northland Chronicles now spans three books.

I wouldn't have made it to book three without the support of these people:

David Bates
Brendan Beltz
Charles Borchert
Andrew Browne
Carol Cheng
Chris Garland
John Maresco
Gary Olsen
Gaila Olsen
Hillary Olsen
Richard Olsen
Jean Replinger
Stephen Robak
Stanley Serkosky
Judy Serkosky
Elaine Smith
Claude Smith
Clayton W.

If you cross paths with any of these amazing people, be sure to pat them on the back!

Henry J. Olsen was once a quiet kid in a small Wisconsin town. Now he travels the world and writes tales of adventure. As of August 2015 he is living in Kaohsiung, Taiwan.

You can catch up with him at: http://simplyunbound.com

Book and Stories by Henry J. Olsen

Grab a coat.
Winter is coming.

www.ingramcontent.com/pod-product-compliance
Lightning Source LLC
Chambersburg PA
CBHW071242170626
46809CB00001B/47